A True Witch

Book 2

L.J. Fox

I wish to acknowledge the Traditional Custodians of the land upon which we live and work and pay respect to Elders past and present.

"The world is full of magical things, patiently waiting for our senses to grow sharper." W.B. Yeats

Chapter 1
NIAMH AND EMMA

"Don't do it, Niamh," Emma warned, but it was too late.

The low humming sound which Emma had initially mistaken for the purring of the plane engines, had grown louder, more intense and more menacing. Her eyes had been closed as she leaned back in her seat relaxing, but within a few minutes she recognised the deep rumbling sound as one she had heard on one awful occasion before. Her eyes snapped open and she quickly turned to Niamh beside her.

Growling rumbling from her throat, Niamh unbuckled her seat belt and turned, kneeling to look over the back of her seat at the guy in the seat behind. He grinned at her with smug arrogance, having achieved his goal of antagonising her, a goal he had been working toward for hours now. Emma peered through the gap between the two seats at the perpetrator, soon to be victim and realised that he did resemble Justin Grimm with his blonde spiky hair and was approximately the same age. With a growing sense of dread, she realised that couldn't be a good thing.

"I've asked you several times to stop kicking my seat, and you have ignored me," said Niamh, sounding surprisingly calm.

The man shrugged his shoulders nonchalantly. "It's a free world."

Niamh glanced at the passenger seated next to him in his premium economy seat and was pleased to see they did not seem to know each other. The other passenger was gazing out the window, appearing to ignore the situation though Niamh could see he was subtly listening.

She sighed and her eyes glowed with anger, the iris flashing amber. She saw the startled look on the seat kicker's face; his pupils dilate and heard the intake of breath. To scare him a little further, she growled softly, an animalistic, guttural growl.

Niamh felt Emma gently tugging at her arm to distract her from whatever she intended for the seat kicker. Having already sent her invisible gift to him, she smiled sweetly at the guy and calmly turned back to resume her position in her seat, clicking her seat belt back into place.

"It's ok," she said to Emma, smiling innocently as a terrible sound and odour suddenly filled the cabin. Rustling sounds and groans emitted from the seat behind as the seat kicker frantically unfastened his seatbelt and made a dash for the toilets at the back of the plane, which were both occupied. Distressed groans could be heard and fists beating on the cubicle door, and before long, whispers from other passengers grew to exclamations of alarm and horror as they were assailed with the stench of someone who had soiled his pants.

"Oh Niamh. That's not nice," said Emma, but couldn't help a slight grin from escaping, followed by a few stifled giggles. It took her a few more minutes to compose herself and stop the sneaky giggles.

"Where do you think that growling comes from? Do you think that's a witch thing?" Emma asked.

Niamh frowned. She had wondered the same thing since that fateful day over six months earlier when the two Grimm brothers, her half-brothers, had managed to infiltrate May's house and she had confronted them. In the altercation that followed, she had growled in rage after May had been killed. She had not even been aware of the growling at the time, but Emma described it afterwards to her.

"No. I don't think so. I can't imagine May ever growling and she never mentioned that aspect to me," Niamh responded, thinking back to the death of her mentor, her teacher and friend.

"So, you think it's a Grimm trait?" asked Emma.

"Well, it must be, but I don't really know anything about the Grimm's. I don't remember hearing those two Grimm brothers growl at all during our fight. Maybe it's just me and something I do." Niamh shrugged and shivered.

"You haven't asked Tarren ... your father, about the Grimm's history or genetic background then?" Emma asked.

A few minutes passed before Niamh responded to the question and Emma had begun to think she was not going to answer.

"No. I haven't been able to bring myself to ask him that sort of detail. I still can barely believe it's true that he's my father or that I have any Grimm blood at all, but I guess I'll have to face facts. Maybe one day I will be able to ask him." Niamh looked away, finding the conversation difficult and confronting.

Emma, realising Niamh was struggling with the line of questioning, brightened the mood by changing the subject. "Hey, do you realise we might love Ireland so much that we won't want to return to Australia?"

Niamh looked back at Emma and smiled, aware of how important this trip was to both of them after the traumatic events of six months earlier. This was a chance to relax, recover and spend time sight-seeing and exploring.

"I'm sure we're going to love it, but I have a little sister due in January and I wouldn't miss that for the world, so three months in Ireland is plenty."

"Oh, you're so lucky. I'd love a baby sister," said Emma, wistfully.

"You've always had a younger sibling," said Niamh.

"Oh, but he's a boy. Boys are not the same. A sister would be awesome."

"I don't want her to grow up like I did, not knowing I was a witch or any of our history. I'm going to teach her how to use magic and look after her," Niamh said with a firmness to her voice.

"So ... she's going to be a witch? How do you know that?" asked Emma, puzzled.

"She's magic. I can feel it. I felt it as soon as I knew my mother was pregnant," said Niamh.

Emma looked at Niamh with concern. "But what if ... what if ... she's magic but not a witch?"

Niamh's head snapped around to look at Emma and Emma saw a flash of something in her eyes, a shift in colour. Immediately, the eyes softened and Niamh exhaled to relax. "You wonder if she will be a Grimm?"

"Don't you?" asked Emma.

Niamh pulled a face as her mind fought with itself over what the answer would be. Would the baby be born with the red hair and grey eyes of her witch heritage, or the blonde hair and dark eyebrows of the witch's arch enemy, the Grimm family. The looks appeared to indicate whether the magic was of the good-natured witch side or the cruel and evil Grimm side.

"I have thought about it and I know it's a possibility, but I can't even contemplate my baby sister being a Grimm. She must be a witch," said Niamh and shuddered involuntarily.

Emma could see Niamh's eyes were watery as if threatening to tear up and she knew how emotionally invested Niamh was in her mother's pregnancy. She put her hand on Niamh's hand which was on the arm rest.

"I'm sure she'll be a witch. Don't you know, good always wins over evil."

A hostess raced down the aisle past their seats on her way to the back of the plane as the whispers and complaints from other passengers became louder and more insistent. Groaning could still be heard, and Emma wasn't keen to turn around and check whether the seat kicker was still waiting for a free cubicle or whether the groans were coming from inside the cubicle.

"Niamh," Emma said in a serious tone, turning back to her friend. "Please never do that to me, ok?"

Chapter 2
LUCINDA

Lucinda felt arms envelope her waist as she stood at the kitchen sink, peeling vegetables for soup. She looked down to see the strong hands and arms of Tarren, and she knew she would never tire of his touch, his affectionate gestures, of just being with him. With a drought of love and affection for twenty years, she never thought this day would happen where they could be together again. She watched his hands caress her small bump where their baby grew and felt his breath on her neck, his whisper in her ear, "How's our little girl this morning?"

Parsnips dumped and forgotten, Lucinda turned around and wrapped her arms around his neck, tiptoeing to reach up to him. "She's doing just fine."

"I'm sure our big girl is doing just fine too," he said after a moment's pause.

Her arms collapsed to her side, and she turned back to the sink and the parsnips. "I know … I know … I'm just being an over-protective mother, but she's never been away from home before for more than one or two nights. Now, she's half-way around the world and she's only nineteen years old."

"Babe, she's not your average nineteen year old." Tarren chuckled as he stated the obvious.

"She's still my baby," said Lucinda, defensively.

He looked at his watch, calculating the time difference between Melbourne, Australia and Ennis, Ireland. "She would be just arriving in Ennis about now, I think."

He could see Lucinda was nodding as the back of her head was moving, and he was also aware she was crying quietly hoping he wouldn't realise. He could smell her tears and almost taste them.

"She's ok, Lucinda. She's a strong and intelligent girl, she has Emma with her, and she'll be back before you know it."

Lucinda nodded again and sniffed, parsnips completed and on to the turnips.

Tarren paused, reluctant to tell her his plans for the morning, aware of how fragile she was feeling with Niamh away and not wishing to add to her stress or worry. "I'm off to the remand centre this morning." He uttered the words simply and without detail.

She nodded again, still sniffing.

"Babe, are you ok? You know I must visit them, don't you?" He noted her still nodding, head down. He sighed, trying to decide how to proceed. Gently, he turned her around to face him and saw her damp, tear-kissed cheeks. Tenderly, he lifted his hand and wiped away a wayward tear.

It was a difficult time for them both, as only months earlier, his two sons had tried to kill their daughter, Niamh, and succeeded in murdering Lucinda's godmother, May. Both boys were currently being held on remand awaiting trial, and he had blocked their bail attempts. Tarren wanted them to face punishment for the crimes they had committed and had no choice but to block their magic or they would have simply used magic to let themselves out of prison.

The rest of his family were furious with him as a Grimm family member had never been held accountable for any crime committed and none of them accepted that killing a witch was a crime. They had been hunting and killing witches for centuries and they couldn't understand why this should be any different. The Grimm family were untouchable, and Tarren was forcing them to follow the normal person's laws.

"Sorry, Tarren. I just miss Niamh and have my mind on her right now," Lucinda said, apologetically.

He had noted that she never mentioned Justin and Beaton, his two sons on remand. It was as if the topic was too difficult to tackle, and he understood. Despite the terrible things his own two sons were guilty of, they were still his sons and he loved them. He owed it to them to visit and ensure their safety and keep the ball rolling with the legal proceedings. In many ways, he wished they were still children and he could kick their backsides and send them to their room, with a stern parental talk about what they had done wrong, but these were grown men. They were fully capable, responsible and needed to face the consequences of their own actions.

The two of them had conspired, with help from their sister who was also facing charges, to attain access to the house of an old witch, stab her so she died a slow death and then attacked Niamh with the intention of possibly killing her, or at least harming her. Could it get any worse for a father? Niamh was his daughter from an affair with Lucinda twenty years earlier, and Justin and Beaton were sons from his marriage to Marion, as was their sister, Monica and another son, Anton.

In the absolute joy of his reunion with Lucinda after twenty years and the impending birth of their new daughter, he was besieged with the horror and sorrow of what his sons had done. He refused to show his distress to Lucinda as he knew she was worried about Niamh and the last thing she needed was for him to be anything but strong. The fact was that he felt a tremendous amount of guilt as a father for the events that had occurred and was under immense pressure from the Grimm family to release the boys. He was on a daily emotional roller-coaster with no end in sight.

"What are you doing today?" he asked, trying to change the subject and lighten the mood.

"Oh, I thought I would visit with Bella and we'd shop for some clothes that are a little larger. I'm struggling to fit into my clothes," she responded, indicating her growing stomach.

"Good idea," he said, and kissed the back of her head. He breathed in her scent, the scent of Lucinda. He remembered this so well from twenty years ago when it had captured him the first time. His beautiful red gold girl that he had fallen in love with despite the many obstacles they faced.

Letting her go reluctantly, he headed for the door, pausing to look back. She was so beautiful and vulnerable, standing at the sink and looking at him with eyes that haunted him. How could he ever resolve this dilemma? How could he ever make things right again? She didn't even know the latest devastating news regarding his son, Justin. How could he tell her that Justin had suffered a traumatic brain injury during the murder of May and assault of Niamh and that Niamh had caused it? He was committed to spend time with doctors and Justin at this time but couldn't bring himself to confide this to the love of his life.

He blew her a kiss and turned to open the door, off to see his wayside sons.

Chapter 3
EMMA

The taxi driver zoomed away after wishing the girls all the best. Well … that is what they thought he was saying. It was going to take time for the two of them to become accustomed to the local dialect and they were struggling to understand what was being said.

"I think it was in English," said Niamh as they watched the back of the taxi disappear down the lane.

Having mastered a stopover at Heathrow Airport in London, and flown on to Shannon Airport in Ireland, the two girls were fortunate to encounter a friendly taxi driver to transport them the last thirty minutes to Claureen, near Ennis. The driver was fascinated they were from Australia and chatted away. They loved his sing-song voice with a strong brogue but acknowledged to him they didn't understand much of it.

It was mid-afternoon when they arrived and the day was still sunny though the temperature was slowly dropping. Emma waved at the departing taxi then turned toward the beautiful stone cottage they had glimpsed from the back seat of the taxi. It sat as it had for hundreds of years on top of a slight hill with nothing in sight except rough fields, a few fences, hedges and the laneway up to the cottage.

"Oh, it's beautiful," said Emma, captivated by the cottage where Niamh's ancestors had lived.

She suddenly noticed that Niamh was hanging back as though not in a hurry to inspect their home for the next few months. She appeared to be anxious and was practically hopping from one foot to the other as if agitated and uncomfortable.

"What's wrong with you?" Emma asked, puzzled.

"I need to pee," Niamh answered, looking more anxious and beginning to pace in tight circles. Even her response was cut short as though giving more of an explanation may cause further discomfort.

"Ok. Well, I'm sure the cottage has a bathroom," Emma replied, shaking her head at her friend's silliness.

"Nope. I need to go pee around the fence line," Niamh responded, pulling down her jeans and kicking them off along with her boots until she was standing in just her pink pants on her bottom half.

Emma blinked a few times, thinking she was imagining things. "YOU WHAT?"

"Witch urine works better than any charm to ward off evil. It worked a treat in Ringwood to keep the Grimm's away and we don't know what nasties are lurking around this place. I'm going to pee around the fence line," Niamh said in all seriousness.

Emma's mouth fell open in surprise and she looked around at the fenced yard of the house which seemed an incredibly large area, even by Australian standards.

"Oh my God," said Emma, clapping her hands across her eyes. "You're not serious, are you? "You can't pee all the way around this fence. You won't even have enough."

Niamh raced to the front gate of the property to pee at the gate and commenced a squat before moving a little further down the fence and squatting again.

Emma giggled. "I'm not watching," she called out then peeked through her fingers which were still covering her eyes. "Can't you wait until it's dark? What if someone sees you?"

"No," Niamh called back. "Can't wait. Have to do it now." Niamh continued her mission squatting to pee then moving to the next position.

"I can't believe you are doing this. Hey, I don't have to do it too, do I?" Emma caught the giggles.

"Nope," Niamh called out to her. "Your pee is no good."

"What do you mean my pee is no good? How do you know that? You've never seen it," Emma yelled back, indignant that there may be something wrong with her urine.

"Well, you're not a witch so it won't work, but if you really want in on the action, why don't you start at the gate and start peeing in the other direction? Can't hurt," Niamh shrugged as she squatted at the next location.

Emma realised that for a moment, she had contemplated joining her crazy friend in this endeavour, shook her head to clear it. She also became aware that she really did need to pee and very soon.

"I'm going in the cottage to find a bathroom," she called out and disappeared through the old wooden front door.

Chapter 4
TARREN

Tarren sat uneasily on one side of the small table waiting for the guard to bring Beaton in for the visit. The room was sparse, simple and unfriendly, like everything else in this remand centre, and why should it be any different, he reasoned? The residents here were not staying for luxury treatment at a five-star hotel.

He hadn't visited Beaton for two weeks and felt anxious about this visit. Beaton was openly hostile toward his father as he knew Tarren was the one delegating him to prison life. A Grimm had never been incarcerated and Beaton considered it below his standard to be expected to comply with the law of the common people and was indignant that his own father could treat him this way. Tarren had achieved a block on their magic abilities that none of the Grimm's had even known existed and Beaton was helpless to use his magic in any way. The rest of the Grimm family had tried magic to overwrite the block, but no one had been able to achieve it. The general consensus was that only Tarren could reverse what he had done.

The door opened and Beaton stepped in to the room, his face eager and excited as he anticipated a visit from his family. Tarren watched the transformation as Beaton realised his father was the visitor, eager anticipation turning into contempt and anger. Tarren stood up and Beaton reluctantly approached, shuffling his feet and sat on the other side of the table, ignoring Tarren's outstretched arms, seeking to embrace or at least shake hands.

Beaton was dressed in his own casual clothing with his hair longer than he normally wore it. He sat sidewards in the chair, refusing to face Tarren in a show of defiance, with his legs stretched out in front of him and crossed at the ankles. His expression was bordering on outright anger and it broke Tarren's heart to see.

"Beaton ... son ... how are you?" Tarren knew it sounded lame, but he had to start the conversation somewhere.

Beaton glared at him and looked away. "How do you think I am?" he countered.

"Well, are you healthy? Do you need anything?" Tarren asked, again knowing it sounded lame.

"I need to go home to my family," he said, gruffly.

"Have your lawyers spoken to you recently? I wondered how the case is shaping up," Tarren asked, vying for conversation.

Beaton pulled his legs in and turned in his chair to face his father, his movements fast and angry. "Look, I don't know why you bother to visit. You obviously don't care. YOU are the reason I'm in here. If it weren't for YOU, I would be home with my wife and children where I should be. YOU have done this to me, and to Justin. I can't even use magic to improve anything, like the food or how I'm treated. I have no magic at all. Do you know how that feels?" His voice had risen in his angry tirade and he sat back, breathing deeply to calm down. "Why are you doing this? I don't understand."

Tarren stared at his son, aware that Beaton's sentiments mirrored how all the Grimm family felt, and how they had always felt, that they were beyond the law and beyond any form of punishment or remorse.

"Beaton, you were all told to stay away from the witches and from Niamh and you ignored my direction. You and Justin ... and Monica to a lesser extent, all conspired to kill that old witch and to harm Niamh, and now, you will face the consequences," Tarren said calmly.

"What are you even talking about, Dad? That is what we do, what our family has always done. We hunt and kill witches. NEWS FLASH ... the Grimm's hunt witches. What did you expect? We were just doing what nature intended. I can't believe you could even think it would be any different." Beaton shook his head in disgust.

"I AM THE HEAD OF THIS FAMILY AND YOU OBEY ME!" Tarren had jumped to his feet in anger at the patronising tone and stared into his son's eyes. "Niamh is your sister and you were both going to kill her."

"Half-sister, you mean. What are you doing with the witches anyway? Weirdest thing I've ever heard. You've left your family to go live with a bunch of witches. A BUNCH OF WITCHES. HAVE YOU LOST YOUR MIND?"

Tarren stopped himself from saying there were no 'bunch of witches' and that Niamh was the only witch left. He didn't want the Grimm family to have that much information and to be aware that if they eliminated Niamh, there wouldn't be any witches left in Melbourne ... for now. The least the Grimm family knew about Niamh's family, the better.

"That's none of your business. I may have a new life now, but I'm still your father and I care about you and Justin, and all my children and grandchildren," Tarren said as he sat down again, feeling emotional and still hoping to get through to Beaton.

"So, you are just going to sit back and watch Justin and me, get tried at court like common criminals and go to jail? Is that right?" Beaton asked.

"We'll let the system run its course to judge what you and Justin have done. I hope you learn that there are repercussions and show some remorse," Tarren said quietly.

There was an uncomfortable silence for a few minutes, eventually broken by Beaton, his voice back to calm.

"What is going on with Justin? Is he ok? I haven't spoken to him since we've been here and last week I saw him across the yard but he just looked at me as if he didn't know me. Is he mad at me?" Beaton asked, appearing less angry and more concerned with this line of conversation.

Tarren looked down at his hands, contemplating the question. He had been putting off talking to anyone about the situation with Justin, even Lucinda. Now, confronted with this question straight up, he needed to be honest.

"There have been some complications with Justin," Tarren paused, unsure how to continue. "He ... well ... it appears he suffered some trauma on the day you guys attacked the witches."

"What trauma? What are you talking about?" asked Beaton, leaning forward intently.

"The doctors say he has a traumatic brain injury," Tarren started but Beaton jumped to his feet in shock.

"WHAT?"

Tarren put his hand up toward Beaton for him to calm down. "It's ok. He's fine but he suffered some damage, and the scans show that there are some parts of his brain that no longer function."

Beaton sat again, eyes wide as he analysed the words his father had just told him. No longer function ... no longer function. He blinked a few times, recalling the incident and running through it in his mind. Niamh, the young witch had sent magic to fry Justin's brain. He remembered it well and saw what was happening to Justin, but he'd been unable to stop it. The old witch had sent her old straw broomstick to attack him and he had been distracted, trying to avoid being hit. He hadn't realised that Justin had been seriously hurt at the time and now he felt guilty that he had not been able to protect his little brother.

"What does this mean? What's going to happen to him?" Beaton asked, voice low and worried.

"He can talk and function but he's quiet, doesn't make conversation or ask questions. He just answers what you ask him. He's ok but he wouldn't be able to look after himself for some time," answered Tarren.

"Does that mean he will improve? You said, 'some time' so he will get better?" Beaton asked.

"We are hopeful. The neurologist tells me that the brain finds ways of working around what no longer works. Other parts of his brain will compensate for the damaged areas."

Beaton took some deep breaths and Tarren could see his anger building again. The rage built within him until he jumped to his feet again, the chair banging as it slid backwards.

"That young witch did this. She did this to Justin. Is she being punished like we are? Where is she? Is she in jail too? How can you take her side over your own kind? We are your sons. Justin is your son. DON'T YOU CARE?"

Beaton's eyes were wild and his face flushed with anger. Just before he turned his back on his father, Tarren could see tears fill his eyes.

"I'm ready to go," Beaton said to the guard.

Tarren called out to him. "Of course you are my sons, and of course I care."

The guard opened the door and Beaton exited the room leaving Tarren sitting at the table, staring after him.

Chapter 5
NIAMH

Hey Niamh," called Emma from the front door of the cottage. "There's a food hamper on the kitchen table. Guess what I found inside?"

There was no response and no sign of Niamh, although she could still see her jeans and boots discarded on the grass where Niamh had left them. She walked around the outside of the cottage looking for her bare-arsed friend.

"Niamh, where are you?"

Toward the back of the cottage where a vegetable garden had been established, a dark red head popped up from where she'd been squatting at the back fence.

"Oh, there you are," said Emma, giggling. "There's a food hamper in the kitchen and look what I found." She held up the wine bottle.

"Great!" Niamh said heading toward Emma. "My bladder's empty. Time to fill the tank. What sort of wine is it?"

"Ummm ... Bunratty Mead," Emma read from the label. "Where would the hamper come from?"

"My mother would've organised it. She knew we weren't arriving until afternoon with no time to buy groceries," answered Niamh, reaching Emma.

Emma looked down at Niamh's white legs and pink underwear. "Niamh, get in the cottage before someone sees you. I'll go retrieve your jeans and our suitcases."

Niamh laughed as she casually strolled around to the front of the cottage and in the front door. Emma shook her head, finding it hard to believe Niamh was so comfortable semi-naked out in the open, in daylight.

As night fell, the two girls felt cosy in the cottage, wine bottle empty and hamper food devoured. They had investigated the small stone cottage and fenced yard area but would leave further exploration until the next day. The cottage was tiny and consisted of one main room with included a kitchen area, one bedroom with two single beds and a reasonably modern bathroom had been added at the back, accessed through the back door. It was quaint and old, and the two girls loved it. Especially appealing was the fact that Niamh's grandmother had been born and lived in this cottage up until she immigrated to Australia, and possibly many generations before her. Niamh felt the essence of her ancestors in every inch of the cottage.

In the middle of the night, Niamh awoke, quietly slipped on a jumper and ventured out into the night. Dozens of animals of the night waited out the front of the cottage for her – owls and bats sat on the fence, foxes, rabbits and mice milled around, eyes flashing in the moonlight, and a few cats and dogs sat quietly. They had not gathered to hunt or fight each other, but to greet her and she giggled at their little excited sounds when she walked among them. She remembered how the animals in her neighbourhood had greeted her after the bestowment from her grandmother back when she lived at Ringwood and again when she moved to May's house after her death.

After a breakfast of coffee from the hamper minus milk as they had consumed everything else, the girls decided they needed to buy groceries urgently. The taxi driver yesterday had informed them the town was only a twenty-minute walk from where they lived and as it was a fine day, they headed out the door for the walk. Niamh halted suddenly just outside the cottage, viewing the surrounds cautiously.

"What's wrong?" asked Emma.

"I don't know. I feel like we're being watched," said Niamh quietly.

Emma looked around, seeing only the picket fence line around the cottage and its newly painted appearance. "Come on," she urged and the two of them set off walking, down the dirt lane toward the bitumen road.

Niamh repeatedly glanced back over her shoulder at the little cottage, expecting to see something or someone to explain her unease but the sight of the quiet, lonely little cottage made her marvel at their good fortune.

"I just can't believe my family lived in this cottage and would have walked this way to town hundreds of times," said Niamh.

Early that morning, she had finally managed to urinate the entire distance around the fence line so was happy to leave the property, feeling the cottage was secure, borders fortified.

"Unreal, isn't it? Such a beautiful place," said Emma. "We are so lucky."

The cottage sat isolated without nearby neighbours, among fields of once ploughed fields but now rough grassland, and as they turned left and started down the bitumen road, a few houses came into view and further on, the houses increased until they were side by side.

Niamh continued glancing back over her shoulder and at one point, she thought she glimpsed a flash of white low to the ground but dismissed it as her imagination.

Although appearing isolated and rural, the cottage was not far from civilisation and as they walked, the town came alive before their eyes with people undertaking their daily activities, cars transporting their occupants to work, voices of neighbours chatting, dogs barking, children playing and music. A distant church bell rang, musical and magical. After heading into the centre of town they finally located a shopping area. The grocery store was tiny and the size of a single shop but they hadn't planned to buy very much, only sporting two backpacks to courier the groceries back to the cottage.

The girls left the store with the essentials - milk, bread, butter, honey, fruit, vegetables and a small amount of meat. Feeling pleased and established now they had accumulated the staples of life, they headed back the way they had come. Again, Niamh felt eyes on them and stopped, spinning around to view the area, but saw nothing.

"You still feel we're being watched?" asked Emma.

"I do," Niamh replied and turned to keep walking.

"I think we'd better buy a car soon. We're going to need it if we want to look around the area and buy more than just a few things," said Emma.

"Agreed," said Niamh, feeling a slight prickling on her skin and distracted by the sensation.

They walked another block when Niamh suddenly spun around to look behind them. Fifty metres back on the footpath, a dog stopped in its tracks and stared back. It was a medium sized dog, mostly white with large brown patches including a patch over one eye. Emma, realising that Niamh had stopped, walked back to her and gazed at the dog.

"Is that who was watching us?" she asked.

"Hmmm … maybe," Niamh said.

"It looks like a bulldog, maybe a cross with something. It's got a flat face like a bulldog," added Emma. Puzzled, she looked at Niamh who always loved animals and wondered about the strange look on her face and the fact that the dog and Niamh were in a type of staring stand-off.

"Niamh?" she queried.

"There's something strange about that dog," said Niamh quietly.

Chapter 6
MONICA

Monica, you MUST do something about this." Beaton's face was white and tense with worry and frustration.

"Like what?" Monica asked.

"Well … try talking to Dad on your own. You were always his favourite so he may listen to you. Make him understand that this is ridiculous, letting me rot in here, away from my family, and poor Justin, he should be in a specialist hospital receiving proper treatment, not caged like an animal." Beaton threw his hands in the air as emotion overtook him.

"I will. I'll talk to him but … I don't know if it will do any good. We barely hear from him, and he seems so different. He's not the Dad I know anymore. What if he won't listen?" Monica asked.

Beaton thought for a few minutes. "You … will have to call a family meeting. Get everyone there." Beaton's mind was racing as the idea formed and spread. "Tell them what's happening … and ask them to intervene."

"But Dad is the head of the family …"

"NO! He is only the head of our family. He's not the head of the Grimm family so if he won't listen to reason then we need to involve the entire family. Dad was the youngest in his own family so Uncle Hardy is his older brother and the head of the Grimm's in Melbourne, and if it comes to that, the family in Sydney will eat Dad for breakfast." Beaton's voice had risen in his enthusiasm for the new plan. For the first time since his father's visit, he felt hope.

"You're right. I agree. I just don't like going against Dad even if I think he's wrong," Monica said.

"Oh, you would leave poor Justin to turn into a fucking vegetable and me to have my life wasted while my family is forced to live without me?"

"Calm down, calm down. No, of course not. I will see Dad this week in person and talk to him. If I don't have any luck with him then I'll call a family meeting. OK?" She put her hand out and placed it over his in a show of support.

He looked over at her and smiled. "Thanks Monica. I've got no one to turn to except you or Anton and you are so much smarter than him."

"Now, I'm going to go see Justin. I need to see for myself what his condition is and what you are talking about," Monica said and stood from the table.

"Good. Go see him. You'll see. Don't let me down," Beaton said as he stood as well.

"I won't," Monica said and signalled for the guard to let her out.

An hour later, she strode out into the carpark and headed toward her vehicle with tears rolling down her face and gentle sobs breaking free and escaping. She could not believe her baby brother had been affected in such a catastrophic way.

When they brought him into the visiting room where she was sitting, she jumped up and raced over to embrace him but he stared at her expressionless, as if he didn't recognise her at all. Seeing the blank look on his face, she paused and gave him a moment to register her appearance. Expecting his face to light up, to say something inappropriate and to give her a bear hug as he always had, none of that happened.

"Justin? It's me, Monica. Are you ok?" she asked, quietly, trying to keep her voice from breaking up with emotion.

He blinked a few times and peered at her, as if waiting for his memory to register who she was. After a moment, he repeated her name in a voice that was way too quiet for Justin, "Monica, hello." He smiled a small, weak smile and she still wasn't sure he recognised her or was just mouthing the words expected with a greeting.

Monica stepped forward toward him and placed her arms around him in a gentle hug. He stood still, not hugging back for a minute and then slowly raised his arms and hugged her back.

"Come on, let's sit," she said and led him over to the table.

She noted the guard standing silently on the inside of the door and watching intently. Was Justin dangerous in any way?

Examining Justin closely, she noted he had lost weight from his chubby boyish face and his hair no longer sported the short sides and spiky top that he favoured. He was looking at her, waiting for her to speak with a small polite smile on his face.

"How are you, Justin?" she asked, peering at his eyes intently to determine his understanding.

He digested the question and then his smile grew a little broader. "I'm fine, thanks."

"Are they treating you well here?" Monica queried.

Again, a slight pause before he responded. "Yes. It's good here."

Monica looked up and addressed the guard at the door. "Hey, can I gel up his hair? You know, spike it up a little?"

The guard looked at her, raised an eyebrow and nodded. Monica stood and walked around behind Justin so the guard's view was the back of her and he had no view of what she was doing. She placed her hands near the top of Justin's head, pretending to play with his hair. Using magic, she arranged his hair to spike and gel, as it had been for the past few years.

"There," she said as she returned to her seat. Now when she looked across at him, he looked more like the Justin she knew, without the sparkling, smart-arse expression.

Monica spent the next thirty minutes asking Justin questions and telling stories of how the family were faring. He answered questions she asked after a moment's pause and listened attentively to the family stories, nodding his head occasionally, but did not initiate any conversation or ask any questions of her.

Monica could identify there was no way Justin would be in a position to care for himself without constant prompting and direction from someone. She struggled in Justin's presence not to cry or show how upset she was, instinctively knowing the importance of him seeing life as easy and carefree.

Once the visit concluded and she headed outside, the pent-up emotion boiled over and the sobs and tears began. Her anger grew as she walked across the carpark and she swore vengeance. The young witch had damaged Justin, perhaps forever and she was still walking around fully functional and free, and not in prison like her brothers. She would not and could not let this stand, not now and not ever. No matter what her father said or restrictions he placed on them regarding the witches, she intended to fulfil her ancestral obligations and destroy every witch she could and especially, that young witch.

Chapter 7
NIAMH

He's just a dog," said Emma dismissively and turned away from the squashy face of the bulldog.

Niamh felt uneasy as she watched the dog, knowing that animals were irresistibly drawn to her and how easily she befriended them. Yet, this animal stood back, wary with his tooth snagged over his top lip, looking like he was baring his teeth. He was seriously watching the two girls and did not want to be friends or get too close.

Eventually, Niamh turned back and the girls continued walking and chatting. Niamh could feel the dog watching with every fibre of her being but refused to look back at him. She knew that eventually he would show his true colours.

The town bustled with cars, people and bicycles on the streets going about their daily business. The girls walked along the route they had come, feeling a little intimidated and anxious on their first day in Ireland. Emma reminded Niamh that they had mastered a stopover at Heathrow, and if they could achieve that, they were capable of anything.

As the girls walked, the sound of acoustic music reached them and as they drew closer to the sound, they realised it was live music, not a radio or recorded sound. It was gentle and intricate finger picking on an acoustic guitar and a male voice quietly singing a song neither of the girls knew and weren't even sure was in English. His voice was smooth, deep and perfectly in tune, and the girls slowed down to listen. Ahead of them on their right, a tall green hedge stretched across the front of a house, a two metre tall privacy screen, and the music was coming from the other side of the hedge.

Not wanting to miss the rest of the song, they stopped on the footpath when they reached the hedge to listen, hidden from view by the thick greenery. For a few minutes, they were captivated by the guitar and voice and both smiled, losing the anxiety that had plagued them and feeling warm and fortunate to be where they were. With no one else in the street at that moment, they remained on the footpath, listening and enjoyed the moment.

The song ended and with shock and horror, Niamh realised that Emma was clapping. Quickly, she grabbed at Emma's hands to stop her, but it was too late. Whoever was singing would have heard the applause. Niamh felt her face blush with embarrassment.

Neither girl moved, standing like statues waiting to see if the singer would ignore the applause, and for a minute Niamh thought they could safely continue their journey. Signalling to Emma, they had only walked a few steps when a figure suddenly appeared ahead of them on the footpath through the gap in the hedge. Both girls froze, shocked at the sudden appearance and slightly embarrassed.

"Good morning to you," a very strong Irish voice called to them. "Thank you for your applause. You liked the music, did you not?"

The voice had the sing-song depth of the Irish voice and it took a few seconds for each girl to translate the words - 'thank you' sounded like 'tank you'.

"Oh yes. Such a lovely melody. I've not heard it before," said Emma.

"Tis an Irish ballad, The Dawning of the Day. Where are you from?" he asked, curious about their accent.

Niamh studied the man in front of them, twenties, dressed casually and with black wavy hair down to his shoulders, kind and interesting face and friendly disposition.

"Australia," Emma replied.

"Ah, Aussie." He nodded his head thoughtfully. "I'm Collins." He extended his hand toward the two girls. Emma immediately took his hand in hers, clasping it and gazing at him smiling.

"Emma, and this is Niamh," she said, turning to Niamh who was standing back a little.

Collins offered his hand to Niamh. "Niamh, good Irish name," he said.

Niamh paused and looked at the hand cautiously. She was not as trusting as she had been prior to the events of seven months ago. She looked up at his face and his blue eyes which held firm with the welcoming gesture. Finally, she reached out and took his hand, gently shaking it and nodding her head in greeting.

"Are you a musician?" asked Emma. "You're very good."

"I am indeed a musician. I teach at schools and I play at the pub some nights," he answered, pleased with the compliment.

"We're here for a few months on an extended holiday before uni," Emma responded.

"Uni?" Collins asked.

"Oh, university. Sorry. I forget that other people don't shorten words like Aussie's do." Emma gave a little giggle.

Niamh noticed Emma was waffling, almost nervously rushing her words with her face blushing a little. She looked at Collins' face and noticed his attention was riveted on Emma, little hint of a smile touched his lips. Emma, with her dark brown hair almost reaching her shoulders and her warm, engaging face was a beautiful girl. Oh no, Niamh thought. We only arrived in Ireland last night and Emma has already lost the plot and fallen for the first man she meets. She sighed as she listened while Emma rabbited on without thinking.

"Yeah, so … we thought we'd stay about three months and were lucky to be able to stay at Niamh's …"

"EMMA!" Niamh interrupted, stopping her from telling a stranger where they were staying. It was the first time Niamh had said a word in front of Collins and it was a reprimand to Emma. She felt embarrassed and blushed, turning away just in time to see the bulldog disappear behind the laneway about fifty metres away.

Emma looked at Collins apologetically, "Oops," she said.

Collins smiled good-naturedly. "Perhaps you could come to Marta's Bar one Friday night to see me play?"

"Oh yes. That sounds lovely," said Emma, turning to her friend. "Doesn't it, Niamh?"

Niamh was still looking toward where the dog had disappeared. She turned back to face Emma and Collins. "Umm … well, once we have a car."

Collins reached into his pocket, pulled out a black leather wallet and rummaged around until he found a card which he handed to Emma.

"Here. This is my number. You call me if you would like help with finding a car or getting around. We, Irish are friendly folk." He gave her his most charming smile.

"Thank you. Ok. Well … I guess we'd better head back. We've groceries in our backpacks," said Emma.

They said their goodbyes to Collins and headed down the street, aware that Collins was standing watching them walk. Emma looked down at the card in her hand.

It was a simple white business card with black print.

Collins O'Brien
Musician and Tutor
7863 489 712
cobrien887@gmail.com

Niamh was silent as they walked, disappointed that Emma had been so chatty and open with a complete stranger and almost told him their address. Two young girls on their own needed to be careful and they both knew this. Collins seemed a nice guy but could be a secret serial killer for all they knew.

"Niamh, did you have to be so rude?" asked Emma, crossly.

Niamh looked at her for a moment. "Rude? That wasn't rude. I can be a lot ruder than that."

Chapter 8
LUCINDA

How did your visit with the boys go?" Lucinda asked Tarren when he returned late in the afternoon.

She had noted his glum face and weary countenance as he entered the house, but he smiled when he saw her and feigned contentment. She knew him better and been aware for weeks there was something troubling him and it most likely concerned his two sons on remand. Although a difficult topic to discuss due to the obvious conflicts on both sides, she wanted to be supportive.

"Oh, ok, I guess. Beaton is not happy with me. In fact, he is downright pissed off and made sure he told me what he thought," said Tarren, touching his forehead to hers as they had always done, and then kissing her on the cheek before noticing the new dress she was wearing.

"You look nice," he said, appreciatively.

"Thank you. So, Beaton's not happy they are being forced to face charges? He wants you to agree to them being released?" she asked.

Tarren had said before that the Grimm's never faced the laws of normal people. It was the first time she had asked him questions regarding the boys and she tried to keep her tone casual and not make it an inquisition.

"He does, and there are ... complications with Justin that has Beaton super angry."

"Oh, what's that?" asked Lucinda.

Tarren paused wondering how to tell her, what words to use. Should he soften the explanation or say it how it is? He decided to be honest and direct.

"Justin sustained a traumatic brain injury and has been undergoing a ton of tests and is closely monitored. Beaton didn't know until today when I told him."

"What? Traumatic brain injury?" Lucinda stared at him wide-eyed, trying to analyse what he had just said, then it dawned on her. "From what Niamh did? Is that it?"

He nodded.

"Oh my god! Really? Is this a permanent thing?" she asked, wide-eyed and shocked.

"Well ... we don't know. The neurologist is conducting scans regularly and tests to determine if there is any change, but it appears there's tissue in his brain that's been damaged and will not repair. We hope he may find a way of bypassing the damaged areas in the future and becoming fully functional."

"Fully functional. So, he's not functional?" Lucinda asked, shocked.

"He's ... he's ... functional, sort of ... but he needs care. He couldn't look after himself," said Tarren.

Lucinda put her arm around Tarren's waist and her head against his chest. "I'm sorry to hear this. You should have told me. What will happen with the trial now? Does he understand the whole thing, the charges, being locked up and so on?" she asked.

"I don't think he does ... and they won't be able to take him through a trial if he doesn't understand what's happening. I think he will probably be held in some sort of medical care unit until they determine if there are any long-term neurocognitive, behavioural or psychiatric issues," Tarren said, reciting what the specialist had told him about Justin's injury.

Before Lucinda could respond, his phone rang in his pocket. Both jumped at the sudden shock of the loud sound and Lucinda pulled her head away as Tarren retrieved the device to see who was calling.

"It's Monica," he said and walked out to another room to take the call in private.

Lucinda was aware Monica didn't contact Tarren often, so she wondered if it was a result of Beaton finding out about Justin's condition. She thought it coincidental that Monica would phone him on this day, after his visit with Beaton.

A few minutes later Tarren returned and confirmed that Monica had visited Beaton and Justin after Tarren that day, and she would like to meet with him to discuss the situation. They had agreed to a 10am coffee the next morning at a coffee shop at Northcote.

"Good. You need to talk to her and work together for the sake of Justin," said Lucinda. "I wanted to go to Northcote tomorrow to pick up a few groceries and visit the Post Office. We could go together. I'll disappear to complete my shopping and we can catch up after?" she suggested.

"Perfect," Tarren responded distracted. He was keen to see his daughter but already rehearsing sentences he would use to convince her that he was looking after the boy's best interests.

Chapter 9
NIAMH

Niamh decided today she would locate her family cemetery which was on land they owned but a short distance from the cottage. Neither Niamh's mother, Lucinda, or Niamh's two aunts had ever visited the cottage at Claureen near Ennis, so they only had memories from their mother, Agatha to go on. Agatha had been born in the cottage and immigrated to Australia at nineteen years of age, the age Niamh currently was. At some point in her life, Agatha had managed to repurchase the cottage after it being sold when she immigrated. It passed on to Agatha's three daughters when she passed on the previous January.

The weather remained fine although clouds were threatening to unleash and rain wouldn't be far away. Emma suggested the Irish summer was similar to a Melbourne autumn day and Niamh agreed. She was glad they had packed coats and jumpers in anticipation of the infamous weather.

Emma chose to stay at the cottage aware this excursion to the cemetery was an adventure Niamh needed to accomplish on her own. She was still cross with Niamh from the day before feeling Niamh had been rude to Collins and in a foreign country where they didn't know anyone, they should be making friends, not alienating people. The two friends had barely spoken to each other since the incident the day before. Emma always knew when Niamh was unhappy with her, because small annoying things happened which had witchy hands all over it, such as the honey refusing to exit the squirt bottle, or only cold water coming out of the tap. These little witchy shows of displeasure made Emma the more furious with her and her childlike behaviour.

As Niamh left the cottage, Emma pulled out the business card with Collins' details on it and tapped it against the table, deep in thought. She could show her displeasure as well in other ways.

Niamh stood at the back of the cottage on the outside of the fence and scanned the countryside. The cottage and small fenced garden sat on the top of a slight hill and all around, the fields had once been cleared and a few trees, hedges and gullies remained. She wondered how it had looked like hundreds of years ago, whether the fields had been harvested for grain or been utilised as pasture for animals.

Heading down the slight slope toward a small thatch of trees at the bottom of the hill, as it was the only place she could think of where there may be a family cemetery. As she walked, she wondered why she thought the cemetery would be so far down the slope but couldn't imagine a family cemetery being on the side of a sloping hill. It seemed logical to be at the bottom where the land levelled.

The thought crossed her mind that perhaps the farmer who had bought the farm from Agatha's mother may have bulldozed the cemetery years beforehand and her mother and aunts were unaware. She fervently hoped this was not the case as the thought of the cemetery completely destroyed made her feel nauseous.

The gully exhibited erosion from hundreds of years of rain flowing down the hill after the land had originally been cleared so she carefully jumped over a shallow part of the gully and on to the other side where the trees stood. She immediately knew she was heading to the right area as she could feel something strange within her. Not a tingling like when another magical person was nearby, but a light humming or vibration in her head, drawing her closer, calling her.

The trees formed in a group as if sheltering and guarding what lay within. As she walked into the treed area, she felt she had walked into another world. Immediately darker, silent and surreal, even the temperature felt warmer. The ground thick with leaves and debris, created a warm blanketed and cushioned ground covering. From within, she felt surrounded by thousands of trees and yet, she could only remember seeing a dozen or so.

Right in the centre of the trees, she halted, tilted her head up and closed her eyes, feeling the place, opening her senses to allow the essence of this location into her very being. She breathed in the atmosphere and invited the place to share its history with her. Immediately, she could hear distant sounds of animals, rustling sounds and detect the earthy scent of livestock, along with the joy of renewal and new life. This was a haven which animals congregated to give birth, possibly cows or sheep belonging to the original farmer. The animals had sought the isolation, protection and privacy of this little wooded area for hundreds of years.

She inhaled a deep breath and heard muffled shouts, saw flames of torches being carried in the night, and felt the panic and fear that more than one of her ancestors had experienced. Her eyes snapped open as she realised there was a time where villagers had herded a witch to this spot and captured them. She exhaled and looked around, forcing her body to relax and accept what had happened long before she was born.

After a few minutes, she continued her walk to the other side of the trees and found the family cemetery. Once a wooden fence had surrounded the area but it had deteriorated and disintegrated, falling to the ground and embedding in the dirt. The cemetery appeared to be around the size of a large room and she could see five standing headstones and a few lying on the ground.

Commencing with the closest headstone, Niamh read the inscription, wiping off dirt and moss with her hand. This one was grey stone with black writing and was inscribed:

Bridget Conlon
1927 – 1969
Beloved mother of Agatha

This headstone belonged to her great grandmother who had died of probable cancer at 42 years of age, leaving enough money for her daughter, Agatha, to immigrate to Australia. This woman lived a hard life, surviving in the cottage where Niamh and Emma were currently residing, though it would have been a different dwelling back in that time without the modern fixtures and renovations. Bridget and Agatha would have experienced a dirt floor, cold stone walls and a leaking thatch roof. Her mother had told her this only a few months ago after she discovered she was descended from witches in Ennis, Ireland.

Niamh placed her hand on the headstone, feeling a connection with this witch who had left the world before her time. She had been the one to set the wheels in motion for the Australian witch family. As she touched the hard and rough surface of the headstone, she felt a shiver, and heard voices singing, saw a large bonfire and heard the jeering voices of others. She snapped her eyes open, realising that she had heard and felt similar when her grandmother, Agatha, had held her hand on her deathbed. It was as if she was seeing tiny snippets of her witch ancestry that her dead family member wanted to show her. Is that what had happened that day Agatha had died in front of her? Had Agatha tried to show her where she had come from?

Niamh walked to the next headstone and struggled to read the inscription which had worn down with age, the text under the death date illegible.

Aine Conlon
Died 1949

Niamh placed her hand on the headstone and again, experienced the whispers of the past although less intense. After a few minutes she withdrew her hand and moved on to the next. She could not read the inscriptions on any of the other headstones as they had worn away to rough stone, many covered in moss, and a few broken off and damaged from trespassers or storms. She could still detect small whispers from these older ancestors, despite lack of inscriptions. In one area where there were no headstones or plaques, only a few weeds, she felt whispers as she walked through and knew there were a number of ancestors buried without headstones.

Looking around the cemetery, she wondered how many men or boys were buried here. Although her family always seemed to be female, logic suggested there must be men involved. She knew they would have been normal people so would not be passing any whispers on to her after their death. The men in her family were the silent dead, the enablers of the witch bloodline.

Standing on the outside of the broken-down non-existent fence, Niamh scanned the cemetery, closed her eyes and gave thanks to those who had come before her. For the first time in her life she felt a strong connection, a belonging that she had never felt before. For the first time she was not an only child of a single mother, but the product of a long line of strong women and one of the flock.

With one more important task to perform, she closed her eyes, lifted her head with hands to the sky and concentrated, pushing her energy out. She could hear the voices of the dead singing in her ears as she concentrated and pushed. It took nearly all her physical strength and energy, but she kept pushing, kept her mind focused.

BANG!

A loud thunderclap crashed, deafening the wooded area for a moment as she opened her eyes and saw treetops above her and grey skies. Her eyes flashed amber momentarily and she was mildly aware of movement around her and the air swirling as if caught in a tornado, whipping her dark red hair around.

Gradually, the world calmed and the air became still as Niamh lowered her head and blinked a few times. The cemetery had transformed with headstones clean and upright, the wooden fence around the cemetery restored and whole, although still rustic, and the area within the cemetery was neatly mowed and weeded.

The cemetery was loved again and Niamh stood gazing over it, pleased that it was the least she could do for her own family. Feeling physically exhausted, she turned to walk back through the wooded area the way she had come when something caused her to halt. She held her breath, eyes scanning for a visual of what had caught her attention. All was still and silent, but she could detect a slight odour in the air and her witch senses picked it up. She twitched her nose and breathed in the slight odour just moments before she saw movement beside a tree and eyes peeking out at her.

It was the white bulldog with the brown patches.

Chapter 10
MONICA

"Dad, I've missed you so much. Why don't you come home?" asked Monica, sitting at the coffee shop in a Northcote shopping centre and looking across at her father, voice pleading.

"I've missed you too, sweetheart and I really want to keep up with what's going on, but … I can't go back to where I was. I've moved on. You know I have and life is different now. You don't even live at your childhood home now," said Tarren, holding her hand across the table and gazing at his pretty daughter.

"A life that doesn't include us?" asked Monica, her lip pouting in just the right measure as had worked on her father in previous times.

"Of course not. You're my family. You will always be my family, just as Anton, Beaton and Justin are, and all your children."

"Then, how can you turn your back on us, on Beaton and Justin … like you are?" she asked, voice quivering.

"I'm not turning my back on anyone. I visit Justin at least twice each week and Beaton once a week or fortnight. How often do you think I should be visiting?" he asked, eyebrow raised.

"That's not what I mean," Monica said, looking away and regrouping.

"How can you leave them in jail? Really? This has never happened in our family before. Why are you doing this?" she asked, eyes piercing into his.

"Come on, Monica. You know why. I told everyone to leave the witches alone. You were there and heard it. Beaton and Justin ignored me and attacked the witches, killing the old one and attacking the younger one, probably with a view to killing her. You were instrumental in helping them gain access if I remember rightly."

"But ... you do know, don't you Dad, that we are Grimm's and killing witches is what we do? Right?" said Monica, feeling justified and focusing on him for his answer.

Tarren sighed. "That is what we've done in the past, what we've been brought up to believe, instructed to do. True ... but times have changed and we have suffered terrible losses due to this stupid feud with the witches, just as they have. It needs to stop, and I ordered that it stop. The boys went against my decision and there are repercussions."

"So ... this is a punishment for disobeying you rather than because they broke a common person law or hurt any witches?" she asked, jumping on his wording.

"No. That's not what I mean."

"But Dad, don't you care that Justin is now permanently injured and will never be the same? Does that mean anything to you?" she asked.

"Of course I care about Justin. I'm in touch with his doctors and specialists almost daily and we are trying to determine what is best for him," Tarren responded.

"Is it best for him to be in prison forever?"

"He won't be in prison forever. The doctors think he won't go to court and face a trial due to his brain injury. He will remain in care where they can monitor him and find ways of helping him."

Monica let a tear slide down her cheek, turning her head to show the glistening tear to her father at its best angle. "What about Beaton, Dad? Can you really just sit back and leave him in that place? I just can't believe this is happening. You are punishing your own sons for performing something that's in our DNA and we are bred to do. Do you realise that? Do you?"

Tarren looked across at his angry and distressed daughter and understood her argument. He had grown up with the same principles and understanding that witches were the enemy and if they were to ever encounter a witch, their primary task was to eliminate. What was it that had changed him? He had thought differently before he met Lucinda all those years ago. Though a born and bred Grimm, he had a more logical mind that analysed the situation and could see where fault may lie and how futile the witch-hunt was.

"I do understand what you're saying, Monica. I really do, but we cannot continue to live like this forever. There is a time where we must let it go. We are in a modern and inclusive world and the witches have as much right to life as we do. Not only that but Justin and Beaton tried to kill their own half-sister, my daughter ... even after I told them not to."

"Yes ... your daughter. Your witch daughter." Monica let the words hang but her face showed disgust and a tinge of jealousy.

"She is a witch, yes," Tarren answered.

Monica pursed her lips, not saying anymore. She didn't need to.

"Please, Dad. I want you to seriously think about what you're doing. Will you do that, for me? Think about my brothers and how you're blaming them for doing what comes naturally to them. You wouldn't blame a cat for killing a mouse, would you? Please, Dad," Monica begged.

He looked at her, his pretty daughter with her shoulder length blonde hair, dark eyebrows and blue eyes. She had been involved in the attack on the witches as far as phoning the old witch, May, and pretending to be from an electrical company seeking to gain entry to the property. She had gained the invitation that led the boys to attack and kill May and try to harm Niamh.

"Monica," Tarren said gently, holding her hand in his. "I think about it all the time and I want to be there for the boys and support them, but they need to understand what they have done and at least show remorse."

He looked down at his watch, noting the time. "Oops. I must go. I have ,,, an appointment." He rose from the table, his coffee only half finished. Monica rose as well and put her arms out to halt him.

"Please think again about this situation, Dad. I'm counting on you to reconsider your position," she said calmly.

Tarren stepped over to her and kissed her forehead. "See you soon sweetheart. Say hello to the kids for me."

Monica watched him walk out of the coffee shop and in a snap decision, she followed, curious to see where he may be going and what appointment he had. She barely knew this man she had grown up, though he was barely ever home, quiet and ineffectual when he was and barely sober. He had always been tender and loving toward her and her siblings, but this man at the coffee shop was imposing, self-confident and dare she say, happy. How could he be happy when he had left the family, admitted to an affair twenty years ago that had resulted in an illegitimate child that was a witch? How could he be happy while his two sons were languishing in a prison cell? She needed to understand why this was happening and why he had changed so much.

She watched him stride along the arcade and she discreetly followed, keeping close to the shop fronts in case she needed to duck into a door to hide. He would sense her nearby but not assume she was following him. He would assume he was still sensing her because she was still in the vicinity of the shopping centre. If he walked out to his car then she would lose him as her car was probably parked nowhere near his, but he turned down another section of the shopping centre and she followed. She noted that he even walked more confidently, striding out as if he owned the world, a handsome man for forty-three years old.

They were near the supermarket entrance when she saw him raise his hand in greeting to someone. Quickly stepping behind a sunglasses display stand, she peeked out and saw him embrace a woman and touch foreheads together. This shocked her and she shivered involuntarily. The woman was wearing a long dress of some sort of oriental looking fabric and her hair was quite long at the back and a soft reddish colour. Then she saw that the woman had a trolley of groceries which her father started wheeling toward the carpark with the woman next to him.

Monica couldn't believe her eyes. Her father ... doing something domestic like wheel a shopping trolley of groceries? What had happened to him? Who was that woman? They obviously were together and intimate. She felt sick and took deep breaths to control the feeling that had overtaken her and the strong urgent desire to send magic to harm that woman.

The woman was not magic or Monica would have sensed it but what completely blew her mind was when the woman turned sidewards and Monica could see her outline.

This woman was pregnant and the baby was magic.

Chapter 11
NIAMH

The white bulldog trailed Niamh as she trudged back up the hill toward the cottage after her visit to the family cemetery. The dog was sufficiently behind that it could easily escape if she turned on it but was no longer attempting to hide as it had the day before. Niamh contemplated the dog as she walked, perplexed at the strange behaviour which seemed very undoglike. It was as if the dog was keeping track of what she was doing and where she was going, trailing her every move. She wondered about the owner.

It took her longer to ascend the hill than it anticipated as she felt physically exhausted from her time at the cemetery. Restoring the cemetery had proven to be the most intense magical feat she had attempted, and she felt the after-effects, her energy depleted.

As she reached the summit and walked around to the front of the cottage, a compact white van sat parked beside the cottage front fence and she couldn't see any sign of a driver. The fact that no one could be seen inside the van could only mean the driver was inside the cottage. She wondered who it could possibly be as they didn't know anyone yet and were not expecting any deliveries. Since the attack on May, Niamh had an anxiety about leaving a friend or family member alone where they were vulnerable. Even feeling secure in the knowledge that a magical person would not penetrate her urine fence border, it was totally useless against a normal person and she knew normal people could be more evil than magic ones.

Feeling a sense of panic, Niamh swung open the gate, raced down the path building speed, threw the front door open and entered the cottage, primed and ready to zap the offender if need be. Her hair had fluffed and was standing up through static electricity with small sparks igniting around her and her eyes had momentarily turned amber.

CRASH!

Dead silence ensued and shock as two faces stared back at her, eyes wide with alarm at her sudden appearance. Emma sat at the small kitchen table and with her was Collins O'Brien, enjoying a cup of coffee. The two of them stared at Niamh as if she were an alien newly arrived on earth and it took several minutes for the shock to wear off. Niamh had eyes on Collins trying to determine why he was here, how he knew where they lived and what he wanted. Everything looked innocent but she held her position silently, until Collins spoke.

"Good morning to you, Niamh. Nice to see you again. Emma invited me over to say hello and she tells me you need help purchasing a car. I'm happy to be of assistance."

His Irish accent made her smile with its melodious tone and she had to admit he did have a captivating smile. His intentions seemed genuine, yet she was still hesitant to be his friend. She knew the issue was her own and not of his making. Relaxing and summoning a smile, she walked over to pour herself a coffee.

"Hi Collins. Sorry I startled you. I was worried Emma may be held prisoner by some mentally deranged asylum escapee," she said in jest.

Collins gave a small laugh and Emma, who had been holding her breath waiting to see how Niamh would react, relaxed and laughed too. The tense standoff over, the three of them spent the next hour chatting and deciding how to proceed with the purchase of a small car.

"I can pick you up tomorrow and take you to a few car yards to look at what cars are available. I know a few in the area. I'd also like to show you our beautiful town," said Collins.

"Don't you work?" asked Niamh.

"I do, indeed. I teach music at schools, but in July we have summer holidays, so I have a few weeks break," Collins replied.

He glanced around the room and studied the aga stove. "You know, I've never been inside this cottage, but I know it well. When I was a small lad, my great grandfather used to tell me stories of this cottage and that witches lived here. I think he was trying to scare me but I was fascinated and used to ride my bicycle out here to sit and watch the house. Maybe I thought I would see magic or witches. Of course, there was just a family renting the place at that time but I had a good imagination and used to dream about the witches every night."

Emma glanced at Niamh and noted she had a funny grin on her face, trying not to laugh at his recollections. She turned back to Collins feeling confident Niamh was ok to share her heritage with him. "You know ... Niamh's family lived in this cottage for many generations. Maybe your great grandfather knew some of them?"

"Really?" He turned to look at Niamh, his eyes wide and childhood fascination rekindled.

She laughed. "My grandmother was born here and moved to Australia when she was about twenty years old. Her ancestors lived here for many years before that."

"So, you are an Irish girl after all. You look Irish. Oh, sorry about the witches' comment," he said apologetically, feeling guilty that he had mentioned it.

Emma laughed loudly and Niamh giggled.

"What?" asked Collins looking from one laughing girl to the other.

Neither said anything but looked at each other trying to contain their giggles. Emma nodded to Niamh, a secret signal to indicate she should show Collins some magic. Niamh nodded her head silently and looked down at his coffee cup. Within a minute, it started turning around in circles on the table. The slight sound and movement of the cup turning on the wooden surface brought Collins' attention down to the cup where he saw the cup slowly spinning on the spot. He blinked and stared for a few seconds, then jumped to his feet.

"JAYSUS! What the … ?"

The girls giggled again. Suddenly, the cup levitated off the table and hovered in the air then slowly lowered to sit on the table again. Niamh relaxed and looked at Collins.

"My family who lived in this cottage, they were witches, just as I am," she said.

A few minutes of silence followed as Collins stared from Niamh to Emma, and back to Niamh. No one needed any magic to see that he was trying to determine if what he was seeing was real or if he was being played. With a slight nod of the head, he moved forward and slowly sat down at the table again, staring at the cup suspiciously and then at Niamh.

"Ok. Convince me. Tell me the story," Collins said, not quite ready to accept this explanation.

"Well … only seven months ago, my mother talked me into visiting my grandmother on her deathbed to say goodbye," Niamh began.

"Didn't she bribe you with pizza?" asked Emma.

"She did. I only vaguely knew that I had a grandmother. I don't really remember having any association with her. Anyway, she was in this bed and suddenly, my mother and aunts left the room and I was alone with this dying old lady."

Niamh glanced across at Emma and could see both she and Collins were invested in the story, leaning forward slightly to listen. "So, she made this weird noise and I walked up close to her to see if she was ok. She grabbed my wrist and said something about bestowing on me and that I was the one, then she died, right there in front of me."

Emma had heard this tale before so she concentrated on watching Collins for his reaction.

"After that, my mother and aunts kept asking me if the dying grandmother had given me anything and I had no idea what they were talking about. Anyway … it turns out my grandmother was a witch from Ennis who came to Australia when she was about twenty years old. Her family had been here for a long time and always been witches. Her mother wanted her to move to another country because the people in the town were cruel to her and she wanted a better life for her daughter." Niamh took a sip of coffee.

"My grandmother made a lifelong friend with another witch in Melbourne called Maybelline … May. So, my mother and aunts told me that my grandmother had bestowed her magic on me before she died. I thought it was total bullshit but May taught me how to use my magic although I'm not very good at it. It seems I was born with magic but never knew and after my grandmother bestowed her magic on me … I guess it became too powerful to hide anymore."

"Your magic abilities seem to be very tied to your emotional state of mind," said Emma. "When you are angry, your magic is very powerful and … not always in control." Emma started giggling.

Collins looked at Emma puzzled at her sudden fit of giggles.

"On the plane over here, there was a guy kicking Niamh's seat and wouldn't stop, so she caused him to shit his pants," said Emma.

"Jesus, Mary and Joseph!" said Collins, looking worried and frowning.

"It's ok," assured Niamh. "I only do that to arseholes, and you're not an arsehole."

Collins grinned at the half compliment. "What do you mean, the town were cruel to her?"

"Well, I'm not really sure. I think the word my mother used was 'ostracised', so I guess being a witch was seen as a bad thing many years ago." Niamh shrugged her shoulders. "Did your great grandfather say anything bad about the witches?"

Collins shook his head. "Not at all but I know my mother is superstitious and grew up that way. Many of the town people would be the same, and the town is known to have witches such as the famous Biddy Early who was a healer. I guess witches were a feared thing."

"I wonder if she was a relative of yours," said Emma, looking at Niamh.

"I'm sure there are other witch families living around this area," said Niamh.

Chapter 12
LUCINDA

Dark had descended outside as Lucinda busied herself in the kitchen about to plate up dinner when she heard Tarren's phone ring. He fished the phone out of his pocket and frowned at the call number before walking across the room to answer. Lucinda could hear the rise in his voice and see from his body language that the call was causing him distress.

When he turned and walked back to her, his face was lined with concern and he appeared to have aged ten years.

"I'm sorry, Lucinda. Can you put my plate aside for later? I must go to the hospital at the prison. Justin has been beaten up by another prisoner."

"WHAT?" asked Lucinda, shocked.

"I don't know all the details yet, but I must go and see him and find out what's happened," said Tarren, looking around for his jacket.

"Yes, of course. Go," urged Lucinda.

It was after 11pm when he returned, tired and stressed. Lucinda had waited up for him, concerned about his emotional state. She heated his dinner plate as he relayed what had occurred.

"A guard found Justin in his cell, beaten up and sent him to the hospital. When they viewed the CCTV footage, they saw another prisoner open the door, walk into Justin's cell, beat him black and blue and then leave. He has a black eye, broken nose, a few cracked ribs, split lip and bruising. He's ok but doesn't understand what has happened," Tarren said, voice rushed from the stress of the situation.

"How can another prisoner just walk into his cell? I thought he was in remand and in isolation," asked Lucinda.

"They shouldn't be able to. Not at all. This guy was in prison for murder and yet, it seems a guard turned a blind eye and let him in, or was possibly bribed to let him in. I don't know." Tarren shook his head in frustration. Lucinda could see the pain in his eyes and knew of his battle with the Grimm family regarding the fact that Justin and Beaton were in jail at all.

"Justin told me that his attacker kept saying he was doing it for May. He didn't even know what 'May' meant."

"So, there's a prisoner in there who was possibly a client of May's, and he did this out of revenge. Is that what you think happened?" Lucinda asked.

"Yeah. I think so. With all the publicity surrounding what happened to May, the boys are well-known, even to the other prisoners. I don't know what to do. How can I leave Justin in that place the way he is? He's a sitting duck and doesn't even know what he did. This injury has taken away his memory of what happened, and I just can't see how he could face justice when he doesn't understand anything."

"I understand," Lucinda said, and she did. For weeks after the murder of May and attack on Niamh, she had wanted to personally strangle both Justin and Beaton, wring their skinny pale necks for taking away her godmother and trying to harm her daughter. She still wanted revenge in so many ways, but if it were true that

Justin had suffered a traumatic brain injury and lost memory and brain function, how could he be held responsible for his actions?

"Wait until your family find out what has happened. That is one heck of a storm brewing," she said.

"I tried to see Beaton to tell him what had happened, but he refused to see me. He obviously already knows. Maybe prisoners talk or maybe someone knew what was about to happen. He will be on the phone to the rest of the family tonight and there'll be mayhem tomorrow." Tarren shook his head in despair.

"What do you think will happen?" asked Lucinda.

Tarren put his arm around Lucinda and stared into her eyes. She was so innocent, so vulnerable and he felt so protective of her and their unborn child. His family were furious his two sons were being held in captivity but once they found out Lucinda was pregnant, and the baby was another witch, mayhem would hardly touch the surface of what they were capable of.

"I really don't know but I think things are starting to get serious with the family."

Chapter 13
NIAMH

Collins chauffeured Niamh and Emma to several car yards in the county to inspect the second-hand cars available. The morning was wet and miserable, their first wet day and after two hours of searching, the girls reached the conclusion that their budget did not extend to the purchase of a vehicle, even a second-hand one. Both parents had been generous with an allocation of money for the Irish adventure, but cars were more expensive than they had expected. The last thing they wanted was a super cheap lemon of a car that they would have trouble with. Neither girl wanted to ask their parents for more money as they felt fortunate in the generosity they had already been shown.

Feeling disheartened, they agreed to tour the town with Collins as tour guide. After driving around for thirty minutes with Collins spruiking the features of the town in a comical parody of a tour guide, their moods had lifted. Ennis was such a fascinating and beautiful town, and Collins enthusiastically pointed out the River Fergus, the old bridges and gave a detailed history of the town. Eventually, they parked in town and Collins led the girls to the Ennis Friary, a Franciscan friary from the 13th century. The rain eased as the three of them explored the ruins and marvelled at the history and character and then on to the Clare Museum. As their mood lightened, so did the weather and they wandered through narrow cobbled lanes and inspected the quaint shops. For two girls born and bred in Australia which was not settled until late in the 18th century and Melbourne not until 1835, the history and age of buildings and town was fascinating.

Stopping at a little café in a busy laneway, they sat inside, ordering coffee and fruit scones. Collins talked enthusiastically about his town and all the other sights the two girls should try to visit in the time they were staying including the Clare Abbey, Cliffs of Moher, Bunratty Castle and the Mill Water Wheel. They joked they would need a few years to investigate all the places Collins mentioned.

"Thank you for your help with the car yards and showing us around," said Niamh, in a rare show of appreciation. Her face blushed at the rarity of the occasion.

"You are most welcome," replied Collins. "I won't say too much yet, but I might know of the perfect car for you both, but I need to check with its owner first."

"Ooh, that sounds exciting," said Emma.

Collins smiled secretively,

"I hoped we didn't scare you off too much yesterday telling you about Niamh and her family," said Emma.

"Not at all. I'm fascinated. I was asking my mother some questions about witches last night. She's always been so superstitious, I thought she may not want to speak of it but it turns out she's a bit fascinated too," he responded.

"She said there's a witch living at a town very close to here who is popular with the locals and lives openly as a witch, but my mother hasn't met her. A few of her friends have visited for herbs and gifts. She also mentioned one in town here that everyone is afraid of and seems a bit nasty, like a bad witch."

"Oh, really? Like an evil witch?" asked Niamh.

"With a wart on her nose and a black pointed hat?" asked Emma and giggled.

Do you know where she lives?" asked Niamh.

"Not the evil one, but the one who sells herbs and gifts is Molly Byrne from Inagh, not far from here. Were you planning to visit other witches while you're here?" Collins asked.

Niamh paused. "Maybe ... I think so. As we mentioned, I only found out I was a witch after my grandmother died and May, the old witch who was mentoring me has also died so I have no one to ask questions or teach me anything. This might be an opportunity to learn more. I'm not sure I want to come across an evil witch though." Niamh shivered. "I'm not sure how to handle her."

"Do you think the one at Inagh is a true witch?" Emma directed her question to Niamh.

"What's a true witch?" asked Collins.

Emma turned back to answer Collins' question. "It's someone who is born magical and is naturally a witch, as opposed to someone who is normal but learns how to make potions, charms and even cast spells."

"Ok. I'll see if I can find out any more information on the evil one. By the way, my mother really wants to meet you both," Collins said.

Niamh noticed his face had blushed, and he was trying to downplay it. She looked across at Emma to see if Emma had noticed and it seemed not. Emma was blissfully watching Collins and hanging on his every word. She saw Collins look up at Emma and a little smile escaped. It dawned on Niamh that he was keen for his mother to meet Emma as they seemed to be developing some sort of relationship. She sighed and sat back, watching the two of them and pleased because despite only knowing Collins for a short time, she had a good feeling about him. He radiated a calm, warm and friendly persona and he already felt like family.

Chapter 14
MONICA

Monica's eyes scanned the room and she nodded to each person present in acknowledgement. The entire Melbourne side of the Grimm family had heeded her urgent call to a family meeting and arrived on time. Her mother, Marion and grandmother, Doris sat at the far end of the table. The glass doors between the dining room and the living room had been opened to accommodate the large number of people. She'd never seen everyone assembled such as this before. It was a tribe, her tribe.

On one side, she noted her immediate family, husband, Jonty, and her two young children, her brother Beaton's wife, Gwenda with their three children, her older brother, Anton, his wife, Carina and their two children. On the other side and spilling out into the living room was her father, Tarren's family consisting of his sisters, Shera and Annastacia plus their husbands, children and grandchildren and his brother Hardy, his wife, children and grandchildren.

The children were too noisy for such a serious family discussion so after some deliberations, it was determined that all children under seventeen years of age would be relocated to the sitting room and the older teenagers would care for the babies and younger children. Once this had been accomplished, Monica looked around at the serious faces and was felt ready to commence the meeting.

"Thank you everyone for attending at such short notice. I don't remember ever seeing everyone in one room before and it's pleasing to see how we've grown in numbers." Monica scanned the faces as she welcomed everyone, noting their attention was on her, wondering what this was all about.

"I'm sorry but I have not called you all here for a pleasant family reunion. In fact, it is with great distress that I am here before you tonight to fill you in on the current situation."

The faces in front of her were showing concern as they waited.

"As you know, my brothers, Justin and Beaton, are being held on remand for the murder of that old witch and my father, Tarren, is allowing this to happen and even encouraging it. You all are aware of this, but tonight … I'm here to tell you what you don't know."

A few grumbles could be heard in the room and Monica hesitated, with the intention of building the drama. She had always delighted in her drama queen status and being the only female child in her immediate family of boys, enabled this.

"On the day the old witch was killed, my baby brother, Justin, suffered a traumatic brain injury which occurred when the young witch used magic on him. She tried to fry his brain. This brain injury has affected him to the extent that he cannot remember the incident, barely knows who he is anymore and cannot function without assistance."

The room suddenly erupted with people talking, groaning and asking questions. To the great majority in the room, this was the first they had heard of this situation. Monica held up her hand to quieten the noise.

"He is being treated in the remand centre, tests are being performed and at this stage, we do not know if he will be like this forever or not. Yesterday, another prisoner broke into his room and beat him up and he is now in the prison hospital with facial injuries and broken ribs."

Again, the room erupted with shock and horror. She saw her aunt, Shera addressing her mother, Marion. "Marion, did you know about this? Did you know about Justin's brain injury?"

Marion had been sitting quietly, and Monica detected a sheepish look on her face. "Umm, yes but I knew he was being treated," she said weakly.

"Did you know he had been attacked by another prisoner?" Shera asked.

Marion nodded. "I received a phone call but they assured me he was ok."

Shera turned away, her face angry and furious whispers could be heard. Marion's excuses were not winning her any fans in the family.

"You may also have heard that my father, Tarren, has put a block on their magic abilities and is refusing to allow them to be released. He is insisting they are punished and jailed." Monica looked around at the faces and could see angry looks.

"Punished for what?" asked Hardy's wife, Helga.

"He ordered our family to leave the witches alone and he is angry that his orders were not followed," Monica responded.

"Why would he order the witches to be left alone?" asked one of Shera's sons. "Isn't that what we are known for? Hunting witches?"

Monica who had been seated at the head of the table, slowly stood up. She wanted all attention to be on her as she told her family the news as she knew it.

"Ok. There are things you don't know about my father and you need to know." She paused dramatically and shook her head tossing her blonde hair to the side. "Twenty years ago, he had an affair with a person who was the daughter of a witch and they had a child who turned out to be a witch."

She could hear gasps of horror from the side of the room that had been unaware of the situation.

"My father ordered us to leave the young witch alone because she is his daughter. Technically, he didn't tell my brothers they couldn't kill the old witch. Now, he wants to punish his own sons for doing what comes naturally to them. Not only that, but his own witch daughter has damaged Justin's brain with her magic and now poor Justin is just a shell of who he used to be. The witch daughter is not being punished but he is punishing his own family. Justin and Beaton can't even use magic anymore because my father has blocked them."

She could hear angry murmurs and knew that her aunts and uncle had probably heard rumours about her father but this was the first time they were hearing the truth.

"You were right to call a family meeting, Monica," said Anton. "Something needs to be done about this situation."

"It gets worse," said Monica. The entire room fell silent, watching her and waiting to hear what could be any worse than their beloved Tarren betraying his own sons and producing a witch daughter from another woman outside of his marriage.

"Six months ago, my father left our family to go live with the witch family. He has resumed a relationship with the woman who is the mother of his witch daughter and ... she is pregnant with a magic baby."

The room erupted into chaos as everyone jumped to their feet, angry and yelling. The fury in the room became tangible with light bulbs shattering and small fragments of glass tinkling as they landed on the large dining table. The air felt electrified and eerie growling could be heard.

Hardy, being the most senior male of the Melbourne Grimm family and technically in charge, walked over to where Monica was standing at the head of the table and raised his hands to quieten the room. Tarren was his little brother and he had also heard rumours but now it was time for him to take control of this meeting.

"SIT!"

Hardy called out the order and the room obeyed, quietening down instantly. Monica sat to his right, happy that she had accomplished what she set out to do and now, Uncle Hardy would take charge.

"Thank you, Monica for bringing this to our attention. You've done the right thing and been the dutiful sister," he smiled at her, dismissed her and then turned to Marion at the other end of the table.

"Marion, I am disappointed to hear what amounts to your neglect of your own sons, neglect of your marriage and with-holding important information from the family. I will be speaking to Sydney and we will decide what should be done."

Marion tried to open her mouth to speak but he raised his hand and dismissed her. She sat staring at the table after this rebuke. Speaking to Sydney was the worst possible outcome for her.

"There are a few major concerns here that we need to address." Hardy counted them on his fingers.

"One ... Justin's brain injury. He is to be released immediately and treated at a proper hospital and with specialist care. I want to see the reports on his injuries." Monica nodded, knowing Hardy was powerful enough to over-ride her father and have the boys released.

"Two ... Beaton is also to be released immediately on bail for now with a view to having the charges dropped."

Beaton's wife burst into tears of relief. She pulled out a tissue to blow her nose.

"Three ... I need to talk to Sydney about this blocking of magic. I was not aware of it and I don't know how to counter it. Does anyone in this room know about a magic block?" He looked around and everyone was shaking their head negatively.

"Four ... Tarren, my baby brother. He needs to be called to account for his actions. Once again, I will be speaking with Sydney and we will decide what is to happen to him and how he will be punished. I am very disappointed with this state of affairs and agree, something needs to be done. Tarren can live his life however he sees fit, but he is not to disrespect the Grimm family, and he cannot breed witches."

Hardy held out the fifth finger on his right hand and everyone's attention riveted to his finger.

"Tarren's woman, unborn child and young witch cannot be allowed to exist. I will confirm this with Sydney but they will be eliminated."

Chapter 15
NIAMH

"What are you doing?" asked Niamh, noting that Emma had her head buried in a notebook and had been writing for hours, obviously concentrating.

Emma looked up and across at Niamh silently, and there was something about the look on her face that made Niamh feel nervous. "What's wrong?" she asked, worried.

It took another minute for Emma to answer. "Well … you know I studied genetics and Mendelian theory in the last year of school?"

She saw the blank look on Niamh's face. "You know, the breeding possibilities based on genetics. I was fascinated with it and studied it, even visiting horse studs to talk about the possibilities of certain colours of foals from different coloured parents?"

Niamh nodded but pulled a face, indicating she vaguely recalled but hadn't paid that much attention to it.

"So … I was playing with some possibilities of your family … with dominant and recessive genes."

"My family?" asked Niamh. "What do you mean?"

Emma hesitated then stood and walked over to sit on the floor near Niamh, notebook and pen in hand. "A few things are interesting with your family, such as your grandmother being a witch, but she had three daughters who were not witches, and then suddenly, a granddaughter is a witch. How does that happen?"

Niamh blinked a few times and silently acknowledged that she had wondered the same thing.

"Do you want me to show you what I was working on?" Emma studied Niamh's face. Niamh nodded.

"Ok. Well, everyone gets a pair of genes from their parents, right?"

Niamh nodded. She at least knew that much.

"So, my theory is that the human gene is dominant over the witch gene. So, we can write normal people as Hh and witches as Wh." Emma wrote on a blank page of the notebook.

"Huh? Why Hh for normal people? Why not HH if humans are dominant?" asked Niamh.

"Well, if normal humans were HH then there would never be any witches because normal people would always be dominant. So, the normal genes are Hh, dominant and recessive, and every offspring of a normal person will carry the H or the h. Ok?"

Niamh nodded.

"Witch is always W." Emma saw the frown on Niamh's face.

"Why aren't witches Ww then?" Niamh asked.

"Witches don't breed with other witches. There is no such thing as a pure witch as there are no male witches. They always breed with a normal person so always have a normal human gene. Is that correct?" she asked.

"It is," said Niamh, realising this for the first time. Witches were always female so needed a male to reproduce, a normal person.

"Therefore, the offspring of a witch with a normal person can be WH or Wh. My hypothesis is that anyone inheriting the WH genes would end up a normal person as the human gene H is dominant over the witch gene and anyone inheriting the Wh would end up a witch because the witch gene is dominant over the recessive h gene." Emma continued.

"So, my grandmother, Agatha would have been Wh?" she asked.

"Yes. Now, when Agatha had children to a normal person, we look at the four possibilities of Wh and Hh. The possibilities are WH which would be normal person, hH which would be normal person, hh which would be normal person and Wh which would a witch." Emma halted and watched Niamh catch up.

Niamh sat up in her chair. "Three out of four would be normal and one would be a witch?" she asked and saw Emma nod. Suddenly, she was very interested in what Emma was relaying. Her mother and two sisters were normal people and yet, her mother had produced a witch. "So, chances are if Agatha had a fourth child, it could have been a witch?"

"Yes, technically, though the one in four theory is averaged over a large sample." Emma saw Niamh's face go blank. "So, if Agatha had twenty baby girls, the chances are that five of them would be witches but not necessarily baby number 4, baby number 8, baby number 12, baby number 16 and baby number 20. The order may be jumbled up. Do you understand?"

"Ok. I get it. So, how does this work with me? What about Grimm genetics?" asked Niamh.

"Well, that is an unknown. I can only tell you the possibilities." Emma said, cautiously.

"Go on."

"Grimms do not breed with normal people, as a rule, so they are homozygous which means they are pure GG not Gg or Gh or GH."

Niamh nodded.

"A witch must be dominant over a Grimm because you are living proof. You are a witch and not a Grimm." Emma said.

"But … my mother is not a witch. She is a normal person," challenged Niamh.

"Ok. So, I think your mother is WH and with a normal person being dominant over a witch, then she turned out normal, but she carries the W – witch gene. When she produced a baby with Tarren, the possibilities are: WG, HG, WG and HG." Emma paused and watched as Niamh looked at the writing on the notebook.

"WG is witch because you said witch is dominant over Grimm."

Emma nodded.

"Two out of four would be witches?" she asked.

"Yes," answered Emma.

"Ok. So, what is HG going to be?" asked Niamh, looking at Emma with a worried look.

"I don't know. We don't have any data to be able to determine if the normal person gene H is dominant over Grimm or Grimm is dominant."

Niamh stared into space for a few minutes. "Potentially … if my mother and Tarren have more babies, they could be Grimms?" she asked, her voice raising slightly.

"Possibly," Emma admitted. "Or they may be normal … but you already know this one is a witch, don't you?"

"Yes. It's definitely a witch." Niamh turned away, suddenly worried. Could she be wrong? She knew the baby had magic but was it the right sort of magic? She assumed it would be a witch as well but now, she had concerns.

"There's one other thing ..." said Emma, quietly.

"What?"

"Well, it's also possible that when the witch gene W is crossed with the Grimm gene G it could create a mutation," Emma said.

"A MUTATION? You mean me?" Niamh's voice rose.

"It's all unknown of course," said Emma, smiling weakly.

"So, what are my possibilities if I choose a normal person as my partner? What will my children be?" she asked.

Emma paused, looking down at the notebook. "Umm ... if you are WG and have babies with a Hh then the possibilities are WH, Wh, GH and Gh ... umm ... normal, witch, unknown and unknown but possibly normal and Grimm."

"GRIMM?"

"Maybe not. We don't know. If you are a mutation then it will all be different."

"In what way?"

"Well ... you could be dominant with a mutation gene and have witchy Grimms."

"WITCHY GRIMMS?"

Emma smiled at her friend. "Niamh, I do think you are a witchy Grimm."

Chapter 16
TARREN

Tarren had been busy for the past few days with the sale of a few properties from his portfolio and attempting to finalise a property settlement with Marion via a solicitor. Marion was proving difficult to deal with and ignored every letter, email or phone call from his solicitor. He had no desire to see her in person but was starting to think it was the only way to negotiate a settlement in lieu of a divorce once the twelve months of separation was over.

He paused and looked at his phone, smiling at the text message Lucinda had sent only moments earlier.

Going to make charms with my sisters. Our little girl very active today.

If only the rest of his life could be as happy and content as his new life with Lucinda and the impending birth of their second child. He stared across his desk at a photo of his four children when they were younger. Four confident and good-looking children stared back at him from the picture frame, feeling they owned the world. Now, Beaton wouldn't speak to him, Justin didn't seem to know him, Monica was not happy with him and he hadn't even spoken to Anton in many months, almost six when he thought of it. Feeling guilty, he reached for his phone to speak to Anton and ask how his family were. The call rang for a few seconds and cut out. The person at the other end killed the call. Tarren reasoned he must have called at a bad time for Anton and he'd try again later in the day.

He phoned the doctor at the prison hospital for an update on Justin.

"Dr James, Tarren Grimm here. I was looking for an update on Justin. How are the facial injuries going? Is he back in his cell now?"

There was a dead silence on the other end of the line and Tarren waited for a minute. He glanced at his phone, wondering if the call had died but it was still active.

"Dr. James, are you there?" he asked.

"Err … yes. Umm … Justin is not here anymore."

"Oh, he's back in his cell then," said Tarren.

"No. No. He's gone. He … was released into the care of his family. You didn't know?" asked the doctor, confused.

"No. I didn't know. Can you tell me when this happened?" asked Tarren.

"The day before yesterday I believe. I've got his test results and reports here but haven't heard where to send them yet."

"Ok. Ok. Leave it with me and I'll find out where you should send them. Thanks Doctor."

Tarren hung up quickly and stared at the phone. He repeated the words the doctor had just told him - Justin was released into the care of family. How was this possible? Who? Which family member? Could it have been Monica?

Quickly, he tried to phone Monica, but the call went unanswered which seemed strange as she always had her phone nearby and was quick to answer. Suddenly, Anton not answering and Monica not answering rang alarm bells in his head, along with the fact that someone in the family had disobeyed his orders and released Justin.

He left the office and drove across town to the remand centre to visit Beaton. If Justin had been released, had Beaton as well? He had to see for himself it Beaton was there and if he would agree to a visit. As he drove, his mind jumped to various scenarios that may have occurred and all of them worried him. Someone in the family had over-ridden his orders again and used magic to secure a release for Justin and possibly, Beaton. To expressly go against his orders was a bad deal in the Grimm family and was seen as war-like.

Thirty minutes later, he climbed back in his car and sat staring out the windscreen. As expected, Beaton was no longer in the remand centre, having been released into the custody of family. The charges were still outstanding but suddenly, bail had become available and Beaton had been bailed. The person who signed Beaton out was Hardy Grimm, Tarren's big brother.

Now, Tarren knew there was trouble brewing as Hardy was senior in the wider family to Tarren and could over-ride almost everything Tarren did. For Hardy to have the two boys released meant that Hardy knew all the details, did not agree with what Tarren was doing and was outwardly declaring war with Tarren. This was almost unheard of in the Grimm family with everyone respecting the views and family of each other.

No doubt Hardy was now aware of Tarren leaving Marion and living with Lucinda and he could imagine the absolute repulsion Hardy would have felt. He was unsure what to do at this point and the last thing he wanted was the entire Grimm family at war with him, especially with Lucinda's pregnancy.

He fished his phone out of his pocket and phoned his mother, Dora. She answered within a few rings, her voice not as loud as it usually was, and he could tell she was stepping into another room before she said much.

"Tarren. What on earth are you up to?" Her voice was whispered.

"Hello, Mum. How are you?" he said, trying to sound casual.

"Well, I've been better. You've upset the whole family now," she said as if chastising a schoolboy.

"Have I? Why is that? Who's upset?" he asked, feigning ignorance.

"Monica called a family meeting with all of Melbourne here and told them about you forcing Justin and Beaton to stay in jail, and about Justin having something wrong with his brain. Everyone was upset and Hardy ordered their release," she informed him.

"He shouldn't have done that. It's none of his business," said Tarren.

"Of course it is. He's head of Melbourne. Not only that but he's been speaking with Sydney and I think my father is coming down to sort things out in Melbourne. Everyone's upset about your situation with the witch family."

She said it so casually and simply, but Tarren's heart almost stopped at those words. Her father, his grandfather was Gunther, an eighty-two year old man who was the head of all the Grimm family in Australia and was legendary for his ill temper and magical abilities. He was recognised in the Grimm world as a formidable character with a huge amount of power. If Gunther was coming to Melbourne, then Tarren was in serious trouble.

"Ok. Thanks for letting me know," he said, trying to keep his voice calm.

"Word of advice. You might want to think about fixing these problems before he gets here."

Chapter 17
LUCINDA

Lucinda retrieved the two bouquets of colourful flowers she had gently laid on the back seat of the car. Carrying them across her left arm, she headed across the cemetery to the site of her parents and May's headstones. She hadn't visited the cemetery for a few months and felt guilty that she was neglecting her loved ones.

May had been gone for six months and she had only visited her once since the funeral. She made excuses to herself that she had been very busy in the past few months but she also acknowledged that she found the visit distressing. The trauma from the incident was still very raw and when she had visited, her mind pictured May struggling to breathe, blood down her chest and hear her last words before she died.

'Loved you girls like you were my own.'

The shock of walking into May's house that day and the panic that ensued remained with Lucinda and she relived the scene at night when she tried to sleep and wondered if there was anything she could have done that would have changed the outcome.

She reached the two plots side-by-side and removed the old, dried flower bouquets that were still sitting in urns placed just in front of the headstones. One of her sisters must have brought these ones as they didn't look familiar to her.

Humming a tune May used to sing to her when she was a child, she bent over and pulled out a few small weeds that dared to grow too close to the headstones and then, satisfied all was in order, she placed the flowers neatly in front of the headstones.

In between the two graves, there was just a large enough gap for her to step sidewards down and then sit on the concrete edging as she always did. From this vantage point, she felt the closest to both parents as well as May. She read the epitaphs as always when visiting.

AGATHA CAITLIN FLYNN
1950 – 2018
A True Witch

CIARAN SEAN FLYNN
1948 – 1979
Beloved husband and father

MAYBELLINE SARAH CONNOR
1952 – 2018
Loved by everyone

Pocketed between the graves of her loved ones, Lucinda hummed and thought about the three people lost to her. She wished she had a memory of her father but he died when she was so young. May always told her what a wonderful man he was and how different her mother had been before he died. All Lucinda remembered was a quiet, sullen mother who never seemed happy and went about daily tasks with such grief and distress etched on her face.

The Grimm family had taken so much from her, including killing her father, eliminating him from her memory, and they had taken May, the godmother and pseudo mother to her and her two sisters. Although it was cancer that ultimately killed her mother and not the Grimm family, in many ways they had taken her away as well, because her mother was a different person after the death of her husband. The Grimm's robbed the three sisters of a happy mother who loved life.

Lucinda felt the baby moving inside her and smiling, she gently touched her stomach. As much as the Grimm's had taken from her, Tarren Grimm had in return, given her so much. He had given her Niamh, her daughter twenty years ago and now he was giving her love, happiness and another child, and this time, the child would grow up in the love of both parents. There was so much to look forward to and she wished May was still alive to enjoy this time. The only downside was that Tarren was a Grimm, and there would always be issues with his family, and in particular, his sons upcoming court case and imprisonment.

The baby kicked with such ferocity, that it took her breath away. She wondered if the baby knew it was in the presence of two deceased true witches, Lucinda thought to herself. Was it possible that an unborn child or an unborn witch could perceive that?

Lucinda stood and leaned out to touch her parent's headstone and then May's as her way of saying goodbye for now. She stepped out of the gap between the graves and slowly began her walk across the cemetery when she felt eyes on her, a creepy feeling with her skin crawling and hackles raised. She stopped and scanned the cemetery around her slowly but no obvious sign of anyone who was not a visitor.

Lucinda continued walking but she was more aware of her surroundings and could feel the baby still kicking furiously inside her. Was the child trying to tell her something? She reached her car in the carpark and as she opened the door, she again felt she was being watched. Quickly turning, she caught a glimpse of a blonde head as it disappeared behind another parked vehicle. She wondered if her imagination was running away with her but felt her skin crawl as she entered the car and shut the door.

Chapter 18
NIAMH

BEEP! BEEP! BEEP!

Niamh and Emma raced to the front door of the cottage wondering what the honking sound was and opened it to see a small black car parked at the front gate. The door to the driver's side opened and Collins stepped out grinning and gave a little wave. Puzzled the girls walked over to meet him on the outside of the gate.

"What's the craic?" Collins said, grinning at the two girls.

"Huh?" said Niamh, glancing at Emma to see if she knew what he had just said. Emma shrugged.

"This car belongs to my great grandfather and the oul fella's going to live in an aged care home so he's agreed to sell. It's grand, a Ford Fiesta and in great condition, not driven much," said Collins.

The girls walked around the car, admiring how neat and tidy it looked and so much better than the cars they had recently viewed at car yards.

"Yeah, but how much does he want for it?" asked Niamh, guessing the price would be well out of their range.

"€4,000. A bargain," replied Collins, grinning broadly.

"€4,000! What? That's too cheap. Why would he only be asking €4,000?" asked Emma.

"Well … money doesn't mean much to him. He's ninety-two years old now and won't be driving anymore. He said because you're my friends, he's happy to sell the car for a good price to you."

"Can we take it for a drive?" asked Niamh, feeling excited.

"G'wan," replied Collins and they piled into the small vehicle, Niamh driving, Emma in the passenger seat and Collins in the back.

It was the first time Niamh had driven since arriving in Ireland and she was relieved to find the car so easy and smooth to drive, even easier than Lola, her own old car that May had given to her. It was as if this car was meant to be theirs. Niamh drove through town and turned around, with Emma driving back to the cottage.

Emma had only received her driver's licence just before they departed Australia so was nervous in an unknown vehicle and drove slowly and cautiously. When they reached the gate to the cottage and turned off the car, Emma looked at Niamh and the two of them silently agreed the car was perfect.

"Oh, we'd love to buy this car, Collins. Are you sure he's only asking €4,000?" asked Niamh.

"Yep. I'm so glad and he will be too. He's coming to our house tomorrow so if you want to drop by then you can pay him then and take the car home with you," said Collins. "He'd love to meet you and so would my mother. She's been nagging me to meet you both for yonks. What do you think?"

Niamh and Emma again glanced at each other and a silent agreement was made.

"Sure. Sounds perfect. That gives us time to go to the bank and withdraw the money, or would he prefer a bank transfer?" asked Niamh.

"He's old school. They all work in cash. Is that ok?" asked Collins.

"Yes. Of course. We'll call by about 10.30?" asked Niamh.

"Grand," answered Collins.

The girls watched as Collins climbed back into the driver's side of the Fiesta and drove away, giving a short wave as he turned. They watched the back of the small black car as it drove away down the lane, both feeling elated to have found their ideal car.

Standing ten metres away near the corner of the front fence, a small face peered out at them. The white bulldog with brown patches snuffled as it watched them, one tooth snagged over its top lip, giving it a snarling expression. Niamh watched silently for a moment, then bent down to pick up a stone and threw it toward the dog. It hit the fence post near the dog with a BANG and the dog jumped and disappeared behind the corner.

"I can't believe you just did that," said Emma, horrified. "Throwing stones at a dog? Have you lost your witchy Grimm mind?" She stared at Niamh with her mouth open.

"That's not a dog," said Niamh.

Chapter 19
LUCINDA

"Being pregnant when you're thirty-nine is so different to being pregnant when you're twenty years old," said Lucinda, unpacking the contents of the bag she had brought on to the table and rubbing at her lower back.

"I can't even imagine being pregnant now," said Bethany. "It was hard enough when I was younger."

Bethany and Arabella glanced at each other; both having completed their pregnancies well over twenty years ago. Bethany had two sons and Arabella was the mother of one son.

"Pregnancy does suit you though and you look gorgeous. We are so happy for you," said Arabella, fondly and Bethany agreed.

"This time you have Tarren's support and that must be such a relief for you," said Bethany.

"Oh, it is and he's so excited about our little girl," Lucinda replied.

"Little girl. He's certain about that?" queries Bethany.

"Yes, and he says it's a magic baby," she said.

"I don't know if that is good or bad, really, after what happened to May and Niamh with the Grimm's. I hope you're being safe, Luce," said Arabella. "Do the Grimm's know about you and about the baby?"

Lucinda pulled a face. "I don't know. I guess not."

The sisters began collecting items that were grouped on the table and weaving them together to form bracelets, necklaces and wreaths. The room smelled of a combination of herbs, earthy ingredients, oils and spices and was illuminated by a myriad of burning candles. They worked through the orders they had received for good luck charms to be worn and a few for mounting on the front door. A few local gift shops often placed orders and lately, they had created an online shop and sales were progressing well. The plan was that ultimately, Niamh would return home and open her witch consultancy business and they would work behind the scenes to make the love potions, candles, charms and jars of herb remedies that the public ordered.

Bethany looked over at Lucinda and noted her bare neck. "Luce, why are you not wearing a charm? Of all times, you really need some protection, don't you think?"

"I can't really. If I wear a charm then it makes it impossible for Tarren to come near me," Lucinda answered.

The two sisters stopped what they were doing and stared at their youngest sister. The thought of Tarren not being able to be near a charm had never crossed their minds.

"So, you don't have any charms in the house either?" asked Arabella.

"No. I had to remove the ones on the house at Ringwood North when Tarren and I reunited. I never put out anything when I moved to Liddle Street. How can I? Tarren lives there too and I can't ward him off now, can I?" she said with a little giggle.

The two older sisters looked at each other with concern, both feeling amiss that they had not realised this fact sooner.

"Luce, can you wear a charm and remove it when Tarren is with you?" asked Bethany.

"Well ... yes. I suppose so, if I remember," she said casually.

Bethany reached out and grabbed Lucinda's wrist so she would stop what she was doing and pay attention.

"It's important. We know what the Grimm's are capable of. I want you to be safe. Ok?" said Bethany.

Lucinda smiled at her sisters, appreciating that they were showing concern for her but also feeling they were overreacting. There had been no Grimm's anywhere near her and Tarren never mentioned any of them unless it was in reference to his sons at the remand centre. She thought briefly of the sensation of being watched at the cemetery but shrugged it off as her imagination.

"Does it concern you that Tarren can't cope with charms ... you know ... does that mean he's evil?" asked Arabella.

Lucinda pulled a face. "No. I know the rest of his family are evil. That's for sure, but you know him now. He's the sweetest and most caring man I've ever known. He can't help having Grimm blood and I guess it's a genetic intolerance why he can't handle charms." She shrugged to indicate she didn't really understand the complexities of evil versus good in this situation.

"But Niamh is ok with charms, isn't she?" asked Arabella.

"But that's because she is a witch," said Bethany.

"I'll tell you something funny," Lucinda said, giggling. "Before Niamh left Australia, I got her to pee into a sterilised jar and placed it in the freezer, just in case."

"You WHAT?" said Arabella, wide-eyed.

"You have pee in your freezer?" asked Bethany. "Why would collect and freeze Niamh's pee?"

"It's potent to Grimm's apparently, and they can't go anywhere near it. Weird thing is that it won't freeze." Lucinda giggled again.

Arabella and Bethany stared at each other, wide-eyed, then grinned.

"I hope you have labelled it sufficiently. You wouldn't want Tarren thinking it was wine or something and drinking it in the middle of the night," said Arabella.

The three sisters pealed into fits of laughter.

Chapter 20
NIAMH

Niamh and Emma walked down Cusack Road on their way to meet with Collins' great grandfather to pay for the Ford Fiesta and drive it back to the cottage. Niamh kept a tight hold of her handbag marvelling that she had never held so much money in her life. In Australian money, €4,000 was over $7,000 and seemed a fortune. Although they had been enjoying their walks into town regularly, it was exciting to think they could purchase a week's supply of groceries rather than only buying a small amount to fit in their backpacks, and they would be able to start investigating other towns and sights in the area.

As they rounded the corner, they came into view of the black Ford Fiesta parked out the front of Collins' house looking clean and shiny as if newly polished. They walked through the tall hedge and up to the front door where Collins was standing with the door open waiting for them, all smiles.

"Good morning to you both," he said, cheerily. "Come in."

This was the first time they had entered Collins' house and it smelled of freshly baked scones. In the kitchen, a woman was placing plates on the kitchen bench with her back to them. She turned to greet them as Collins introduced her as his mother. Her face broke out into a warm welcoming smile and she moved closer to inspect the new arrivals.

"Nice to meet you, Mrs O'Brien," said Emma, putting her hand out to shake the woman's hand.

"Ach, call me Janie," she said laughing and took first Emma's hand and then Niamh's, lingering over Niamh's hand and stroking it with her other hand.

"Collins has told me all about the two of you and your visit here to our area. I'm so glad to make your acquaintance and I just know you're going to love it here," she said, still holding Niamh's hand and peering up into her eyes. Niamh grinned, enjoying the warmth and transparency of Janie.

A beeping noise sounded and Janie jumped. "Ach, Jesus, Mary and Joseph, my scones are ready. Go on in to see your Granda, Collins and I'll be in shortly with scones."

Collins led them to the back of the house where a large porch had been enclosed to create a sunroom and this morning, it was capturing the warm rays. An old man sat in a comfortable lounge chair, staring out the back yard and enjoying the view. He looked every bit his ninety-two years with lines etched all over his face and neck, his frail, withered hands resting on his knees.

"Granda," called out Collins. "The girls are here."

Collins had previously told the girls that his great grandfather had been a large part of his life, once living only a few doors down. He had stopped in to visit his great grandfather and great grandmother every night after school for many years. Once his great grandmother had passed on, his great grandfather came to live with his family but now he needed more assistance with his well-being and care than what his family could provide, so had agreed to live in a care home.

The sunroom was only small and with a low ceiling, so as Niamh entered the room, she stepped to the left of the doorway with Collins on the right and Emma in the doorway. The old man turned toward Collins with a smile lighting up his face, ready to greet his great grandson's friends. His mouth opened as he prepared to call out his welcoming gesture when his eyes drifted from his great grandson to Niamh and slowly, the smile froze on his face and his mouth opened.

His facial expression registered shock and surprise and the smile slowly slipped away, and Collins was momentarily stunned, as was Emma and Niamh. Tears welled in the old man's eyes and he continued staring at Niamh with mouth agape until Collins cleared his throat in an attempt to focus his great grandfather.

"Ahem."

"Bridget?" The words came out slowly and almost in a whisper from the old, lined lips. "Bridget?"

Collins gave a small, embarrassed laugh. "No, Granda. This is Emma and Niamh. Remember, I told you about their visit today?"

"Bridget, I'm sorry … I'm sorry." The words were slow and stuttering as the old man tried to stand to face Niamh but he was weak and struggled to rise. He kept looking back at Niamh and before long tears rolled down his lined cheeks.

Collins looked at Niamh and saw the look of shock on her face, her eyes wide and staring at the old man. He didn't understand but something had just passed between his great grandfather and Niamh, some sort of understanding or knowledge.

Collins stepped forward and guided his great grandfather to lean back on his chair.

"What's wrong, Granda. Are you ok?" he said gently to the old man. He glanced up at Emma and Niamh, unsure what to say.

Emma was also staring wide-eyed, aware that something strange was happening. She stepped forward and addressed Collins. "Bridget was Niamh's great grandmother," said Emma. "She lived here at the cottage and was the mother of Agatha. Could your Granda have known her?"

The old man sniffed, brought a handkerchief out of his shirt pocket, blew his nose and wiped his eyes. He then looked up at Niamh again and this time he saw his great grandson's friends.

"Ah, I'm an eejit, seeing ghosts." He smiled weakly. "Forgive me."

Niamh still stared at the old man, mind racing. This could not be a coincidence that he had thought she looked like Bridget.

"Granda, did you know Niamh's family, Bridget or Agatha?" asked Collins, kneeling in front of the old man.

The old man stared at his great grandson silently, then looked up at Niamh again. "Granda, what's going on?" asked Collins.

Emma and Niamh stepped in to the room, closer to where the old man sat.

"Granda?" Collins repeated.

He nodded after a few minutes of silence. "Yes. I knew them." He said it quietly and with a trembling voice. He looked at Niamh again and smiled weakly. "You look like Bridget."

"Why're you upset, Granda? Did you know Bridget well?" asked Collins.

A tortured look passed his weathered face and he sighed, a long, drawn-out sigh, then looked down at his hands which he twisted back and forth.

"The boys in the village used to go out to the witch's cottage sometimes and throw stones. I was one of them, I'm ashamed to say." He shook his head and pursed his lips, acknowledging his shame.

"When the older witch died, Bridget lived there on her own and she was a looker. Dark red hair and a pretty face, like you." He turned to look at Niamh again.

He looked around at the three faces staring at him and he sighed again. "I have carried a secret for over sixty years." His face crumpled as he fought off the threatening tears again.

"Go on, Granda," said Collins cautiously, worried about what secret was emerging.

"I used to spend time out there at the witch's cottage, just trying to see Bridget or talk to her. I had a schoolboy crush and she was just a few years older. I helped her with the vegetable garden, fencing and fixing leaks in the roof. Odd jobs like that." He cleared his throat, partially to keep his composure.

"We used to chat and she confided her dreams to me, that she wished she could move to a new country and start a new life. I admit I fell in love with her ... completely ... deeply." He stopped in his narrative and Collins prompted him.

"Go on."

"She loved me too and we became lovers."

There was a gasp from Emma and Niamh stared at the old man, unsure if she was hearing correctly. He wiped his eyes with his handkerchief and continued his tale.

"I wanted to elope with her and flee to another country, and I told her I would save enough money for us to go. I was eighteen years old and started working at the mill and saving my pennies."

He looked at Collins and then the two girls who were staring at him, hanging on every word.

"Bridget became pregnant and we planned to leave before my parents found out ... but they did and they forbade me from ever seeing her again."

He looked at the indignant expression on Emma's face. "You have to understand that at the time, the father of the house ruled the house with fist and rod. He beat me black and blue, and threatened to burn down her cottage and drive Bridget out of town if I visited her again. I was terrified he would carry through with his threat and she would be destitute. I promised not to see her again if they would leave her be and we made a deal."

"So, you saying you are the father of Agatha?" asked Collins, incredulous.

"Other boys in the village said that it had to be the devil's child because she didn't have a man, but it was my child," he replied, looking Collins in the eye.

Niamh looked away and out the window, unsure how to feel about this revelation.

"My parents never knew but I used to go out to the cottage at night and leave money on the doorstep to help support Bridget and the baby. I didn't know what else to do. I left money up until she died and Agatha left."

Tears ran down the old man's face and he stared up at Niamh. Collins had also stood and stared from his great grandfather to Niamh, speechless and shocked.

"Is this possible, Collins?" asked Emma. "Does the timing work out?"

"Umm … Granda, Sean O'Brien was born in 1932 so he was eighteen years old around 1950. When was Agatha born?" he asked.

Emma and Niamh looked at each other. "The timing works," said Niamh and she turned and ran.

Chapter 21
HARDY

The black limousine glided to a halt in front of Hardy's house and the driver jumped out to open the back doors. A middle-aged man stepped out dressed in a black suit, followed by an old man dressed casually in a white shirt and dark trousers. The middle-aged man could easily be identified as a Grimm with his blondish/greying hair and dark eyebrows but the older man now sported a full head of silver hair and silver eyebrows as well as being shorter and stouter.

They stood on the driveway and looked up at the fortified house in front of them silently, judging. The old man reached in his pocket, pulled out a handkerchief and cleaned his spectacles, before placing them back on his face.

The electronic gates opened and Hardy and his wife, Helga, studiously watching for the arrival of the visitors. Both were professionally dressed in preparation for the visit with Hardy in a suit and Helga wearing a dress and blazer. Nothing less would be expected by the patriarch of the entire Grimm family in Australia.

Everyone shook hands with the two visitors in greeting then invited them into the house where the maid served tea and lamingtons. Helga then excused herself to enable the three men to talk business. A Grimm woman understood that business was a man's world and she must excuse herself to focus on her domestic duties.

"Hardy, I can't tell you how disappointed I am in this current state of affairs in Melbourne. There have been problems down here for the past fifty years and I don't understand why your family can't get their act together. This witch family seem to rule the roost and now, I hear that your own nephew has brain damage as a result of a witch attack. Is this true?" Gunther's voice had risen as he spoke and his eyebrows raised, knowing this question was superfluous.

Duly chastened, Hardy kept his voice respectful and in truth, he was intimidated by this legend of a man in the Grimm family to the point where he had downed a glass of straight Scotch whisky prior to his arrival.

"This witch is more than just a witch. She is my brother, Tarren's daughter, so she is some sort of hybrid – half witch, half Grimm. I've not met her but my understanding is that she is very powerful," Hardy responded.

"Hmmm," came the gruff reply. "Is it true that Tarren has left our fold and taken up living with the witch family and that the woman is carrying another witch hybrid baby?"

"Yes. I'm afraid so," Hardy admitted. He glanced over at the suited man who had been introduced as Hans and so far, had not uttered a word. He was clearly Grimm but not familiar to Hardy and he wondered what role Hans was playing and why he was present. Was he a hit man?

"You'd better tell me the whole story from the start," said Gunther.

It was another three hours of discussion, questions and possible scenarios before Gunther made his decisions clear to Hardy.

"Regarding the boy, Justin – no hospitals for him. We don't want normal people prodding around in the brain of one of our own now, do we? It may not be safe for us if they found something unusual. I will send Natasha down as my understanding is that they were betrothed before the witch attack happened. They will marry and she can tend to his care and report on his progress."

Hardy recalled vaguely that there had been talk in the family that a young girl in Sydney, Natasha was waiting to turn of age and would be sent down to marry Justin.

Gunther sat back in the chair and closed his eyes as he vocalised his decisions.

"The other boy, Beaton … he's already home with his family, you indicated. Good. I would like a discussion in person with Beaton to find out more about this witch hybrid and her powers. Please arrange it for me."

Hardy nodded.

"Marion, the mother of those two boys is being sent back to Sydney. It seems she needs some reminding of how to nurture and care for one of us. She did not maintain her marriage with Tarren and she has not sufficiently cared for her sons in prison. She needs an attitude readjustment."

"But she has children and grandchildren here in Melbourne," said Hardy.

"Too bad. She may return one day … or she may not," said Gunther, bluntly.

"Hans, here," Gunther indicated the suited man. "He has been in Sydney for twenty years from Germany and is married to one of my granddaughters."

Hans nodded to Hardy in acknowledgement, face solemn and unpliable.

"Hans is our top legal brain and my right arm and we'll need him to sort out the mess that has been created here in Melbourne. There's been media attention since the witch attack, and mountains of paperwork over the charges, too much to use magic to make it all disappear. Hans will handle the paperwork through legal channels and see about dropping the charges."

"Now ... I'm ordering Tarren to present to me and explain his actions. I'll have my secretary send him a formal invitation to appear this week while I'm in Melbourne. He needs to explain to me why he has allowed his sons to be jailed like common people, why he has left his marriage, why he has blocked his sons from their magic, why he has taken up and is having children with a witch family and where his witch hybrid daughter is. I understand you have not been able to locate her ... the witch daughter?" Gunther leaned forward to ask the question directly to Hardy, eye to eye.

"Umm ... no. We have not," Hardy replied. "What will happen to Tarren?"

"Good question. This is not something I have dealt with in all my eighty-two years and I never thought I would. Tarren has betrayed and acted against his own kind and his own family with the witches. This is unforgivable and there is no coming back from this dark place where he has scurried. In all fairness, I will allow him to explain his reasoning to me, but it is clear to me that he will be executed, along with every member of the witch family. There can be NO witch hybrids born. Do you understand that?" He glared at Hardy fiercely.

"I do. I do, but Tarren is my baby brother," Hardy said, weakly.

"Too bad. He is a bad apple and must be tossed out. Your family will be stronger as a result. Now … Hans," He turned to the suited man. "Use your investigators and find that witch hybrid. I'd like her brought before me. I'd like to see personally how powerful she is. I may be in my eighties, but I would enjoy out-powering her and seeing her physical body collapse in on itself with the fury of a Grimm." Gunther ground his hands together as if squashing an unseen enemy in his bare hands and uttered a strange guttural laugh. Hans followed suit and the two Sydney men's eyes gleamed as an animalistic longing erupted from their mouths.

Hardy looked away, slightly disturbed.

Chapter 22
NIAMH

The sound of a car pulling up outside brought Emma and Niamh to their feet. They opened the front door to see Collins walking through the gate and up the path, looking at them silently for a moment. Behind him, outside the fence, the Ford Fiesta was parked. His face looked cautious as if expecting to be sent his marching orders, not the usual happy and cheery Collins.

"C'mere to me. Can I come in and speak with you?" Collins asked quietly, his face tensed and ready should they tell him to leave.

Niamh stepped aside and signalled for him to enter. He strode over to the table and sat with Emma sitting opposite and Niamh choosing to stand. Emma nodded at him in greeting but kept quiet, waiting to hear what he had to say. They had not heard from Collins in over one week now, since the fateful day at the O'Brien house when it was discovered that Collins' great grandfather was also Niamh's great grandfather, after an affair with Bridget, Niamh's great grandmother over sixty years earlier.

Niamh had bolted, running from the house with Emma racing after her. Niamh had run the entire 1.2 kilometres back to the cottage whereas Emma had slowed to a walk, unable to keep up. When Emma arrived at the cottage, Niamh had been in her bed with the covers pulled up high over her head, hiding and shielded from the world and the painful secrets hidden in the depths. Emma sat on the edge of the bed and comforted her friend, rubbing her back through the covers.

The revelation from Collins' great grandfather was still a shock and Niamh needed time to analyse and accept what had happened so long ago. There was nothing she could do to change the past and she reasoned that this secret had unfolded at this time because she was supposed to know for some reason. She had laid in her bed that first night after the discovery, staring at the ceiling and realising that Sean O'Brien and Bridget Conlon had been in this very cottage when they had conceived Agatha so many years ago. It all felt surreal, arriving in Ennis, meeting Collins and then discovering the truth from his great grandfather.

Collins being a no-show that week was baffling, but the girls reasoned that this was a shock to him as well. His beloved great grandfather, his Granda had deserted his pregnant girlfriend, leaving her to fend for herself and live in poverty.

Collins looked across at Emma and up at Niamh, his hands quietly clenching and unclenching.

"I'm sorry I haven't been to see you. Are you ok?" he asked.

Niamh nodded.

"I've been wrestling with what Granda did, abandoning Bridget like that."

Collins' face looked tortured. "My mother took him back to the care home that afternoon and I kept away from him, just played music all week. My release, you know."

"Today, I visited him and asked him questions. You see, I know he's a good man. I know he is. This secret has eaten away at him for all those years. He was a coward, not standing up to his father. I didn't understand why he didn't just take what money he had and they both run away, go and live somewhere else. I asked him today and he said it wasn't enough money for them to live more than a few weeks, but he agreed he should have done that anyway. He couldn't face Bridget again but she saw him in town a few days after his father beat him up. He turned away from her but she saw his battered face and she knew. He was so ashamed and remorseful that he left money for her every week until she died."

Collins looked again at Niamh to judge her reaction but she was just slightly nodding, face unreadable.

"Although I don't condone what he did, and wish it were different, he is still my Granda and I love him."

"Of course, you do," said Emma.

"Today I made peace with him, and I hope we're still friends." He looked at each of the girls and they both smiled and nodded. His body relaxed after a week of anxious reflection and deep thoughts. He breathed a sigh of relief and smiled for the first time during this visit.

"Granda wants you to have the Fiesta ... as a gift," he said, fishing the keys out of his pocket.

"No," said Niamh firmly, shaking her head.

"Please take it. It will make him feel that he is making amends with you."

"No," repeated Niamh. "It's blood money. He doesn't need to make amends with me."

"He really wants you to take it. He'll be offended if you say no and he'll feel more guilty about what occurred long ago."

"Niamh, take it. We do need a car and taking it is acceptance of the past, a compensation of sorts," said Emma. Collins nodded in agreement.

Emma and Niamh held eye contact with each other, silently and invisibly conversing. Eventually, Niamh dropped her head and nodded. "Ok," she said. "Thank you."

Collins' face broke out into a grin as he ceremoniously placed the car keys on the table as if placing an expensive royal crown.

"So, now that we're cousins, can you drop me off home?" he said with a laugh.

Chapter 23
TARREN

Tarren read the text message repeatedly as his brain reacted to the message. It seemed surreal, like someone was playing a joke on him. It couldn't possibly be real, could it?

TARREN – WARNING – GUNTHER IN MELB – DEATH WARRANTS IMMINENT

The number was not one in his contact list and when he tried to phone it, it just went straight to message bank. He had no idea who could have sent this message as he knew his mother was not technically savvy enough to type a message on what he suspected was a burner phone. It surely wasn't his daughter, Monica, as she was the one who had called a family meeting to start with.

His mind raced on who the sender could be, Anton, his oldest son? Hardy, his brother? One of the others feeling bad about what was happening. It could be anyone and he wouldn't know. He sent a message back to the number in the hope that someone would answer.

PLEASE TELL ME MORE. DEATH WARRANT FOR ME? OR OTHERS AS WELL? APPRECIATE THE NOTICE.

Tarren could feel sweat breaking out on his forehead as he waited for his phone to ping indicating a message had arrived. Sitting in his office now, having read that message, he felt like a sitting duck. He rose from his desk and walked over to the door, scanning the office but all he could see was his secretary, Jade, sitting at her desk typing an email.

"Everything ok, Jade?" he called out.

She stopped typing, turned and smiled at him. "Yes. Mr Grimm. All fine."

He walked back and peered out his window cautiously at the street below in Doncaster but nothing caught his attention, just the normal volume of cars parked on the sides of the road and people walking about, tending to their groceries or everyday tasks.

Where was Lucinda?

He clutched his phone frantically and clicked on her name, exhaling relieved when she answered within a few seconds, sounding happy.

"Hey, Tarren."

He tried to sound calm and casual. "Just thought I would check how your day was going and where you are."

"Oh, you're so sweet. I'm with my sisters and we're having a bit of fun making these charms. They think it's hilarious that I have Niamh's urine in the freezer." She giggled and he could hear other giggles in the background.

"That's potent stuff. It could burn the very hair off your head," he said jokingly and he could hear laughter at the other end.

"Well, babe. How about I pick you up this afternoon and we'll have a nice dinner somewhere?" he said.

"How lovely. I'm not dressed for anything fancy," Lucinda said.

"That's fine. We won't be going anywhere fancy. Are you at Arabella's or Bethany's?" he asked.

"Arabella's house. Do you remember where it is?" she asked.

"I do indeed. I'll pop by in about thirty minutes. Will you be finished by then?"

"Yes. We will. See you," Lucinda said and hung up.

Tarren stared at the phone. She was fine for now but what was going to happen from here on and did it include her sisters? Should he be warning Arabella and Bethany? What about their husbands and their children? He walked over to his desk and shut down his computer, packed it in his laptop carry bag and headed out of the office.

"Jade, I'm off early today and I may take the rest of the week off. I'll be in touch," he said as he was leaving.

He went immediately to the bank and withdraw $20,000 in cash, much to the surprise of the bank teller. In a world where everything is digital, he didn't want to leave a trail of credit card transactions and decided cash would be a good option.

Next, he stopped at an electrical appliance store and bought two burner phones, paying for them in cash. Pulling up at their house in Liddle Street, he raced inside to the freezer and removed the jar of Niamh's urine, gingerly carrying it, terrified of dropping the lethal liquid. He placed it in a shopping bag and returned to his car, checking the street for any sign of activity. Satisfied no one was following or watching, he drove across to Warrandyte to pick up Lucinda from Arabella's home, still unsure exactly what they would be doing next.

His primary goal at this point was to protect Lucinda and their unborn child.

Chapter 24
NIAMH

"Are you sure you don't mind staying here?" Niamh asked Emma, again.

"No. I'm all good. I'm planning to binge watch *The Bold and the Beautiful* while you're gone," said Emma.

"Eww. Yeah. Finish it before I get back," Niamh responded, pulling a face of distaste.

Since Collins had told her about Molly Byrne at Inagh, Niamh couldn't wait to venture out and try to find her. According to Collins' mother, Molly Byrne was a mother, living happily in a small community and was well-liked and accepted by the locals. She didn't know her exact address, but Niamh was confident that if her grandmother, Agatha could find May in busy Melbourne back in 1970, then she could find another witch in a quiet town.

Collins' mother had also given him information about another woman living on the other side of Ennis who was considered a bad witch. This threw Niamh as she had never heard of a bad witch and never knew they existed, other than the green witch in *The Wizard of Oz*. She wondered if a bad witch was just a normal witch with a bad personality or whether a bad witch was a totally different type of creature to her or May. This bad witch's name was Anne Riley and Niamh was not keen to meet her at all. The thought of her was terrifying and her knowledge of other magical people was so limited, she hoped Molly Byrne might be someone who could educate her.

Climbing into the Ford Fiesta, she drove the fifteen minutes from the cottage at Claureen, with Google Maps instructing her on directions. She had also googled Inagh and knew it was only a small town of about 228 people. Surely, a witch could find another witch with only 228 people around abouts. In many ways she felt she had imposter syndrome, feeling that Molly Byrne may be a real witch whereas she was a pretend witch. With over eighteen years of not being a witch and suddenly, six months of being a witch, it sometimes didn't feel real.

She located the main part of town which consisted of just a few colourful buildings and parked the Fiesta. Stepping out and admiring the lovely small town, set in such a scenic place, she could see a few people milling around, shopping or tending to gardens. Should she ask someone? How did a witch go about detecting another witch? Where exactly was her witch radar?

Without warning, she felt a tingling sensation that initiated in her neck and ran down her spine. It was such an intense feeling that she knew it could only come from another witch. She looked around trying to determine the source but there were no obvious leads. She walked closer to the shops and could hear children playing and laughing. She turned the corner into a side street and beside the building, could see a metal fence with three children playing, laughing and bouncing a red coloured ball, throwing it to each other. She stood at the fence watching the children, still feeling the tingling when one of the children, a young girl approached her. The girl looked to be around seven years old with red wavy hair tied back in a high ponytail. The girl walked slowly toward Niamh at the fence and with a sudden shock, she realised the little girl was a witch.

"Other than mummy, grandma and my great grandma, you are the only other witch I have met," the little girl said in her lovely melodical Irish voice.

"Well, you are the youngest witch I have ever met," responded Niamh.

The girl tilted her head on the side as she studied Niamh, reacting to the Australian accent. "Are you from a faraway country?"

"Yes. I am from Australia and visiting for a few months," Niamh answered.

"I'm visiting my friends." She turned to look at the other two children then turned back to Niamh. "You should visit my mummy," she said.

"I would like to do that. Where is your mummy?" asked Niamh.

"At home, down that street." She pointed down to the right past the town.

"I'll go visit her now. My name is Niamh. What's your name?"

"Maureen. Bye then." The little girl turned and ran back to her friends.

Niamh drove down the direction she had indicated, slowly until she reached a group of houses that were nestled together on the stretch of road. She parked the Fiesta and stepped outside, hoping her witch sense would help her out.

Immediately, she felt the tingling that started at her neck and ran down her spine, causing her to shiver in sweet delight. She looked at the group of four houses and wondered which house belonged to Molly Byrne. She walked over to the front gate of the first house and stared at the front door. The tingling sensation continued but was no stronger or weaker so she moved to the next house.

She didn't need to wonder any longer as she could see a figure walking out the front door of the third house and looking her way. Slowly, Niamh stepped toward the third house as the figure made her way to the front gate, both meeting at the same time. The tingling sensation was intense and Niamh wondered why she had never felt this before in such a way, considering she had been around May.

The figure was a woman in her thirties, dressed in casual attire, with an attractive face and dark auburn hair scrunched up into a bun at the back of her head with wispy pieces falling around her face. The woman stood staring at Niamh with a neutral expression. Niamh had no idea how witches were supposed to interact with each other when they had never met but she stood still mirroring the older woman's expression and waited.

After a few minutes, the woman's face relaxed and she smiled. "Welcome."

Niamh smiled shyly and nodded her head. "I'm sorry to arrive announced but I needed to find you. I'm Niamh. I've met Maureen." She offered her hand to the older woman and the two hands touched and gripped.

"She told you to come and see me? I'm Molly. Come on in," she responded warmly and opened the gate to invite Niamh to enter.

Chapter 25
TARREN

Tarren halted abruptly in his walk up to the front door at Arabella's house and looked up at the charm above the door frame. It had stopped him in his tracks before he even saw it. Like an invisible shield that blocked his entrance, the charm worked as it was intended, making him uncomfortable and prevented him from entering the house uninvited. Even invited, it was still uncomfortable but tolerable.

Months ago, the Brigid's Cross above the door on Lucinda's house had prevented him from entering until he was invited to enter, then when he became a regular visitor, Lucinda had removed it and all the other charms around the house. The house they lived in together at Liddle Street was charm-free, although Lucinda still burned candles, incense and had various herbs and oils all over the place. They didn't bother him like the charms did.

He had planned to collect Lucinda and for the two of them to go into hiding but on the drive across to Warrandyte he was rethinking. If she could stay here with Arabella and fortify the house, then this would be the safest place for Lucinda to be. The Grimm's didn't know where Arabella or Bethany lived as far as he knew, and no Grimm would be able to enter the premises with the charms guarding the entrance, and there would be no invitation forthcoming. This was a much better idea than spiriting her away to a dodgy hotel or hidden accommodation where she would be alone, and it would also give him the opportunity to try and resolve the situation with the rest of his family.

He sent a text message to Lucinda's phone.

Charm outside house. Can your sister invite me in?

The door opened and he could hear Lucinda laughing as Arabella and Lucinda appeared on the front porch. Arabella stepped forward and played her part with a theatrical flair.

"Tarren, please accept my invitation to enter my house. Won't you come this way?" said Arabella with added pomp and ceremony.

Tarren grinned at the charade and walked up to the two sisters, touching foreheads with Lucinda as he drew close enough. He followed them into the house, greeting Bethany on the way. They had been so afraid of him the first time they had met him at Lucinda's house but in the months since then, had grown to admire him, trust him and were genuinely happy that he had reunited with Lucinda.

"Ladies, I have something important to discuss with you," he said, and all eyes turned to him at the serious tone of his voice.

"I have received a disturbing warning from someone in my family, and I think we need to take precautions."

"What? What do you mean?" asked Lucinda.

"Gunther, my grandfather is in Melbourne. He is the patriarch who lives in Sydney and would only be here if he is unhappy about something. With my insistence on Justin and Beaton facing justice for their crimes, that has probably been enough for him to come down here and reverse it."

"Has it been reversed?" asked Arabella.

"Yes. I have discovered that both boys have been released."

There was an audible gasp as the three sisters looked at each other, unsure what to say.

"He would also be unhappy that I blocked their magic. Neither of them have magical abilities on a temporary basis and I am the only one that can remove that block," he added.

"Why did you block their magic?" asked Bethany.

"If I hadn't then Beaton would have released himself and Justin on the first day." Tarren looked at the three sisters and wondered how much he should say. "I don't know who in the family sent me the warning but I am concerned that it may be more serious than the situation with the two boys."

He paused to study the three faces to determine if they were comprehending what he was trying to say but they looked puzzled.

"It's possible they have discovered that we are living together and having a baby." He looked at Lucinda who was staring at him wide-eyed.

"You are concerned for Lucinda's safety?" questioned Bethany.

"Yes, and the baby," Tarren responded.

There were gasps again as the realisation of what he was saying dawned.

"I thought I was being watched a few days ago when I went to the cemetery," said Lucinda, remembering that strange feeling.

"Arabella, I wondered if Lucinda could stay here with you. You have the charm above the door which prevented me from entering uninvited. If you could add extra charms all over the place, you will be safe here," he said looking at Lucinda.

"Of course she can," said Arabella without hesitation.

"No. Wait … what about you?" Lucinda said, voice trembling. "Are you in danger? What will they do?"

Tarren pursed his lips and shrugged. "I don't really know. First, I must find out what they know and why Gunther is here. Hopefully, it is just about the boys, and I may need to unblock their magic to bring peace." He smiled at Lucinda to reassure her and lessen the shock of a threat.

"I want you and our little girl to be safe. That's my number one priority." He leaned forward and wrapped his arms around her. Lucinda immediately broke into tears and clung to him.

"We'll look after her," said Bethany.

"Bethany, same with you. Charms everywhere and around your neck and your other family members. Do you understand?" he asked firmly.

They all nodded.

Tarren reached into the shopping bag and passed a burner phone to Lucinda with a piece of paper. "In case they track our phones or calls, I want you to use this phone in the future. Here is my new number. I'm using a new phone too."

She took the phone and paper without looking at them, eyes on Tarren. "They won't hurt you, will they?"

"I'll be ok. Trust me. Oh, hang on." He reached back into the shopping bag and gently and cautiously drew out the jar and placed it on the kitchen bench. "I nearly forgot. I got this out of the freezer for you. Dab some on the front gate, the door and even on your charms. I must go. I love you."

With not another word, he kissed the top of Lucinda's head, turned and left before they could see the worry in his eyes.

Bethany picked up the jar and peered at the golden liquid. "This isn't Niamh's urine, is it?"

Chapter 26
EMMA

Emma was on her third episode of *The Bold and the Beautiful* when a strange feeling overcame her. She paused the episode and listened but couldn't hear anything. Feeling a little spooked and being on her own with Niamh away, she slowly got to her feet and peeked out the window. The landscape looked eerily dark with heavy clouds hanging low in the sky.

She walked over to the front door and opened it slowly, peering out to see if a car had pulled up or anyone was around, but there was nothing there. She was about to close the door again when a slight sound drew her attention to the right side of the front fence. She stepped outside a few steps, peering at the tall picket fence when she saw something white through the gaps. The white object was moving so she stepped to the right to take a better look. Two eyes peered back at her and with a start, she realised it was the white bulldog with the brown patches. She hadn't seen it for a while but here it was again.

Feeling relieved that it was only the dog, she turned to head back into the house when another noise caught her attention. She spun around to the front gate and a woman stood there. Emma jumped in fright at the sudden sight of this person. Where had she come from? She hadn't been there just moments ago.

The woman looked to be possibly in her fifties, with dark shoulder length hair streaked with grey. She wore a black straw hat and a grey trench coat that hung straight down hiding whatever clothes she was wearing. She looked very much like Emma imagined a homeless person would look. It was her face that stood out to Emma, unsmiling, pale and with dark eyes that bore into her.

"Can I help you?" asked Emma.

The woman looked at Emma and moved her head sidewards to peer around her to the open front door. "I heard there were two girls living here."

Emma stared at her, waiting for her to finish but that seemed to be the end of the sentence. "Well, you heard correct. There are."

The white dog walked up and rubbed itself against the woman's legs. Looking at the dog and the woman, Emma felt uneasy but could not identify why.

"Is your friend not here?" she asked, again trying to look around Emma.

"No, she's not," replied Emma.

She could see the woman's nose wrinkling and her eyes blinking and then she stepped back a few steps, looking from left to right. Emma had been considering whether she should invite her in or ask more questions, but instinct held her back. Something about this woman rang alarm bells and now Emma realised that this woman could smell Niamh's urine and was unable to enter the property. She instinctively knew then that this woman was magic but not the type of witch like Niamh or May but something else entirely.

Feeling more courageous now that she knew this woman could not enter the property, Emma strode closer to the gate. "Do you live nearby? What's your name? What do you want" she asked the woman.

The woman was still stepping backward with the dog at her heels. She didn't want to look Emma in the eye and was turning trying to walk away, flustered.

The rain started and the woman stopped to fish out an old tattered black umbrella from her hessian bag over her shoulder. She fumbled as she tried to open the umbrella, finally succeeding. Once up, the dog moved in closer to her legs seeking shelter from the wet.

The woman glanced back at Emma, just a quick glance as if holding eye contact was too difficult.

"Errr ... umm ... Anne Riley. Tell her I called."

Chapter 27
NIAMH

Molly was a busy mother of three young children under the age of ten years, running a house littered with toys and clothing items complete with cooking smells, burning incense and drying herbs. Messy and disorganised but so delightful, Niamh instantly felt at home. Molly continued washing the pots she had been cleaning and Niamh sat on a stool at the island bench.

"Sorry to arrive unannounced like this, but I heard you lived nearby and I really wanted to meet you. I only found out I'm a witch in January when my grandmother died and bestowed her magic on me, so I'm still learning," Niamh admitted.

"You didn't know your grandmother was a witch?" asked Molly, surprised.

"No. My mother is normal and she kept me away from my grandmother," said Niamh.

"But … you would've already had magical abilities before you were bestowed if you were a witch," suggested Molly.

"Well, I guess I did but I never knew I was any different to anyone else, and I never knew how to use it. I probably used magic without knowing when I lost my temper but my mother hid this and made me think it was just normal behaviour. After my grandmother died, her best friend, May, taught me how to use my abilities. Then May died and bestowed on me as well."

"You must be quite powerful then," Molly stated.

"Hmmm, well I guess so but I'm still learning. I can do amazing things when I get angry. I'm not always good at controlling it," Niamh admitted.

"Maureen sometimes loses control, so it's definitely an ability that takes practice. My other children are not witches, just Maureen."

"Is your mother a witch?" asked Niamh.

"She sure is and she lives just over in the next town with my grandmother who is also a witch."

Niamh clapped her hands together. "Oh, how fabulous. Three of you. You must know so much about being a witch."

"I'm sure they would love to meet you. It's not often a witch turns up on our doorstep. We witches need to stick together. Would you like to meet them?" asked Molly.

"Oh, yes. I would. My mother's family came from Claureen near Ennis and I'm staying at the cottage where they lived. I'm only here for a few months and hope to learn as much as I can. I don't know anyone magic in Australia who can teach me ..." Niamh stopped suddenly as she realised her own father, Tarren, was magical but there was nothing he could teach her.

Molly picked up on her sudden halt in mid-sentence and raised her eyebrows. Niamh looked at her and shrugged. "It's a long story. I do know of another family who are magic but they are evil and not witches."

"Oh yes. We have a number of different entities around who are not nice and have magic," said Molly.

"Around here?" asked Niamh.

"Yes. There's one who lives in Ennis. The town folk call her a witch but she's not one of us. I'm not too sure what she is exactly, but her aura is … murky, not colourful like ours. My mother has met her briefly and could see who she was. I'm surprised she hasn't come looking for you," said Molly.

"Oh, really? Why? What would she do?" asked Niamh, feeling a little alarmed.

"I think it's a territorial thing. Good versus evil and all that," said Molly.

"I've experienced the good versus evil once before," Niamh admitted.

"She may even send her familiar to check you out."

"What's a familiar?" asked Niamh.

"Oh, it's usually an animal. I believe this woman has a white dog," said Molly.

She saw the look of alarm cross Niamh's face. "You've already encountered the familiar, I see."

"Yes. Umm … my friend, Emma is here with me. I left her alone at the cottage. Should I be concerned?" asked Niamh.

"Have you protected the place with charms?" asked Molly.

"No, but I did pee around the boundary. That works better than any charm," said Niamh.

"Really? I never knew that," said Molly, eyebrows raised. "Did your grandmother's friend teach you that?"

"No. It was just something I instinctively felt and it worked on an evil family I met," said Niamh.

She took her phone out of her bag and sent a text message to Emma. Receiving no reply, she tried phoning Emma and the call went unanswered. Feeling a panic building inside her that this evil woman had kidnapped Emma or worse and maybe Emma was now floating in a cauldron of boiling water about to be turned into a casserole, Niamh apologised to Molly but said she needed to race home and check on Emma.

She left her phone number with Molly and they agreed to set up a meeting with Molly's mother and grandmother. Trying hard not to speed in the Ford Fiesta, Niamh hurried back to the cottage, her heart racing and feeling a dread in her soul.

As she halted the Ford Fiesta at the gate, she could see the front door was ajar, and Niamh's alarm intensified. Racing toward the front gate, it opened before she reached it and she shot through and down the path to the open door, careful not to slip over on the wet pavers. She raced into the house, calling out to Emma. No one there. She checked the bedroom, nothing.

Feeling more of a panic that Emma had certainly been taken by the evil witch, Niamh ran back outside, calling Emma's name. No sign of her.

Lightning flashed across the sky as her panic grew and claps of thunder could be heard rolling as if the gods were angry. She raced around to the back of the cottage calling out.

"EMMA, EMMA, EMMA, WHERE ARE YOU?"

She could see nothing but green grass and green bushes, a strange colour in the semi-darkness from the dark clouds above, then down by the vegetable patch, a brunette head suddenly popped up from among the green bushes. Niamh released the breath she had been holding, feeling the relief wash over her.

"Emma, what on earth are you doing?"

"I'm pissing around the fence line. From now on, we do it every day."

Chapter 28
TARREN

Tarren sat in the driver's seat of his car with the envelope in his hand and stared at it. He knew without opening that it was an official communication from the Grimm family. He had seen these envelopes many times in his life but usually they were a wedding invitation or an announcement of some type. The paper was a fawn colour of thick waxy paper and an intricate embossed border around the edges. This one had his name in curved script right in the middle of the front.

Tarren Forsyth Grimm

The envelope had been delivered to his office and handed to Jade by a blonde man in a suit, according to Jade. She had agreed to bring the envelope to a café around the corner from the office and hand-delivered it to Tarren.

"Are you ok, Mr Grimm?" she had asked, concerned about his pale and worried face.

"Oh, yes. Thanks Jade. Just need a little holiday," he'd replied, and smiled at her to reassure her.

Now, he sat in his car and stared at the ominous looking envelope, feeling it was almost burning his hand. With a deep breath, he tore the edge open and removed a single sheet of parched paper.

*Gunther Adolphus Grimm
requests a meeting with
Tarren Forsyth Grimm
on Wednesday 22nd July
2019 at 10am
to be held at Mont Blanc Hotel
Conference Room*

There was no phone number listed on the document and there was no RSVP required as this invitation was mandatory and without choice. Tarren sat back in his seat and stared out the windscreen contemplating the invitation.

He had only met his grandfather once when Gunther made a trip to Melbourne after Tarren's father, George and two brothers had been killed in the house fire that Agatha had conjured. Gunther made a trip to the funeral as a show of support to his daughter, Dora, and the other Grimm's in Melbourne. Tarren had been just a small child of four years old so he couldn't really remember anything about him, except that he seemed tall and frightening to a young boy.

He'd heard stories about incidents involving Gunther and the general consensus among the Melbourne Grimm's was that he was a total control freak, a narcissist and an arrogant bastard. Even Tarren's mother, Dora, had been afraid of him and told stories about his treatment of any Grimm who stepped out of line including perpetrators being exiled to Germany, revoked of magic, tortured and even, terminated.

What hope did he have? It was only a matter of time before Gunther found out everything including his magic baby with Lucinda, Niamh's whereabouts, his magic block on his two sons, and their incarceration. He knew this invitation in his hand amounted to a death sentence for him and for the witch family, and his heart pounded as he frantically tried to think of what he could possibly do to change the outcome.

He picked up his mobile phone and saved the number from the warning text to his burner phone, before turning off his old phone and tossing it in the back seat.

USING THIS NUMBER NOW. RECEIVED GUNTHER INVITATION. HOW BAD?

He sent the text message off to his unknown family member and hoped whoever had sent the first message might respond to this one. He couldn't see any way out of this mess he had made for himself, but he didn't regret anything he had done. He would have trod the same path had he to live his time over. Possibly the only thing he may have done differently was left his Grimm family many years earlier and been with Lucinda these past twenty years. This past six months was the first time he had really known happiness, even though the road had been rocky due to the death of May, Niamh leaving and his sons in prison. He hadn't even touched a drop of alcohol in these past months, having previously drank to excess, but he really felt like a drink now.

BAD. WORST KIND OF BAD. DON'T ATTEND.

He read the response on the burner phone as soon as it alerted him to a new message. Don't attend? He hadn't even considered not attending. That was unheard of, but then again, so was living with a witch family and producing magic witch children.

Don't attend. What would happen if he didn't attend? Gunther would have a limited amount of time in Melbourne and would then return to Sydney, he reasoned. If Tarren could go into hiding for the time being, would Gunther return to his own home eventually? Would Tarren have to go into hiding forever? He may end up losing his Grimm family, including Anton, Monica and his grandchildren. Was he prepared to lose communication with his own family? What was the alternative? Death?

Tarren sat and contemplated his future and the future of the people he loved. Was hiding forever the only answer? There had to be something else, something he could do to change things, to fix things.

Chapter 29
NIAMH

Collins arrived as arranged to babysit Emma while Niamh had plans to meet Molly's mother and grandmother. After the recent scare where she left Emma at the cottage and the evil witch had turned up, Niamh couldn't take any further chances with her friend. Just the thought of Emma being harmed, caused such anger from Niamh that her magic exploded from her body and lightning flashed.

She phoned Collins and asked him if he would stay with Emma while she was away for a few hours. He readily agreed and although she knew that Anne Riley couldn't enter the property without an invitation, she felt safer knowing Emma had company. She instructed Emma to tell Collins about the urine around the fence and what it meant, as the thought of telling him herself was too embarrassing.

Standing outside the front door to the cottage, Emma and Niamh finished telling Collins what Molly had said about the bad witch and her familiar when a snuffling sound caught their attention. Over near the two cars, the white bulldog appeared, peeking through the gaps in the picket fence.

Niamh looked at the dog and furrowed her forehead in concentration. A few grunting sounds issued from the dog, and some movement as he scratched around and then with a whimper, he took off running back down the lane.

"What did you do?" asked Emma.

"I gave him a bad case of fleas," Niamh said, and they laughed.

Niamh left the two of them with a warning to Collins not to let Emma suck him into binge watching *The Bold and the Beautiful*. She drove across the lovely countryside, feeling part of it for the first time, feeling at home and sang as she drove.

Molly greeted her at the gate and climbed in the passenger side of the Fiesta, giving her directions to where Molly's mother and grandmother lived. Molly's husband was in charge of the three children for the afternoon so Molly could take a few hours break for this visit. They all waved to her from the front step of their house, and Molly waved back, blowing kisses.

The house they arrived at was a standalone cottage with a few neighbours spaced several hundred metres apart. The house was an older type of cottage that had been renovated to modernise it, like the cottage she was staying in. It was charming and quaint but not as messy and disorganised as Molly's house.

On the drive there, Molly had explained that they had lost her father to cancer only one year earlier so her grandmother moved in with her mother, and it was working well.

Two women appeared at the door, very similar in appearance to Molly but appropriately aged for her mother and grandmother, one with greying hair and the other with totally grey hair. Niamh thought they looked picture perfect, daughter, mother and grandmother. She imagined Maureen would complete the picture of four beautiful Irish witches.

Molly kissed her mother and grandmother in greeting and turned to introduce Niamh.

"This is Niamh I was telling you about, and this is my mother, Mauve and my grandmother, Asher," Molly announced.

Niamh stepped forward ready to greet with a big smile but hesitated. The women were studying Niamh for a few uncomfortable moments with a serious look on their face, not unlike Molly had at first, and Niamh became concerned something was wrong. Suddenly, they both broke into smiles and offered their hand in friendship, inviting her in.

"Lovely to meet you," Niamh responded and followed the women into a cosy and warm sitting room. They all sat on the large, overstuffed chairs and Mauve brought them a pot of tea where they sipped at the strong tea and talked 'witch' for the next few hours.

Other than May, Niamh hadn't experienced such easy and knowledgeable witch talk before and it was exhilarating. She hung on every word spoken, soaking up the knowledge like a sponge.

"Molly tells us that you only discovered you are a witch recently," began Asher. "How is that going for you?"

Niamh considered the question. These three witches were so genuine and warm and she so desperately wanted friends who could help her with her new abilities. She felt a need to be truthful and to confide in this family. How else would she gain knowledge? She also felt that any untruths would be immediately identified and trust lost.

"It has been a traumatic time, to be honest?" she said quietly.

"Would you like to talk about it?" Asher asked.

"Oh yes. Please do," Mauve responded, a little too enthusiastically. She realised and lowered her head apologetically.

Niamh smiled and nodded. "My grandmother, Agatha lived here at Claureen and moved to Australia when she was about twenty years old," Niamh began.

"Yes. I knew Agatha as a child, and Bridget before her. I occasionally had tea with Bridget and shared stories," Asher said.

"Really? Wow! How amazing is that?" said Niamh, delighted. "She made friends with a witch in Melbourne named May and they remained friends for the rest of their lives. Agatha married and had three daughters, none of them witches. One of them was my mother, Lucinda."

Everyone was listening, nodding and sipping their tea.

"It turned out there was also a family in Australia called the Grimm family. Have you heard of them?" Niamh asked.

"No. I can't say we have," said Molly looking across at the other two shaking their heads.

"They have magical abilities though not as strong as a witch. They all share blonde hair and dark eyebrows and are evil with an overwhelming urge to kill witches." Niamh noted Mauve frown as if something jogged her memory.

"Apparently, they were instrumental during the witch trials across Europe in hunting witches. Anyway, this family found out about Agatha and May and began a vendetta to kill them. One of them stabbed May but Agatha was able to heal her enough for her to survive."

Niamh took a sip of the hot tea. "The Grimm family caused the death of Agatha's husband, my grandfather, I guess as a way of getting to her. She sought revenge and went to their house where she set one of them alight in his car and then set the house on fire. The Grimm father and two of his sons were killed in the fire."

There was dead silence in the room as the three witches stared at Niamh, spellbound. "She allowed the mother and other children to escape and made them promise to leave the witches alone in the future."

"My grandmother was traumatised for the rest of her life. When I was born, my mother decided she didn't want me to be associated with the witch way of life at all so she kept me away from my grandmother and May. I never knew any of this history or them."

"My grandmother died of cancer early this year and my mother took me to say goodbye. During this time my grandmother grabbed my wrist and bestowed upon me. My mother realised that she had no choice but to tell me who I was and then, May was called in to teach me how to be a witch."

"You were lucky to have May," said Molly.

"Oh, I sure was for a short time. I loved her." Niamh took another sip to calm her emotions. She could feel tears threatening as always when she talked about May.

"The Grimm family found out about me and sent a guy to stalk me. I took precautions so he beat up one of my friends and then they decided to attack and kill May."

She heard the intake of breath from the three witches. "Did they kill May?" asked Mauve.

"Yes. I arrived just after she'd been stabbed but was still alive. There were two of them and we had a magic fight. I came out in front but it was too late for May." The explanation was too much for Niamh and she burst into tears. Molly put her arms around her to console her and Asher passed her a tissue. They let her cry for a few minutes.

"Did May bestow on you as well?" asked Asher.

"Yes. I was too late to save her. She did but there is another complication to this story," said Niamh between sobs.

"Go on."

"Well … I found out that my mother had an affair with a Grimm twenty years ago and I was the result," Niamh admitted.

She felt Molly's arm twitch and heard the three witches shock intake of breath again. The three of them stared at her as if she had turned green and sprouted wings.

"I'm half Grimm but I'm a witch," she said. "My father was one of the children that escaped the house fire my grandmother set. He's not … like the others but he's still a Grimm. He's left the Grimm world now and he and my mother are back together and having another baby. It's going to be a witch as well."

Niamh finished her narration with a smile of pleasure at the thought of her mother's baby being a witch. She waited to hear what the other witches thought and realised they were looking at each other with a question in their eyes.

"You sure about that?" asked Molly.

"It's a magic baby," said Niamh, no longer as confident as she was.

Chapter 30
GUNTHER

Gunther was seated in a luxurious overstuffed chair carefully placed to be in the optimal power position in the conference room so that when Tarren entered the door, he would be forced to walk the considerable distance to his waiting chair with Gunther sitting high at the desk in front of him. His secretary, Anya, was seated to one side of the desk with pen, paper and recorder at the ready, and Hans sitting on the other side of the desk.

They waited, primed and ready for this interrogation of Tarren Forsyth Grimm. All were aware that Tarren would not be leaving this office once the interrogation was complete. His fate was unknown and Gunther enjoyed the anticipation of making that decision on the spur of the moment depending on the outcome achieved at the interrogation.

On the desk in front of him, sat a list of Tarren's faults, failings, accusations and atrocities and Gunther glanced down regularly at the list to keep them fresh in his mind. How could someone of his own flesh and blood be guilty of such horrific crimes? He needed to know this information, the reasoning, so he could ensure it never happened again. He was looking forward to this interrogation and had woken up in a good mood, eager to begin the day.

He glanced at his watch again and noted the time was 10.06am, and that Tarren was now six minutes late. No one was ever late to a meeting with Gunther and the sheer brazenness of it ate at his very core. The thought that Tarren may not attend at all had never crossed his mind and it was not until 10.18am that it dawned on him that he had been stood up. His own grandson had refused the invitation for the meeting. It was totally unheard of and totally unacceptable.

SLAM!

Gunther slammed his fist on the desktop. Anya jumped in fright but Hans had been coiled up and ready for Gunther's explosive temper. He had experienced it many times before.

"HE'S NOT COMING, IS HE?" Gunther yelled at his two companions.

Anya picked up the pen and paper and busied herself with writing less she burst into tears at the sudden display of temper. Gunther swung around to look Hans in the eye, his face red in his fury and spittle running down his chin.

"DO WE KNOW WHERE HE IS RESIDING?" Gunther demanded.

Hans looked down at his notes and turned a few pages. "He left the family home and was in a hotel for nearly four weeks then moved to Liddle Street in Coburg with a 'Lucinda Flynn'. He is no longer there and there has been no sign of him this past week."

Hans looked up at Gunther, registered his red fury and that he was not relaying the quality of information that Gunther wished to hear. "Umm ... he has not been at his office but we know his secretary met with him to deliver the invitation. We have her under surveillance. Sooner or later, he will check in with her again and we'll know about it and locate him."

"What about his woman?" asked Gunther. "What do we know about her?"

"She is missing as well …"

Gunther slammed his fist down again.

"WHAT ABOUT THE WITCH DAUGHTER?" He yelled at Hans.

Hans gulped and straightened his tie, vying for composure. "Yes. My contacts said she left the country three weeks ago on a Qantas flight, with short stopovers in Singapore and Heathrow, arriving at Shannon Airport in Ireland. She travelled with another female, Emma Gail Watkins and …"

"WHERE ARE THEY?"

"Err … there is a cottage at Claureen, close to Ennis, west of Dublin that was owned by the grandmother witch and was passed down to the three daughters. We suspect she is staying there with her friend and there are two of our family members enroute to the location shortly. They should be there in the next few days. Hans looked up from his notes to check how this latest information was being received.

Gunther was nodding slightly. "You tell them I want her. They need to bring her back to Australia so I can finish her."

"If she is powerful like we have been led to believe, it may be impossible for them to safely escort her back on a plane. They may have no choice but to destroy her in Ireland." Hans said quietly.

Gunther threw his hands in the air in frustration, knowing this was a true statement and the most likely scenario. He couldn't stand the thought that someone else may take pleasure in destroying this witch and not himself.

"Ok. There are three daughters born of the witch, you said. Have you tracked down where they reside?" Gunther asked Hans.

"Err … yes. We have their homes being watched and if Lucinda Flynn turns up at one of those houses, we will be notified immediately." Hans said, taking a deep breath after this delivery.

Gunther sat back and twiddled his fingers, calculating. "Ayna, please delay my trip back to Sydney. I think I am needed here in Melbourne for a bit longer."

Chapter 31
NIAMH

"Niamh, I'm really glad that you've told us this story and been so honest," said Mauve. She looked at her mother and daughter for agreement. "I'm sure I can say that all three of us felt a little hesitant with you because we could detect something different in you that we have not come across with other witches ... something a little dangerous ... something a little volatile, and now we understand. You have this other family blood in your veins, but you are a witch at heart."

Niamh sniffed and dabbed at her nose with the tissue. "I do feel that I'm a witch and not a Grimm. Emma calls me a witchy Grimm."

"What? A witchetty grub did you say?" asked Molly.

Niamh gave a giggle. "No, a witchy Grimm."

"You said your father is in a relationship with your mother now. How do you get along with your father?" asked Molly.

"Hmmm ... I only found out about him six months ago and I really hate the Grimm's. They killed my grandfather, stabbed May and killed her, ruined my grandmother's life and beat up my friend. I know he didn't do these things, but his two sons did and now they're in prison awaiting sentencing. My father has left the Grimm's and is protecting my family. He wants his sons to pay for what they have done."

"But how do YOU feel about your father?" asked Molly.

Niamh frowned, unsure how to answer. "He treats my mother well and I'm happy about that. I want to like him but he's a Grimm and I can't accept it." She shook her head violently.

"Tell me about the Grimm family and their magic. What can they do?" asked Asher.

Niamh shrugged and then concentrated on her recollections. "I don't know much. I know more what they can't do than what they can. Umm ... they can't handle charms or Brigid's Cross and can only enter a protected house if invited. May once told me that the first Grimm she met, Dora Grimm, tried to give her a headache but Agatha, my grandmother, gave her a worse one. Umm ... they can detect when another magic person is nearby. I know my father put a magic blocker on his two sons that are in prison."

"A magic blocker? What's that?" asked Mauve.

"It's some way of halting or pausing their magical abilities so they are like a normal person," Niamh replied. "May told me the Grimm's are rich so they must have a way of winning lotteries or able to detect the stock market. Also, something weird happened during their attack. When I was bleeding the two brothers smelled my blood and were transfixed or something, then it happened to me when one of them bled. I could detect they were of the same blood as me. What do you think they are?"

"I don't really know but I did once hear about a group of people in Europe that had limited magic abilities but were descended from an animal," said Mauve.

"An animal? Really? Like a dog or cat?" asked Niamh.

"I heard it from a witch visiting from Europe. She said they had some animal characteristics."

Niamh considered these words. Did she have any animal characteristics? She could smell blood and she had growled a few times. That was an interesting thought and one she would have to contemplate. One day she would need to talk to her father about the history of his family and what they were.

"Are you aware of other types of magical beings?" asked Niamh.

"I met a fairy once," said Molly.

"No way. A fairy? Like with wings? What ... like Tinkerbell?" asked Niamh.

"No wings but she was magical and she said she was a fairy," said Molly.

"I think there are possibly many different types of magic out there, and not all of it is good, unfortunately," said Mauve. "You may be still learning but you've been bestowed twice and you have this other blood as well. I wouldn't be surprised if you are very powerful one day," said Asher.

"But how do I beat the Grimm's in a fight if it comes to that?" asked Niamh.

"Hmmm ... I think that is to be avoided at all costs. You may be powerful but there is only one of you and possibly lots of them," said Asher.

"If you have to," said Mauve. "I think you should try this magic blocker. If you can block their magic then they have nothing."

"What if they can block mine?" asked Niamh.

"You need to find a way of preventing that from happening. You are ok with charms?" asked Molly.

"Yes," said Niamh.

"Wear something at all times, around your neck. They can't touch you or do anything magical to you when you are wearing a charm," said Molly.

Niamh thought for a moment. "Yes. I'll make something. Thank you to all of you for listening to me today and being so helpful."

"You're welcome, Niamh. You can always call on us to help you. We've got your back."

Chapter 32
LUCINDA

Lucinda stared at her burner phone, the one Tarren had instructed her to use. Should she call Niamh and tell her what was going on? The question nagged at her, but she didn't want to ruin Niamh's trip to Ireland or cause any stress, and she really didn't know what, if anything, was going on. Niamh had been so protective since the assault in January and May's death, that if she found out there was possibly a problem with the Grimm's and their safety, Niamh would be on the first plane home. Lucinda didn't want to cause a panic with Niamh if and put her life in jeopardy. What was the right thing to do?

She was seriously concerned after seeing the look on Tarren's face as he said goodbye to her. She knew, without a doubt, that this situation was much worse than what Tarren was letting on. She was in serious danger and so was Tarren, and possibly her own sisters. How could this have happened? She felt guilty for dragging her sisters into the situation, but she reasoned they had always been part of the Grimm story after the Grimm's had targeted their parents years ago.

The sisters had spent the morning making new charms for themselves and their family to wear around their neck. With a great amount of precision, she had leaked a single drop of Niamh's urine on each charm hoping that it would be enough to ward off the evil Grimm family. How she wished she had asked Niamh to leave several vials of her urine in the freezer.

New charms were also placed on the door and back door, plus Bethany was instructed to install charms at her own home as well. Everyone hoped it was sufficient and although her sisters urged her to let Niamh know what was going on, she held off.

Lucinda was also reluctant to phone Tarren as she knew he would be busy with trying to resolve the current situation and she didn't want him worrying about her unnecessarily. She was itching to hear his voice though and know he was ok. Arabella brought her a coffee and kissed the top of her head affectionately.

"Have you spoken with Niamh yet?" she asked.

"No. I don't want to worry her if I don't have to, and ruin her trip," Lucinda replied.

"But what if ... what if something happens here and no one let her know there was an issue? What if ... there is something she could do to change the situation? Don't you think she would want to know? Seriously. I do believe you need to talk to Niamh."

The baby kicked and she felt her stomach moving from the pressure as she picked up her phone and stared at the screen, still unsure whether to call or not. The phone rang in her hand, startling her and she glanced at the screen to see it was Niamh calling. She should have guessed with them just talking about Niamh and the baby kicking furiously to let her know, and now Niamh was calling.

Lucinda looked up at Arabella who could tell by the expression on her sister's face who was calling. She looked down at the screen again and touched the screen to answer the call.

Chapter 33
NIAMH

The moment she entered the cottage, Niamh knew something had changed. She could sense a subtle difference in the air, an essence that hadn't been there before. Puzzled, she stopped, looking around to determine whether it was a physical change or her imagination. Emma and Collins had been sitting on the couch, but Emma sprang to her feet as soon as Niamh entered the cottage. She could see Collins with his guitar on his lap so guessed he had been playing music for Emma.

"Oh, Niamh. There you are," Emma said, brightly.

Niamh stared at her and then looked across at Collins suspiciously before it dawned on her. She put her bag down and turned to look at Emma carefully. Emma's face had blushed a rosy colour and she was trying not to meet Niamh's eyes. Niamh looked over at Collins and he had a cheeky smile on his face which he was trying hard to hide as he strummed his guitar.

"Ok," Niamh said, smiling. "I get it. You two are together now. Yes?"

Emma looked back at Collins and giggled. "Yes."

"I'm so pleased to hear that," said Niamh and she truly was. They matched so perfectly, looked great together and both with kind and friendly dispositions. It was meant to be, she thought to herself.

"How did your visit with the witches go?" asked Emma.

"Great. They are lovely people and helpful. They said something interesting about a family from Europe who had animal blood in their veins. I wondered if it was the Grimm family," said Niamh.

"Animal. Seriously?" asked Emma.

"Well, remember how the brothers reacted to my blood, and then it happened to me too. Also, you said I've growled a few times."

"Growled?" queried Collins from over at the couch, guitar strumming halted and looking concerned.

"Yeah, but animal blood?" said Emma, sceptical. "Sounds a bit of a stretch."

"Oh, but the fact that witches exist and other magical people isn't a stretch?" said Niamh, ironically.

A noise startled the three of them, a dog barking and sounding very close by. Niamh was nearest to the door so she opened it and the other two followed her outside. Standing on the outside of the gate stood Anne Riley and the white bulldog.

Niamh stepped forward and made her way over to the gate with Emma and Collins behind her. She felt the hair on her head rise and her skin prickle, as she neared the magical person. The woman was dressed in the same coat and black straw hat that Emma had described to her, and Niamh noted the white bulldog at her heels.

Her eyes met the eyes of the other woman and the two stood staring at each other, evaluating. Emma had recounted to Niamh how the other woman had not been keen to look Emma in the eyes when she had visited the cottage, yet she was openly eye to eye with Niamh.

Niamh noted she had sunken brown eyes with no spark as she had detected in the other witch's eyes. They were only metres apart as they stared down each other. Emma and Collins watched silently wondering who would blink first and what did the staring contest mean. Both unsure what they should do in this situation other than stand by and wait.

"So, we meet," said Anne Riley, her voice a little croaky.

"So, we do," said Niamh, calmly.

The woman looked down at the white bulldog who was snuffling at her feet and then back up at Niamh. "You gave Byron fleas."

"I did," said Niamh. "He was hanging around where he shouldn't be."

The woman continued staring at Niamh. "What are you?" she asked in a serious voice, her voice cocked slightly to the right.

"What are you?" Niamh countered.

The woman continued staring and then sniffed loudly. "I'm Anne Riley."

"Niamh Flynn," returned Niamh.

"But ... you're not a witch," said Anne Riley, her voice unsure.

"What am I then?" asked Niamh, inwardly concerned that this woman could tell she had different blood.

"I'm not sure but I'll work it out. Why don't you come out here?" said the woman, wrinkling her nose to indicate the fortified border of the cottage.

"Why would I want to do that?" asked Niamh, knowing that Anne Riley wanted her away from the protected area so she could really measure who and what Niamh was.

"Oh, just to be friendly."

"I'm not in the friendly mood," said Niamh. The truth was that Niamh was a bit fearful of this strange, magical woman who knew that Niamh was different to a witch. She had to find a way to scare the woman away, a show of muscle and power.

Suddenly, there was a crack and lightning flashed across the sky. Anne Riley ducked her head as if the lightning was about to strike her. She raised an arm up in defence and peeked up at the sky where dark clouds were forming. Then she glared back at Niamh who had a slight smirk on her face. Anne Riley's eyes were wide with fear and panic.

"Better hurry home before the rain hits," said Niamh. "You wouldn't want to get caught in a storm and get soaked through."

The rain began and within ten seconds, it was pelting down torrentially, soaking Anne Riley and the white bulldog who whimpered and tried to shelter close to its master. Anne Riley fished around in her bag that was slung over her arm and eventually retrieved the crumpled, black umbrella. By the time the umbrella had been opened and raised, she was already soaked through.

Emma looked at the ground around her and Collins, then at Niamh standing a few metres ahead of them and noted that there was no rain on their side of the fence. Anne Riley turned and headed back down the laneway with the bulldog at her heels, soaking wet. Niamh turned to look at Collins and Emma.

"I'm not ready to face her one on one yet. I don't really know how to deal with her or what I'm up against. For now, I'm just going to stall the situation."

Emma nodded. "I'm glad you didn't make her poop her pants."

Chapter 34
HARDY

Hardy paced his home office, stopping occasionally to stare out the window, unseeing. He had never felt so torn and distressed in his life and was unsure how to handle the situation. Being the head of the Melbourne Grimm family was a huge responsibility, and he admitted to himself that he felt inadequate in the role. His brother, Tarren had always been stronger and shown more leadership than he ever could.

He had just received a summary of the morning's interrogation meeting from Hans over the phone in a robotic, monotone voice. Tarren had not presented to his interrogation and was in hiding, supposedly. Hardy silently breathed a sigh of relief at this news. He had been heavy hearted all day, fearing that his little brother may not have survived the interrogation, or might be held captive awaiting execution.

No one could know that he was the one who had sent warning texts to Tarren which may have saved his life. If he were found to be the anonymous whistleblower, his own life would be in danger as well, which was why he had bought the burner phone.

The summary report from Hans informed him that Tarren's location was currently unknown. Hardy crossed his fingers that this would remain the case for now; that his woman's location was also unknown. Hardy assumed they were together somewhere in hiding, but there were family members watching the homes of her two sisters.

Also, that they were confident the witch hybrid daughter was in Ireland, and European Grimm family members were on the way to bring her back to Australia, if possible.

Hardy didn't care at all about the witch family and considered it easier if they were eliminated and completely out of the picture. Perhaps then, his little brother could forget this lapse in ethics and immerse himself back in the Grimm fold. Hardy would welcome him with open arms and felt a tear in his eye as he thought of his brother.

The big question for Hardy right at this moment was what should he do now?

Should he let Gunther run the show while he weakly sat back and watched? Should he participate and agree to everything Gunther wished to do, a submissive party to the execution of his own brother?

There was no doubt in his mind that he needed to speak with Tarren in person and try with all his persuasiveness to encourage him back into the fold. If Tarren would unblock his son's magic abilities, or at least Beaton's, and walk away from the witch family and back to his own Grimm family, perhaps that would be sufficient for Gunther to back off and leave them be.

If Tarren would not listen to reason, then at least he had full knowledge of what Gunther was planning and could protect himself as he saw fit.

Hardy pulled his phone out of his suit jacket pocket and looked down at the screen. Suddenly, the door to his office opened and he almost hit the roof in fright, dropping his phone on the floor in the process.

"Oh, sorry. I wondered if you would like a coffee?" asked Helga, smiling that she had startled him.

"Ummm ... not yet, thanks," he answered, feeling flustered.

She nodded and closed the door as Hardy fished his phone up from the floor. Calming his nerves, he sat on his office chair and sent a message to Tarren on his burner phone.

Meet me under the clocks today 12 noon

He waited quietly, barely taking a breath for a response, and it came within two minutes.

Ok

Hardy exhaled with relief and although nervous that he could be followed or that someone may see him, he also felt he was doing the right thing. It was imperative that he see his baby brother and try to talk sense into him before it was too late.

He let Helga know he was off for a business meeting and drove down to Richmond railway station. It would be easier for him to catch a train into Flinders Street Station than drive and try to find a car parking spot in the busy CBD. He surreptitiously parked, and walked into the station, keeping a look out for anyone who may be watching him or following.

In some ways, it felt ridiculous to be worrying about being followed by a Grimm as the Grimm family were all on the same page and all had the same agenda, except Tarren. The Grimm's would never expect that Hardy would do something against the family wishes.

He hoped.

Chapter 35
NIAMH

Niamh and Emma walked into Marta's Bar on Friday night to watch Collins play as he did every Friday night. They had been planning to attend for weeks but without a car, it was difficult to think of walking home in the dark, cold and wet at midnight. Now that they had the Ford Fiesta, a night on the town was not out of the question.

The two of them had spent hours preparing for this outing, applying their make-up to be on-point and using just the right amount of hair lacquer to ensure a bouncy, full head of hair. Their outfits were complete with jeans, boots and a shirt. Of course, they knew spending so much time on make-up and hair was over the top, but it was fun and their first night out in Ireland.

When they walked into the half-full bar on Friday night, they felt like they owned the world. Every head turned to look at them and Collins, who had been setting up cords to his amplifier up on stage, raced over to greet them. He wrapped his arms around Emma and planted a big kiss on her. Niamh looked away, pulling a puke face which made the other two laugh.

"So glad you came. Here … I have these seats for you," Collins showed the girls to two bar stools at a small, round bar table not far from the stage. "Set starts in ten minutes so get a drink and enjoy. The bartender here is Marc and he'll look after you." He winked at Marc who smiled and asked the girls what they wanted to drink.

Emma settled on a Prosecco and Niamh ordered red wine, thinking back to the red wine she had enjoyed the night she stayed at May's house. They took a sip from their drinks and looked around at the growing crowd in the room. Everyone was dressed casually and seemed to be enjoying themselves. There was a good vibe in the air and they both felt pleased to be there.

"Excuse me, are you the two girls Collins has been rattling on about?" asked a voice, and they turned to see a bearded man standing and addressing them. He looked to be in his twenties, light brown hair and beard and a friendly face.

"It depends on what he's been saying," said Emma, joking with him.

"Ach, well … he said one of you is his princess and the other one is a witch," the man laughed.

Emma put her hand out to shake his hand. "I'm Emma and this is Niamh."

"I'm the evil witch," said Niamh, giggling.

"Pleased to meet you. My name is Duncan and I've been Collins best friend since we were lads," he said earnestly.

The three shook hands and as Niamh looked across at Collins, she could see him smiling and happy they had met Duncan. They sat with Duncan for most of the night and listened to the music, blown away at how talented Collins was with the guitar and how good his voice was. He performed with another guy on a base guitar and one on keyboard with the music ranging from Irish ballads to up-tempo dancing music.

The crowd clapped vigorously after each song and particularly, at the end of each set to show their appreciation. As the night wore on, the dancing increased until the floor was full and the venue was vibrant with movement and energy.

A drunken man of about forty years old, slurring his words approached Niamh from behind.

"'S'cuse me. Wanna dance?" he asked, wobbling slightly as he tried to stand on one spot.

"Umm ... no thanks," said Niamh, politely.

"You English?" he asked.

"No. Australian," she responded, leaning away from his alcohol breath and unsteady stance.

"AUSSIE, AUSSIE, AUSSIE, OI, OI, OI," he yelled in her ear and laughed.

Niamh and Emma exchanged looks at the Australian term often used at sporting events which they both hated and found cringe-worthy. In this case, Niamh just smiled at him and turned away, ignoring the term.

The man put his hand on her shoulder and tried to pull her back around.

"Hey, I'm talkin' to ya," he said, staggering to stay upright.

Emma saw Niamh's eyes flash amber and heard crackling noises in the air above. Quickly, Emma stood up and put her hand out to gently push the man away from Niamh.

"Come on, time to go. She doesn't want to dance. OK?" Emma said, calmly.

Duncan had been over at the bar buying a drink and had missed what was happening. He returned just in time to see Emma gently pushing this man away and heard what she said. He immediately put his drink on the table and grabbed the man, pulling him away.

"Come on, Todd. You've had a few scoops. How about you go home and call it a night?" he said.

"Naw, I want to dance, yer dryshite" Todd said, pulling away from Duncan. Duncan tried to turn the man around again, and Todd managed to escape his grasp.

Emma saw a bouncer from the door watching and heading over in their direction. Good, she thought. Best to get this man out before Niamh turns him into a victim.

Too late.

The man groaned and clutched at his belly, immediately followed by some loud wet squirting sounds. Duncan dropped his arms away from the man and stepped back in an automatic response. Todd groaned again and staggered across the room toward the men's toilet with the bouncer close behind him.

Emma looked at Niamh's passive face. "Naughty girl," she said.

Niamh just smiled, conspiratorially.

Chapter 36
GUNTHER

Gunther sat in his over-stuffed chair at his high desk and looked across at the young man sitting in the chair that Tarren had evaded the day before. This young man was nervous, fiddling with his pockets and not knowing where to look. Gunther smiled to himself as this was the sort of behaviour he had come to expect from underlings, and he admitted to himself; he liked the feeling it gave him. This was his own great grandson, but he had so many grandchildren and great grandchildren that he would be hard pressed to even remember what their names were or who they belonged to.

Gunther leaned forward across the desk to appear more menacing to the young man.

"I want to know everything about the witch hybrid. Every detail of your encounter with her. Do you understand?" he asked in his authoritarian voice.

"Yes, sir," answered Beaton, nodding as well to double affirm his acquiescence and sat up straighter in his chair.

Gunther sat back and clasped his hands on the desk in front of him. "Go ahead. Tell me the whole story."

"Ok. Well … Justin and I, we … tied the old witch's hands together and Justin used a knife on her, in her side." Beaton indicated the area on his body. "We wanted a slow death and for the young witch to see her friend die. So, we waited and when the young witch arrived, she had a normal friend with her, shielded behind."

Beaton wriggled in his seat, beginning to feel more confident with the story telling.

"Our father had told us she was our half-sister and we weren't to harm her. None of us were sure that she was definitely his daughter because she doesn't look like us. She looks like a witch with that red hair." Beaton shivered at the revolting concept of a red-haired sister, even a half-sister.

"We decided the only way to be sure that she was our half-sister was to bleed her. Then we would know by the blood smell and if she wasn't family, then we could kill her too."

Gunther was nodding. "What if she was your half-sister? What were you going to do with her?"

Beaton paused and contemplated the question. "We wouldn't have killed her ... I think. The old witch was already dying so we probably would have roughed her up a bit to scare her. If she did fight too much, then we might have killed her ... you know, in self-defence."

Gunther indicated for Beaton to go on with the story. "She used magic to throw things at us, like candles and saucepans, or stuff like that. I remember something hitting me. Justin slashed her with the knife and cut her arm. There was blood and then we knew that she was Dad's daughter, our half-sister. By then, she was really fighting us and using strong magic. When Justin started bleeding from a wound on his head, she got the blood smell and I tried to attack her. She threw something in front of me and I fell to the ground. Next thing I knew, there was this old broom attacking me on its own. The old witch was still alive and sent her fucking broomstick to beat me up."

"There's no need to swear," said Gunther, gruffly, his sense of civility affronted.

"Sorry. When it eventually stopped, I saw that Justin was at the sink putting water on his face where boiling water or candle wax or something had burned him. Dad and a woman walked in and then all hell broke loose. The old witch died and the young witch went berserk … completely nuts. There were windows exploding and thunder and lightning. She tried to fry Justin's brain and it looks like she succeeded because half his brain is now minced meat."

Beaton took a few deep breaths to calm down from narrating this traumatic event.

"Police arrived and we were handcuffed like criminals. Everyone was milling around the dead old witch and Dad wanted nothing to do with us. He was embracing the young witch and the other woman and we were left to be dragged off and thrown into prison."

Beaton sat back, emotionally drained and waited for questions.

"You said, the young witch caught the blood smell?" Gunther asked.

"Yes, she stopped and put her head up and could smell family blood," Beaton replied.

"So, she is more than just witch then, isn't she? She is hybrid. Half witch, half Grimm."

"Yes, I guess so."

"I wonder how powerful she is. The family think the first old witch bestowed on the young witch, don't they?" Gunther asked.

"Yes. They do."

"Is it reasonable to assume that the second old witch, the one that Justin killed, also bestowed on her?"

"She did. I heard it."

"That is a lot of witch power and then to have half Grimm blood too." Gunther's eyes widened and his pulse increased with excitement.

"Boy, you are lucky to have escaped with your life. Your brother is lucky that half a brain is all he lost. Do you understand?" Gunther demanded.

Beaton, taken aback, stared at Gunther not sure what he was supposed to say.

"Umm ... I guess so."

"Ok. I am finished with you. You can go."

Just like that, Beaton was dismissed. He walked out of the room feeling like a chastised little boy who just had an altercation with the principal of the school and needed to go home to lick his wounds.

Gunther turned to Hans who had been sitting silently throughout the questioning of Beaton.

"I want that witch hybrid here. I've never wanted anything so much in my life."

Chapter 37
NIAMH

Niamh was excited to be introducing Emma to Molly, Mauve and Asher, her new witch friends, when they visited the cottage on the Saturday. For Niamh, this meeting of her personal life and her witch life was vitally important and she wanted to know that the three witches would have Emma's back as well if there was ever trouble. She remembered back to taking Emma to meet May on that fateful day, and how excited she had been for them to meet.

She needn't have worried as the three witches thought Emma was wonderful to the point where Niamh felt the one left out of conversations and attention. Emma had a way of conversing with anyone, putting people at ease and was so damned likeable.

"You're so damn nice it makes me want to puke," Niamh once told her.

Entertaining the three witches filled the small cottage to capacity with plenty of laughter and stories. After coffee and shortbread biscuits, Niamh asked them if they would like to visit Bridget's grave. The three visitors were keen so the five of them headed down the hill toward the thicket of trees that hid the cemetery from the world. They kept the pace slow as Asher was a little arthritic but determined not to be left behind. Niamh was surprised Emma wanted to come along but she was also determined not to be left behind and was enjoying the company of the new friends.

When they reached the treed area, Niamh walked through first and halted in the centre where she had felt such intense feelings and flashes of past events on her first visit. She could feel tingling and closed her eyes to again sense the birth of countless livestock, followed by the capture of witches by villagers. She reasoned that these flashes or whispers had been left in this place for a reason and it was only fair that she pay homage.

When she opened her eyes, she saw Emma standing quietly watching the witches as they breathed in the location and drew its history into themselves. Emma could see something witchy was happening and not to speak or distract the women at this moment. The other three were still in the throes of their journey so Niamh smiled at Emma to reassure her and they waited.

Within a few minutes, the three women opened their eyes and sought Niamh.

"Tell me what you sense, Niamh," said Mauve.

"This is a special place where many calves and lambs have been born over hundreds of years. It is a sheltering place of peace, calm and new life."

The other three witches nodded silently and waited.

"It is also the location where a few of my ancestors – witches – were chased and captured in this very spot by villagers with torches. They were dragged in ropes back to the village where they were interrogated and burned." Niamh felt emotional as she said the words out loud.

Emma inhaled loudly in shock at what Niamh had just said and stared at her, wondering if she was joking. "Oh my God, Niamh. How do you know that?"

"I can sense the livestock and the arrests of at least two witches from this place, but the rest I know from whispers that the deceased told me in the cemetery," Niamh answered.

"You can sense more than us because we've not had the whispers, but we can sense the animal births and the fear of the witches captured," said Asher, solemnly.

The five women continued through the treed area to the cemetery which looked neatly kept and freshly weeded. They entered by moving a wooden rail to the side and stood looking at the headstones.

"You've done a good job," said Mauve, realising that Niamh had restored the cemetery.

Niamh was pleased that they had noticed and acknowledged how important it was to her to honour her ancestors. As Bridget's headstone was the closest and she was the one Asher had known, and Mauve had met as a child, the four witches touched the headstone in greeting. Niamh felt the same whispers again and she wondered if it was just her, as a descendent or whether the other three would sense it too.

She opened her eyes and looked to Molly expectantly. "We can feel her but don't receive the whispers," she answered. Niamh thought it amazing that these three knew each other so well and their witch abilities that each could answer for the three of them rather than singularly.

For a few minutes all was quiet as the five women stood around where Bridget had been laid to rest and then Molly, Mauve and Asher broke into song, the three voices harmonising so beautifully. The song was a sad song of death and loss.

> *Why does thou sit upon my grave*
> *And will dead lips to speak?*
> *Why does thou weep upon my grave*

And will not let me sleep?

My breast it is as cold as clay
My breath is earthly strong
And if you kiss my cold clay lips
Your days they won't be long

How oft on yonder grave, sweetheart
Where we were won't to walk
The fairest flower that e'er I saw
Has withered to a stalk

When will we meet again, sweetheart?
When will we meet again?
When the Autumn leaves that fall from trees
Are green and spring up again

How oft on yonder grave, sweetheart
Where we were won't to walk
The fairest flower that e'er I saw
Has withered to a stalk

Emma and Niamh listened in rapture as the three voices sang the deep, sad song and when the song was over, they clapped.

"Oh, that was so beautiful," said Emma. "What is the name of the song?"

"It is part of *The Unquiet Grave*," said Molly.

The five headed back up the hill to the cottage, Mauve holding Asher by the arm to assist her with the gullies and rough ground. Niamh had anticipated that Emma would be bored with this visit but she looked happy and bright, pleased to have been included.

Nearing the peak of the hill just behind the cottage, all four witches stopped dead in their tracks. Emma, who had walked an extra few steps before realising, stopped and looked back.

"What is it?" she asked, nervously.

"We're not alone," said Molly.

"Huh, what do you mean?" asked Emma, looking around concerned.

"Someone with magic is at the gate," said Niamh and she strode on.

Chapter 38
JUSTIN

Justin smiled at the young woman in front of him as she was smiling at him and he felt it was the polite thing to do. He had no idea who she was but that didn't matter. He didn't know who half the people around him were anyway.

She looked at him continually throughout the lunch and he kept glancing back at her and smiling, wondering why she was so persistently watching him. He had gone for a nice drive with his big brother, to pick up this girl at the airport. Apparently, she had flown down from Sydney, wherever that was, and was part of the wider Grimm family. That's nice, he thought. It's nice to have family around you.

"What's her name again?" he asked Beaton, who was sitting next to him.

"Natasha," Beaton answered. "We picked her up at the airport. Do you remember?"

"Yes, of course," Justin said, beaming a big smile.

She was seated on the other side of him which made it so obvious when she was staring at him. Was he supposed to stare back? He wasn't quite sure what he was supposed to do, so he sipped his glass of orange juice and nibbled at his risotto.

Someone spoke to him and he looked over to the woman sitting half-way down the table. She looked familiar but he had forgotten her name.

"Justin, are you looking forward to the wedding?" the lady asked.

Justin stared at her for a minute wondering what wedding she was talking about. It didn't really matter who's wedding it was, he was sure it would be a great day, nonetheless.

"Yes. Sure am," he replied, smiling at the lady.

He felt the girl beside him squeeze his arm and he flinched automatically at the touch. What did she do that for? He looked at her for a reason and she was smiling at him and then leaned her head against his upper arm. He looked down at the blonde top of her head and thought she was a very strange girl and very friendly.

Beaton turned to him and nudged him slightly which was a good thing as it made the girl sit up and stop leaning on his arm. "I'll take you shopping this afternoon for a nice suit to wear at the wedding. How does that sound?"

"Great. Sounds great," Justin responded.

"The wedding is Saturday, so we have a few days to get all your outfit in order. After the wedding you and Natasha can stay in our spare room until you are ready for your own place," said Beaton.

Natasha? Was that the girl next to him? He thought that was the name Beaton had said earlier. Yes. Natasha. That was it. Was she staying in Beaton's spare room? Or was it himself who was staying in the spare room? Yes. It was him. He was the one staying in Beaton's spare room and a nice room it was, too.

He nodded and smiled at Beaton. Beaton looked satisfied as he turned to his wife. Justin heard the whisper even though Beaton was trying to keep a hushed voice.

"See, I knew he would come good. He just needed his family, not the doctors."

Justin had no idea what that meant but he had worked out if he just smiled and nodded at people, as well as be polite, then all in the world was fine.

Chapter 39
NIAMH

Turning the corner of the front picket fence, Niamh immediately saw a figure in a grey coat and a black straw hat standing close to the front gate and next to her, the white bulldog snuffled around the fence halting when it saw Niamh round the corner.

The only other time Niamh had seen Anne Riley, she had felt protected behind her urine bordered fence but now, she was caught out in the open without protection. She wasn't even wearing a charm on her body. She was completely vulnerable to someone who was potentially stronger magically than her.

Rather than show any fear and knowing she had the other three witches behind her, Niamh strode up to the woman and stood with her arms folded in front of her, in defiance.

"Yes. What can I do for you?" she asked, firmly.

Anne Riley stared at Niamh and then looked behind her at the other four women rounding the corner and then back to Niamh.

"I ... I wasn't wanting to cause any trouble," she said, meekly.

"Then what do you want?" asked Niamh, still with arms crossed.

"Well ... I ...I ... wanted to ask you what your intentions are," she said, and Niamh noticed how nervous the woman was. She wasn't holding eye contact and stammered a little when she spoke. Was she nervous because she was standing in front of four witches? That would be enough to make anyone nervous.

"What do you mean my intentions? My intentions in what regard?" asked Niamh, totally confused.

"Will you be staying here at Ennis? Is ... is this where you will stay?"

"Why do you want to know this? I don't even know you," said Niamh.

"Yes ... yes ... I was worried ... you know ... that you might ..." The woman was struggling to speak the words she wished to say. "That you might ... drive me out of town ... you know ... want me gone."

Niamh dropped her arms that had been folded across her chest and stared at the woman. This was the last thing she was expecting to hear. She turned to look at her four colleagues and they were standing back near the corner to give Niamh privacy but were intently listening and looking perplexed.

"Should you be run out of town?" asked Niamh, her voice a little calmer than it had been initially.

The woman looked down at the bulldog who was looking up to her. "People don't like me. They think ... I'm bad. I know they think that. I hear it."

"Are you bad?" Niamh asked.

"No," she answered quickly. "No. I'm not bad. I don't do anything bad."

"Then why do people think you're bad?" asked Niamh.

The woman sighed, a long and painful sigh. She kept glancing over at Niamh's face and then looking away. "I'm ... not ... very good with people. I don't know ... how to be friendly. I don't have any friends." She paused and looked up at Niamh and then across to the four women further away.

"You have magic and you have a familiar. What are you?" Niamh asked, bluntly.

"My mother was a … a … Cailleach … but … I was … I'm not like her. I was … not bad enough and I don't have much magic. She kicked me out of home when I was fourteen and I spent most of my life wandering around … homeless. Here … I have somewhere to live … and I have Byron … and I don't want to go."

She started silently crying with tears running down her face and small sniffs. Byron whimpered and snuffled against her leg.

"Why did you come looking for me and send your dog?" asked Niamh.

"I knew you were here in town. I … I … could sense you and I was scared. I sent Byron to watch you so I'd know what you were up to and if you were good or bad. I wanted to scare you so … you … you wouldn't try to kick me out."

She wiped the tears from her face with the back of her hand and left dirty streaks on her face.

"I saw how strong you are … your magic … it's much stronger than mine. Please don't make me leave," the woman pleaded.

Niamh glanced back at her friends again and they had serious looks on their faces, spellbound by the conversation.

"Do you use your magic to harm anyone or do anything bad?" Niamh asked.

"No, not at all."

"Why do people in town think you are a bad witch?"

"Well … I think it's because … I … I'm not friendly and … just keep to myself and Byron. I just use my magic to buy food because I don't have any money. I guess it's the same as stealing … kind of." She lowered her head and wiped her face again.

"Are you telling me the truth, that you do not use magic to harm any person, animal or event in Ennis?" Niamh asked again.

"Yes. I'm telling you the truth." Fresh tears swelled and spilled over. "Honestly, I'm just a miserable woman … who wants to stay here. This is my home."

Niamh looked at the woman in front of her and thought she could be mistaken for a homeless person with her bland attire and messy hair. Her face and expression didn't look evil but she didn't have a friendly or welcoming disposition in any way. People would steer clear of her and think the worst.

"Anne, would you like to come into the cottage and have a cup of coffee?" Niamh asked.

Chapter 40
LUCINDA

After one week of forced house arrest at Arabella's residence, Lucinda felt stir-crazy. She hadn't ventured as far as the backyard in that time, remaining inside the house, away from windows and unseen. It had been the same for Arabella and her husband, Robbie. They had watched so many movies and television series during the past week that Lucinda felt she would never want to watch television ever again.

Arabella submitted an online grocery order with Woolworths and the bags of groceries had been delivered to her doorstep, so food had not been a problem. The three of them found ways to amuse themselves but underneath it all, Lucinda missed Tarren badly.

They had spent almost twenty years apart and yet, one week without him now and she was feeling tearful and fragile. Thankfully, she had the burner phone he had given her and could converse with him and send text messages regularly, so she knew he was ok.

How would this end? Would the Grimm family harm Tarren? It seems unbelievable to think it possible, but they were evil and she had no idea how they worked. How had Tarren turned out the way he had? What would she do if something terrible happened to Tarren? These thoughts churned around in her head continually and she was constantly apologising to Arabella and Robbie for her tears.

Last time she had spoken with Tarren, he told her he had received a text from his unknown family member with a proposal to meet up. This was the unknown family member who had warned him Gunther was in town and not to attend the meeting with him. She was worried sick about this meet up with the unknown family member but understood Tarren's determination to go through with it. They couldn't continue as they currently were forever and needed to find a solution.

Niamh still was unaware what was afoot in Melbourne which Arabella and Bethany didn't agree with. She knew Niamh would be on the first flight back to Australia if she knew what was happening and Lucinda didn't want to worry her or spoil her trip away if she could help it. Of course, if things became more serious or something happened to Tarren then Niamh would be her first call, but for now, she preferred to keep her oblivious.

"LUCE, LUCE, you'd better get over here," Arabella's concerned voice penetrated her thoughts, and she walked into the main bedroom where Arabella's voice was coming from.

Arabella and Robbie stood at the bedroom window looking out toward the front of the house. The plantation shutters were partially open, just enough to see out and the two of them were peering through a crack in the blinds. Lucinda walked over to them and looked out through the gap in the blinds.

Standing in front of the house on the nature strip, leaning on a black parked car were four blonde heads. The four blonde heads were looking up at Arabella's house with no expression. Lucinda rushed a few steps backward in fright, mouth open and sucking in air. She backed into the bed and ended up sitting on the master bedroom bed, horrified.

"Oh my God, they've found us. They've found us," she cried, shocked and terrified.

Robbie left the room and came back a minute later with binoculars which he used to peer through the blinds and identify details of the four guards.

"There's three males and one female," he reported. "One male and the female look to be in their twenties, and the other two males are older, possibly middle-aged."

It didn't matter as Lucinda didn't know any of the Grimm family other than seeing Beaton and Justin in May's house months earlier in an extreme situation, and she doubted it would be them.

"They've parked on the road and it's currently a clearway until 10am, so I'm phoning to report them," said Robbie and he walked out of the room to find the number for reporting breaches of the road rules.

Arabella's phone rang on her bedside table and she picked it up and answered.

"Beth, we have ... WHAT?" Arabella started and stopped to listen.

"Oh, we do too. Four of them."

"That's interesting. So ... that means that they don't know where Lucinda or Tarren are, doesn't it? If they are staking my house and your house as well, then they are trying to flush them out."

"Ok. Yes. Don't leave the house. Don't let them see you. If they don't know, we won't be giving them any clues."

"Ok. Will do. You too. Bye."

Arabella hung up, tossed the phone back on the side table, and placed her arm around Lucinda.

"They don't know you're here. They only know where Beth and I live so they're trying to scare us and flush you and Tarren out, but it won't work," said Arabella, rubbing Lucinda's back.

"Don't forget, Luce, they can't step foot on our property with the charms and Niamh's urine so we're safe. We all have our charms on too," Arabella said, touching the charm around her neck.

Lucinda pulled out her phone from her pocket and tried to phone Tarren but the call went unanswered.

Chapter 41
NIAMH

Molly turned to Niamh, "Wow! You are amazing. I can't believe how that situation turned around with Anne Riley."

"You did well," said Asher. "I for one, feel ashamed that we live near her and never knew she was a lonely person looking for friends."

Anne and her familiar, Byron, had just departed for home after spending forty-five minutes sipping coffee and making friends with the five women. It was clear to all of them that she had no social graces and no idea how to communicate with others. Her table manners were poor and her choice of words when replying were stuttered and a bit random. She had trouble maintaining eye contact and stammered quite often. Neither her dress sense nor body odour were pleasant, but these were issues that could be overcome with time. She just didn't know any different and all women present felt they could help her.

Even Byron had allowed Emma to pat his head, and Niamh felt guilty for giving him a dose of fleas.

"It should be a lesson to us not to listen to idle village gossip and be judgemental. I guess the town people knew she had magic and with her lack of social nuances, assumed she must be an evil witch," said Mauve.

"She would have been blamed for anything that went wrong in the village and so the rumours spread," said Asher.

"You do think she's genuine, don't you?" asked Emma. "She's not just pulling a 'swifty' to get inside the cottage and inside your head?"

"I believe she's genuine," said Niamh.

"Me too," said Molly.

"I'm confused about something," said Niamh. "She said her mother was a Cailleach and I thought that was what Bridget was, what we are. That is what I was going to call myself to the public back home."

Mauve nodded. "Yes. It has a lot of different meanings depending on where you live, but a Cailleach was also known as the old woman, old hag or old witch, so I guess that is what Anne was referring to."

"Well," said Emma, standing up with a coy smile on her face. "I'd love to keep talking to you all, and I have loved meeting you, but I need to prepare for my date tonight." With that, she disappeared out the back door to the bathroom.

"Ooh, a date. Anyone we know?" Molly asked Niamh.

"His name is Collins O'Brien from Ennis, a musician and it turns out we have the same great grandfather, so he is kin to me," Niamh responded.

"How so?" asked Mauve.

"I just found out recently that Sean O'Brien, a local eighteen year old boy from town was in love with Bridget, and she with him, apparently. They were going to elope to another country and live happily ever after, however she became pregnant and his family found out. He was banned from seeing her or else his father would burn down Bridget's cottage and run her out of town. Agatha is, therefore, his daughter and my great grandfather."

"Oh my God," said Molly. "You seriously have the strangest family."

"Yeah, no kidding," Niamh responded. "Sean O'Brien gave us the car out there as a gift … like a sort of compensation for his perceived crime. I admit it took me a bit of time to accept what he did or … didn't do. I went to the aged care home where he lives and thanked him and I guess, we made our peace." Niamh smiled recollecting how pleased he had been to see her and didn't want to let go of her hand.

Emma appeared, dressed in a lovely red dress with a black jacket and everyone admired how she looked as she jokingly did a twirl around the room. A car beeped its horn out the front, and Emma said her farewell to all and disappeared out the door.

Niamh burst into laughter as the moment Emma closed the front door, the other three witches raced to the window to peek outside at Collins. After checking him out, they all agreed he looked like a nice guy and wished Emma well.

"Ah, you girls. You really are my tribe," said Niamh, and she meant it.

Chapter 42
TARREN

Tarren waited in Melbourne Central Business District, sitting on a bench at Federation Square across the road from Flinders Street Station. The station is an iconic landmark in Melbourne, a majestic old building where a row of clocks displaying the next departure time for each train platform are displayed above the entrance. 'Meet you under the clocks' had been a Melbourne saying for generations and everyone knew it meant to meet at the steps under the row of clocks.

Tarren wore sunglasses and very casual clothes of jeans and a shirt, clothes he was rarely seen wearing. His usual attire consisted of neat casual to business-like clothing. Just before the appointed time of 10am, he calmly sauntered across the road but stayed back away from the steps where he had a clear view. He had no idea who he was meeting and wondered if they would arrive incognito.

For five minutes he waited, wondering if the unknown family member had bailed and would not be attending. Then he saw Hardy and despite the baseball cap and sunglasses, Hardy still wore a business suit, looking obviously uncomfortable and trying to be invisible.

Tarren walked over to the foot of the steps and put his hand up to capture Hardy's attention and with a moment's pause, Hardy walked down the steps and up to Tarren. Without a word, the two men turned and walked toward the right-hand side of Flinders Street Station where the Yarra River runs beside and out to sea. Following a paved path, they found a vacant bench seat in an area designed for people to enjoy the sights of the Yarra River. Both men removed their sunglasses to see each other clearly and embraced, patting each other on the back affectionately.

"Oh, little brother. What a mess you've made," said Hardy.

"How bad is it?" asked Tarren.

"The worst. Gunther knows everything. He knows Justin and Beaton were incarcerated and you blocked their magic, that you left the family and are living with a witch family, that you have a witch daughter from an affair years ago and that you are having a magic baby with your woman." Hardy finished and looked at Tarren, hoping for a correction to something he had said, for Tarren to tell him parts of it were untrue.

Tarren stared at him, shocked that the pregnancy secret was now out. He sighed and stared out at the Yarra River. Although he knew the answer to the question, he had to ask anyway.

"What does Gunther plan to do with this information?"

"Well, apparently he had planned to interrogate you and fill in the details, but my opinion is that he plans to have you executed and the entire witch family," said Hardy.

Tarren exhaled loudly and sat back. He had suspected that would be the case but hearing it was still shocking. He kept repeating the words in his head. Hardy turned to look at him directly.

"Tarren, listen to me. There may be a way to sort this out before it goes any further. If you come back to the family, make peace with your sons and remove the magic blocker then maybe Gunther will let it go at that. You don't have to worry about Marion as she's been sent back to Sydney. Gunther wasn't happy with her lack of mothering skills and felt she had neglected her marriage."

"I can't do that, Hardy," Tarren said, cutting short Hardy's idea for reconciliation.

"Why not? I'm sure it's not too late," pleaded Hardy.

"I'm in love with Lucinda. I have been for over twenty years and we are having a baby. I can't walk away from her," Tarren said.

Hardy leaned back slightly and stared at Tarren for a moment. "Whether you stay with her or don't stay with her, will not make a difference to Gunther. He will have her entire family executed anyway. Don't you see that? She's practically already gone."

"Don't say that."

"It's true," pushed Hardy. "Think of yourself. Think of your family. Make the right decision. There's still a chance to fix this."

"Hardy, I really appreciate that you reached out to me and warned me. I really do. If it wasn't for you then I would've attended Gunther's invitation and I wouldn't have left the meeting." He looked across at Hardy and Hardy was nodding in agreement. "But I have a new life now. I'm happy and have a chance at truly being happy and I can't let that go."

"Gunther will take away your happiness. Even if you manage to survive his visit, your new family won't. You won't have the happiness you crave from this current arrangement. You need to come home."

"I will protect Lucinda and her family. We may need to relocate to another city or another country, but I will do whatever it takes to keep them safe," said Tarren.

"I don't think that will help … moving to another country. Gunther brought down this guy called Hans and he has contacts everywhere. He knows your witch daughter is in Ireland at a family cottage and has sent European Grimm's there to take care of her."

Tarren bolted to standing position in shock. He blinked a few times, heart racing and turned to Hardy. "What did you say?"

"Your witch daughter, he knows where she is and has sent people to eliminate her," said Hardy. As much as Hardy was trying to help Tarren and help remedy the situation, he had no understanding or empathy for a witch whether it be Tarren's daughter or not.

"I have to go," said Tarren, turning in circles, almost unsure which way to walk. This was the last thing he had expected to hear. He thought Niamh was the one who was safe and hidden away. All he could think of now was trying to warn Niamh and he fervently hoped he was not too late.

Hardy stood up and put his arms around his little brother. "Please think about doing the right thing. I don't want to lose you, little brother."

"Thanks Hardy. Thank you for meeting me. I am doing the right thing." Tarren turned and rushed back toward the railway station.

Chapter 43
EMMA

"Do they always give you free drinks?" asked Emma, watching as the bartender smiled and walked away when Collins brought out his wallet to pay for their two drinks.

"Naw. Jimmy gives me a free one here and there," said Collins, sipping his Guinness and exaggerating an expression of bliss.

Emma and Collins sat at Marta's Bar where Collins played guitar and sang on a Friday night. Sunday night was roast dinner night, and the two of them were keen to enjoy a quiet roast dinner and a few drinks. The venue was still quiet but beginning to fill with patrons sitting at tables and a few around the bar. Popular songs from the nineties played quietly in the background, and the atmosphere was relaxed and jovial.

The two of them were seated on stools at the bar, planning to relocate to a table in the next hour when they were ready for their roast dinner. Emma tapped her wine glass against Collins' glass of Guinness.

"Cheers," she said. "Here's to us."

Collins smiled at the toast. "I'll drink to that." They both sipped from their glass.

They chatted for the next thirty minutes, on various topics as they became more acquainted with each other, both feeling confident their relationship would be warm and lasting. Emma felt the most important aspect of a relationship was that they must be best friends, and she found Collins to be easy to talk to and entertaining.

Emma became aware of someone at the bar beside her but paid them no mind as she was turned sidewards toward Collins. It wasn't until she heard a gruff, heavily Germanic accent order a beer that she took note and tried to discreetly glance at the person.

Turning slightly on her stool and casually glanced around to her left, she observed two men standing at the bar beside her and looking out of place in their suits, the ties so perfectly in place. On a Sunday evening no one walked around with suits complete with perfect ties, especially in Ennis, Ireland. Their very attire highlighted the fact that they were not locals.

From the side-view, she could see they both had very blonde, thick hair a little longer and shaggier than what was considered fashionable in Melbourne, Australia. With a shrug, she turned her attention back to Collins and they continued their conversation on Australian Rules Football versus Gaelic Football.

The men were conversing quietly mostly in German with the occasional English word thrown in. It wasn't until she heard the words 'Niamh Flynn' that she halted, drink halfway to her lips and froze. Her eyes widened and Collins noticed the look on her face.

"Is everything ok?" he asked.

She frantically tried to use her eyes, facial expressions and a slight nodding of her head to indicate that he should pay attention to the men behind her. He looked totally confused for a minute or two then gave a slight nod to indicate he understood. The men in suits were speaking in a language he didn't understand which made him more perplexed at why they were listening. To keep up the charade that they were casual drinkers not paying attention, he took a mouthful from his glass.

Emma felt frustrated that she was unable to turn around and face them and that Collins had no idea what was happening. In a sudden light bulb moment, she took her phone out of her handbag and sent a text to Collins.

These men just said Niamh Flynn

Collins retrieved his phone from his pocket, read the message and then quickly snapped a few photos of them discreetly, pretending to be photographing Emma.. Emma lifted her phone up and posed for a few selfie photos, striking poses and pulling faces, ensuring the man were in the background.

Looking down at her phone innocently and invisible to the men, Emma watched as they collected their beers from the bartender and headed over to a table. She watched as they lifted menus and tried to read the unfamiliar English, obviously trying to determine what the meals were.

Emma looked back down at the photos and flicked through them. In one photo, she caught one of the men facing her way and she could clearly see dark eyebrows. Her heart missed a beat with fear as she took Collins' phone to review his candid shots and sure enough, both men had blonde hair and dark eyebrows. In fact, they looked identical as if they were a clone of each other. Identical twins? She looked over at the table again but couldn't tell without them being side-by-side.

Emma leaned over and whispered to Collins that she thought the two men were Grimm's and they must be looking for Niamh. He didn't understand much about the Grimm's as he had not yet heard about the Grimm aspect of Niamh's life, but he comprehended from the expression on Emma's face that this was a bad thing.

Emma phoned Niamh and after what seemed like a very long time, Niamh answered sounding sleepy.

"Hello," Niamh said. What are you ringing me for on your date?"

"Niamh, there are two Grimm guys here in town. I just saw them. They were standing right next to me and I heard them say your name."

"WHAT?" Niamh was awake now.

"They speak in a foreign language, maybe German and look like twins. Anyone you know?" Emma asked.

"No. No one I know. SHIT!" said Niamh.

"I'm coming home," Emma declared.

"NO," said Niamh. "I'm safe. Don't forget I have an invisible piss fence. No one is getting through that sucker. Where are they now?"

"They're here at Marta's, sitting at a table and ordering dinner."

"Stay where you are and watch them. Don't do anything that makes them realise you know me, whatever you do."

"I can't leave you alone," insisted Emma.

"No. I really am fine. I fell asleep but I'll sit up and watch a movie or something. I might call Molly and let her know what's going on. OK?" Niamh assured her.

Emma waivered but then agreed to remain at Marta's and have dinner with Collins. If they were watching the two men at Marta's Bar, then they weren't at the cottage and Niamh was safe.

Emma and Collins stayed, ordered roast chicken meals but Emma barely tasted it. Her focus was on the two Grimm men and why they were here. What did it mean? Somehow, the Grimm family had tracked down Niamh and If they were here, then it could only be something bad.

Collins insisted that he would be sleeping on their couch the night to keep on eye on the situation. Emma thought it sweet that he was being the protector of the two girls and told him the parts of Niamh's story regarding the Grimm family that he had not yet heard.

Emma knew that the whole world as they knew it was about to turn upside down.

Chapter 44
TARREN

Tarren raced back around the corner to Flinders Street, swiped his Myki card through the machine to gain entry and raced down to his train platform. Instead of driving into the heart of Melbourne and struggling to find parking, he had opted to catch a train in as it arrived at the exact location that he was to meet his unknown family member who had turned out to be his brother, Hardy.

Glancing up at the monitor, he could see he had eight minutes before the next train so he pulled his phone out of his jacket and realised there were many missed calls and texts from Lucinda. He didn't have time to read them just yet. It was imperative that he call Niamh immediately.

The phone rang a few times and he hoped she would answer considering he had never called her directly before, and he knew she was still wary of him in her life. Quickly calculating the time difference, he estimated it was after 1am in Ennis. She answered after six rings and her voice didn't sound as sleepy as he expected if waking her up.

"Tarren?" Her voice was a question wondering why he would be calling her at all.

"Niamh, thank goodness. Are you ok?" he asked.

"Yes. Why? Is Mum ok?"

"Yes. We'll talk about that later. Listen, I've just found out that the European Grimm family have sent a few Grimm men to … well … I think they plan to harm you," he started.

"They're already here," Niamh cut him off.

"WHAT?"

"Emma was in town tonight and she saw two men which she is convinced are Grimm's having dinner and she heard them say my name, so we are aware they are here," Niamh explained.

"SHIT!" exclaimed Tarren. His plan was to fly to Ennis, retrieve Niamh and bring her back home to Melbourne but now he realised it was too late.

"A friend of ours, Collins, is staying here on the couch so there are three of us currently here. We all are wearing charms and there are charms on the gate, the front door and the back door, as well as … as … a boundary protection," Niamh stammered.

"I know about the urine border. We had a jar of it in our freezer," Tarren said.

"Ok. Yes. We are well protected, and I have made friends with three other witches who live nearby. I've called them and told them this latest news and they have my back although I wouldn't want to put them in any danger." Niamh paused for a moment. "You said you HAD a jar of my pee in the freezer. Where is it now?"

It was Tarren's turn to pause, unsure what to tell her. "Ummm … your mother took it."

"Took it where?" Niamh asked, puzzled.

"Ok. There are problems here in Melbourne that none of us have informed you about as we didn't want to worry you."

"Well, you'd better tell me now," demanded Niamh, concerned.

"My Grimm family were not exactly happy that I forced my two sons to face charges and remain in prison plus I'd put a magic block on them. They called a family meeting and it involved the head of the Australian family from Sydney. His name is Gunther, an old guy who happens to be my own grandfather. He came down to Melbourne, released the two boys and basically ordered the death of me, and your entire family."

"WHAT? FUCK! ARE YOU SERIOUS?" Niamh was almost screaming into the phone.

"Your mother is hiding at Arabella's house with strict instructions for all of them to remain inside, as is Bethany and her family. They also have charms and your jar of urine protecting them," Tarren responded.

"Oh my God, why didn't Mum tell me?" Niamh asked.

"She didn't want to worry you and spoil your trip. I've been staying elsewhere at a hotel and trying to find a solution. My brother, Hardy has met with me in secret, and told me what is happening. That's how I just found out about the European Grimm's being sent to either kill you or bring you back here. I'm not sure which."

"So, they know about the baby?" Niamh asked but she already knew the answer.

"Yes."

"Fuck! I'm coming home. How long has Mum been at Aunt Bella's for?" she asked.

"Ah, over one week now."

Tarren could almost hear the wheels turning in her head as she tried to plan how everything would work. "I'm flying home as soon as I can but I need to sort out these two Grimm guys that are here. I can't go and leave them where they can hurt my friends. I'll take care of them first and then I'm coming."

"Niamh, I think you should stay away from them. There are two of them and only one of you. What would your mother say?" Tarren asked.

"I'm not leaving my friends in danger. I'm not sure what I'll do yet but I'm positive I'm stronger than they are," she said.

Tarren heard the announcement that his train was due in two minutes time. As he spoke with Niamh, he looked down at the text messages Lucinda had sent him.

"OH NO!" he exclaimed. "Your mother sent me some text messages while I was with Hardy. There are four Grimm's standing outside Arabella's property and four standing outside Bethany's place. They're just standing, watching and waiting, she says."

"They can't enter either," said Niamh. "Does that mean they don't know where she is but they suspect she could be at one of those places?"

"Yes, I think so," Tarren said.

"Tarren, please don't do anything. Mum's ok. She's safe as they can't come in, same as me. I'm going to sort these Europeans out and then I'm flying home. Please let me know if anything else happens but otherwise, I'll let you know my flight details. OK?" she asked.

Tarren's mind was racing and he felt sick with worry about Lucinda. Niamh could hear it in his voice.

"Niamh, please be careful. Think of your mother. I have to go. Train's here."

The train slowed to a stop in front of him, and he entered the carriage, ending the call.

Chapter 45
NIAMH

When Niamh hung up from her call with Tarren, she turned and saw Emma and Collins standing at the door to the bedroom waiting to hear what was happening. She had been so loud on the call that they had heard from the next room and were waiting for the details that they hadn't heard. They both perfectly understood her desire to go back to Melbourne and be with her mother, help in whatever way she could but at the same time, they were terrified for Niamh's safety here in Ennis and on her return to Melbourne.

"What are you planning to do about the Grimm men we saw?" asked Emma.

"I'm not sure yet. I imagine they're staying at a hotel for the night and will be here in the morning if they find out where I am. They won't be expecting our infamous pee border so they would assume they can just come in and take me," Niamh said.

The other two were nodding thoughtfully. "But they can't get past the gate, can they?" asked Collins.

"Nope. Will they sit it out like what's happening in Melbourne right now with my two aunt's houses or, will they try to force me out?" Niamh was tossing around thoughts as they came to her.

"How could they force you out?" asked Collins.

"Can they burn the cottage?" asked Emma.

"Well, I don't really know how powerful a Grimm is. They haven't done it in Melbourne with staking out my aunt's houses. They didn't do it to May or my grandmother, Agatha all those years ago. I have to assume they can't do that."

"They could do it the old-fashioned way, with accelerant and a match," said Collins.

The two girls looked at him, picturing that scenario.

"I especially don't want them to find the other three witches or Anne. They would kill them without a second thought," said Niamh

Emma nodded. "But you've told them these Grimm people are here, haven't you?"

"Yes. I've told them to stay away and protect themselves. I made them promise not to come here until I tell them it's ok. I haven't yet told Anne, of course," replied Niamh, referring to the fact that Anne didn't own a phone.

"Ok. We'll sort out Anne. You still don't have a plan how to deal with these Grimm men so you can leave for Melbourne," said Emma.

"No. I'll think on it overnight and by morning, there'll be a plan," said Niamh, brightly.

Collins and Emma nodded, said goodnight and returned to the lounge room where they'd been dozing on the couch and watching movies.

Niamh lay back in bed, her mind churning with possible scenarios which she quickly dismissed. She knew with absolutely certainty that the issue with the Grimm men needed to be resolved tonight. There was no time to think on it or adopt a 'wait and see attitude. Come morning and those men would be on the hunt for her, like hounds after a fox. A few shop owners knew her and Emma now so it wouldn't take long for the men to locate her, or they could potentially find Molly and her family, or even Anne Riley. There was no doubt in Niamh's mind that they would be killed if discovered.

How to deal with them was the dilemma. Two against one is never a fair fight even with the strength of her magic and she really didn't want to get into another magic fight, the last one leaving such a traumatic scar on her.

The only solution she kept coming back to was to burn them, as Agatha had burned the Grimm house many years earlier. In Agatha's case, she had burned the Grimm father and two children before allowing the mother and three other children to escape the flames. There was no way Agatha would have deliberately burned children, Niamh knew, but reasoned that her grandmother was not in her right mind and the children were terrible collateral damage.

Niamh needed to ensure that if she burned the Grimm men then any other patrons staying in the hotel would be able to escape. This was imperative and the thought of even burning a hotel which was someone's livelihood bothered her, but she couldn't see any alternative.

Niamh waited another twenty minutes until she was sure Emma and Collins were either dozing again or focused on the movie before rising quietly and dressing in dark clothing, tying her unruly dark red hair back and under a dark beanie.

Quietly, sneaking out the back door and out to the Ford Fiesta, Niamh stole away into the night, on her way to burn two men to death.

Chapter 46
TARREN

Fearing the train was too noisy to phone Lucinda, he waited until he reached his train stop and phoned Lucinda as soon as the train departed.

"Oh Tarren, I've been so worried about you when you didn't answer. Are you ok?" Lucinda asked.

"Yes. I'm fine. I've just met Hardy in the city, in secret, and he wanted to warn me about the situation with the family. Now, I have something to tell you and I want you to keep calm and listen, OK?" he said, knowing full well that she would not stay calm.

"Ok, Shoot!"

"The family have sent a few Grimm's to Ireland to capture Niamh or to get rid of her."

He could hear her voice already freaking out and he kept speaking, forcing her to stop and listen. "I've spoken to Niamh and these guys are already in the town near where the cottage is. She knows about them and has plans to deal with them." More hysterics on the phone from Lucinda. "Lucinda ... Lucinda, it's ok. She's made friends with some other witches who can help her if she needs it, and she is protected with charms and her witchy piss."

He heard Lucinda's voice calming a little as she took some deep breaths. He hated terrifying her like this, but he couldn't not tell her. This was not a secret he could keep from her, what was happening with her own daughter.

"You can ring her after 8am Irish time as I'm sure Niamh will not have slept much and will be tired. OK?" he said.

"OK," Lucinda responded and he could tell she was crying.

"Are the four Grimm's still outside Arabella's and Bethany's houses?" he asked, checking his watch and seeing that it was only midday.

"Yes, still there," she answered.

"Can you take a photo through the blinds of them and send it to me?"

"Yes. Hang on." She went into Arabella's bedroom and snapped a shot, sending it to Tarren's phone.

He looked at it immediately and recognised Monica, Anton, Shera's husband, Jock and Anastacia's husband, Antony.

"Ok, two of them are my children and two are my brothers-in-law. I'm guessing they are going to work to a roster so there are a number of them on duty around the clock. Can you ask Bethany to send me a photo of her watchers as well?"

"Are you sure Niamh is going to be ok?" sniffed Lucinda.

"She is a smart and strong girl and she has promised me that as soon as she has taken care of these people who are in town, she will be flying home. She could be home in the next few days." He knew Lucinda would be excited about seeing her daughter again, even though she had been gone only one month.

"She won't be safe here either though," said Lucinda.

"I'll collect her from the airport and take her somewhere safe. Between the two of us, we will hatch a plan to take control of the situation. I'm sure of it. OK?"

"Ok. Tarren. Please take care of yourself. I couldn't bear it if anything happened to you."

"I'll be fine. Nothing's going to happen to me. I'm going back to the hotel now, plan what can be done and wait for Niamh. I'll be in touch. I love you."

"I love you too, Bye."

She was gone, and he stared at the phone wishing he felt as confident as what he let on to Lucinda. He was worried sick about Niamh, but if he told Lucinda that, she would be a basket case of worry. He had to be strong and sound calm and reassuring.

He could still see no way out of this mess.

Chapter 47
NIAMH

Niamh vaguely heard voices in the lounge room but pulled the covers over her head to drown out the sounds. Since her sneaky return to bed in the early hours of the morning, she had slept soundly but just needed a few more hours. The bedroom door opened and abruptly, the covers were pulled off her head. Looking up, she saw Emma looking down at her and she didn't look happy.

"What?" Niamh asked, rolling over to face the wall as if she was going back to sleep.

"Collins just checked Ennis Community Noticeboard on Facebook and guess what?"

"What?" Niamh asked, groggily.

"There was a fire last night at Kings Hotel in town and two tourists from Germany are unaccounted for and feared killed in the fire," Emma said, angrily.

"Really? That's a shame. Much damage?" Niamh asked innocently.

"Turn around. Look at me," ordered Emma. "You did this. You went to town and set that fire, didn't you?"

"How could I do that?" asked Niamh.

"You did. Too much of a coincidence. Two German tourists, huh? You snuck out and found them, didn't you?" Emma was on a roll.

"Why are you so mad?" asked Niamh, turning over to look at seething Emma.

"Cause … cause … you could have been killed. They could have killed you."

With that, Emma burst into tears, big sobbing tears. "Did you think about me? What would I do if something happened to you? NO! You just went off and did this thing and you could have died."

Niamh sat up and pulled Emma's arm for her to sit on the bed next to her. "Emma, it's ok. You don't need to stress. I've no plans to die any time soon." She rubbed Emma's arm. "Thank you for caring so much. You're such a good friend but it's ok. I'm ok. OK?"

Emma nodded and wiped the tears from her face. "Don't do that again, Niamh."

"Do what?" said Niamh, innocently.

"What are you going to do now?" Emma asked.

"I'm going to book the first flight back to Melbourne and try to sort out what's going on there. I hope my mother is ok," Niamh responded.

"Tarren will look after her. He won't let anything happen to her," said Emma.

"Well, they want his arse too. He'll be busy saving his own and can't watch her as well. I'm needed there."

"Niamh," Emma said, looking down at her hands. "Will you be upset if I stay here? I really would like to return to Melbourne to help with all my heart, but I can't help. I can't do anything and I'll just get in the way."

Niamh had been wondering how to politely tell Emma that she didn't want her to come, so she was relieved to hear Emma suggest staying in Ireland.

"No. I think that's a great idea. Collins will look after you and so will the witches. I'd be happy if you would stay here."

The two girls hugged as Collins called out news from Facebook, from the loungeroom.

"Two German nationals are unaccounted for after an overnight fire at the King Hotel which destroyed the entire building. They were on the third floor where a fire is believed to have started in or close to their rooms. Other guests evacuated after the smoke alarms sounded but guests say they never saw the two German nationals during the evacuation. An investigation will be commenced immediately into the cause of the fire. The deceased names have not yet been released pending notification of family members in Germany."

"I wonder if their surname is Grimm?" said Emma.

"Yes. What a coincidence," Niamh said.

Emma looked down at the runners, black outfit and beanie on the floor of the bedroom from where Niamh had tossed them only hours ago and looked at Niamh with eyebrows raised.

Niamh just shrugged. "I got them out because I thought I might wear them on the flight home."

Chapter 48
GUNTHER

"You're not serious, are you?" Gunther asked Hans, wide-eyed and caught off guard.

"I'm afraid so. Reports in state that Carl and Otto Grimm have most likely died in a fire at their hotel overnight. Firefighters are going through the ruins now to locate any remains, but they appear to be the only casualties. All other guests of the hotel managed to evacuate, but for some reason, Carl and Otto did not," replied Hans.

"You got this information from the family?" asked Gunther.

"Yes. Initially it came from the family and then I studied the news reports and contacted the local police in Ireland."

"This is very coincidental. Didn't they only arrive at Ennis yesterday in the evening?" Gunther asked.

"Correct." Hans consulted his notebook again. "They hired a car at Shannon Airport and drove to Ennis, checked in at the Kings Hotel and had dinner at Marta's Bar before retiring back to their hotel at 7.30pm. The fire started sometime around 2am according to the authorities."

"There's no way the witch could have known they were in town yet, could she? Do we have any indication that she was involved?" asked Gunther.

"No. Nothing."

Gunther sat back in his chair and exhaled. This was very unexpected news and deeply disturbing as he had been anticipating the exciting news that they had captured the witch and were bringing her back to Australia. Now he was stunned and unsure what the next step should be.

"It does seem very coincidental, don't you think? I want you to keep abreast of the investigation into the fire. Send someone out there to ensure the investigation is thorough. I want to know why all other guests escaped the fire, but our two men did not. I assume there are smoke alarms installed in the hotel. It's not as if they could sleep through an alarm, is it? There would be doors, windows, fire escapes and so on. Why didn't they leave via the door or break the window and escape? Something is fishy here and I think the witch must be involved."

"I will. Do you want me to also arrange someone else to capture the witch?" Hans asked.

"No. Let's find another way of bringing the witch back to Australia. I don't want us to lose any more family members and I'm convinced she must be involved in this. The surveillance at her aunt's houses hasn't tempted her. How is that coming along? Any sign of Tarren or the woman yet?"

"No. No sign of anyone. They've gone to ground," Hans admitted.

"Hmm maybe it's time we go to the media and call a press conference. Let's tell the world what a bad, evil witch she is and how she has escaped punishment for attacking my great grandsons. It may push the authorities to bring her back or it may push her to come back on her own," suggested Gunther.

"Leave it with me," said Hans.

Chapter 49
LUCINDA

Imprisoned in Arabella's house and unable to venture outside, the occupants watched movies, read books and trawled the Internet to keep entertained. Early on the Saturday morning as Arabella and Lucinda buttered their toast for breakfast, Robbie yelled out to them to come and see what he'd found in one of the online newspapers he read daily.

GRIMM FAMILY HEARTBREAK

At a press conference held today at the Mont Blanc Hotel, the Grimm family, a wealthy Australian family of investors, outlined their heartbreak over an incident that occurred in January this year, and is the result of fifty years of torment.

On 8th March 1980, Gerhard Oban Grimm (37) visiting from Sydney was burned to death in his vehicle at the Grimm's house in Doncaster at the same time as a fire was ignited in the family home. During the fire, Dora Grimm and three children managed to escape but George Sherman Grimm (31) and two sons, Grady (15) and Aaron (13) died in the fire. This tragedy has tormented the family for fifty years and the biggest unanswered question is, who could be evil enough to deliberately burn two men, one a father, and two children?

Suspicion landed on the door of two well-known Melbourne witches, Maybelline Sarah Connor, known as 'Marvellous Maybelline' and Agatha Caitlin Flynn. According to spokesperson, Monica Sable Grimm, her grandmother,

Dora Heidi Grimm had called out the witches for fraud and obtaining money by deception, and a feud had erupted. The Grimm family accused Agatha Flynn of setting the fire that killed her family members. No charges were ever laid.

Agatha Caitlin Flynn lost her battle with cancer in January this year, and two of Dora Grimm's grandsons, visited Maybelline Sarah Connor at her house in Liddle Street, Coburg seeking further information now that her friend had passed on. During this time, Maybelline produced a kitchen knife and attempted to stab the men and during the altercation, Maybelline was stabbed in the chest.

Agatha's granddaughter, Niamh Aine Flynn arrived and attacked the two men, using a broom to assault one man and a saucepan of boiling water to inflict head injuries on the other man. The police arrived and the two Grimm men were arrested and charged with murder, attempted murder, entering a house by deception, assault among other lesser charges.

The Grimm family claim that the incident has never been fully investigated, that Niamh Flynn has never faced justice and fled to Ireland to escape charges. It is since emerged that one of the men, 22 year old Justin Armin Grimm, has suffered a permanent traumatic brain injury as a result of the attack by Niamh Aine Flynn and now requires full-time care.

Recently, Justin Armin Grimm and Beaton Conrad Grimm were released on bail pending a trial date. The family argue the injured man, Justin Armin Grimm, has no memory of what occurred in January and no understanding of the legal implications and they demand the charges be dismissed.

Our legal department at this masthead agree that the charges against Justin Armin Grimm warrant being dismissed following an appropriate report from a qualified doctor.

The Grimm family are requesting from the Victorian Government:

- *charges against Justin Armin Grimm dismissed due to his traumatic brain injury. A defence of mental impairment is not appropriate as Justin Armin Grimm was of sound mind when the offences happened, however he is now unfit to stand trial;*

- *charges against Beaton Conrad Grimm downgraded to manslaughter with a defence of self-defence. The defence of 'self-defence' in Victoria, as articulated in section 322K of the Crimes Act, requires that the accused believed that their conduct was both necessary and a reasonable response to the circumstances as they perceived them. https://galballyparker.com.au/examining-the-use-of-self-defence-for-assault-related-charges-in-victoria/*

- *a thorough and fair investigation to be conducted;*

- *charges be laid against Niamh Flynn including assault and attempted murder;*

Stay tuned and we will report again as more information comes in.

"Goddamned liars," said Arabella, angrily. "May came at them with a knife? As if! May was an incredibly sweet natured person and not at all aggressive."

"I know," said Lucinda. "This is deliberate. It's a strategy to put pressure on the police, have the public feel sympathy for their family and turn the public against us."

Lucinda pulled out her phone and sent Tarren a link to the article. She glanced outside and could still see a shift of four Grimm family members standing out the front. She clicked a photograph and sent it to Tarren as well.

She couldn't help but feel excited today as Tarren had informed her that Niamh was on a flight back to Melbourne. She was thankful the press didn't have this information or the Grimm's. Well, she hoped the Grimm's weren't aware as they could capture the two of them, follow them or even shoot them in public. Feeling anxious, she sent Tarren another text message.

Please take care at the airport. Be on lookout for 'you know who'.

After a few minutes, a reply arrived and she read it and smiled.

Between Niamh and myself, 'you know who' are in deep shit.

Chapter 50
NIAMH

Having cleared Customs, Niamh made her way out of the Tullamarine International Airport to meet with Tarren. She'd notified him of her flight details and he planned to collect her so the two of them could enter into hiding. She looked at the sea of faces and dragged her wheeled suitcase, acknowledging that this was the first time she had ever felt she would be pleased to see him.

He approached her before she saw him, and she realised it was because he was wearing a baseball cap, that she hadn't recognised him, not considering he may be incognito. He tried to wrap his arms around her in a welcome hug but she wasn't ready for that. She stood still and allowed the hug but didn't reciprocate.

"Here," Tarren said and handed her a black baseball cap which she quickly pulled on, her hair already back in a ponytail.

"Are we all clear? No one following?" she asked.

"No. I don't think so but let's just be cautious," he responded as they made their way out the doors to the waiting airport car park bus.

Ten minutes later they had been dropped off at the airport car park and located Tarren's car.

"Where are we off to?" Niamh asked.

"Unfortunately, I can't take you to see your mother as the sentry are still on guard, but I have booked a second room where I'm staying. I didn't want to leave an easy digital trail so I've been using cash and I know someone who owns a hotel. He's agreed. I can rent a room and pay cash, so it works well."

"Hey Tarren, what about the car park ticketing machine? You'll have to use credit card to pay," she asked.

"True, but we will be long gone. The family know you were in Ireland and will assume you are going to return to Melbourne with events happening here. I'm surprised they missed your flight in, but perhaps they were not thinking you would be leaving so quickly. With the ticketing machine, they will know I've picked you up but not where we have gone."

Niamh nodded, it was a fact of life that in today's modern world, there were digital trails everywhere. Even at the airport there were CCTV cameras, speed cameras on the roads and car park ticketing machine which did not accept cash. Leaving no digital trail would be impossible so anything to make tracing them a bit more difficult was worthwhile.

The trip to the hotel took thirty-five minutes due to the heavy traffic on Tullamarine Freeway and Bell Street. Tarren pulled the car into a car park behind the hotel which appeared to be an ordinary long, brick building of rooms in the style of the 1980's.

"Sorry, it's not the Hilton," Tarren joked as she checked out her room. It was clean and neat, but very basic with small bathroom, small kitchenette, bed, tv and desk area.

"No. It's fine, really," Niamh answered as she manoeuvred her suitcase on to the ottoman.

When she turned back, Tarren had retrieved his phone and called Lucinda, placing it on loud speaker.

"Hey babe, I'm here at the hotel with Niamh."

"Hi Mum," Niamh said brightly, realising she really did miss her and could feel tears prick at her eyes at the sound of her mother's voice.

"Oh, thank goodness. I've been so worried. I had visions of the Grimm family kidnapping you both. I can relax now I know you're safe. How are you, Niamh?" said Lucinda.

"I'm good, just a bit jet lagged. Are you ok? Do you still have security out the front?"

"Yes. I'm afraid they're still there. I did hear that Melbourne is due for hail storms this afternoon. That would be a terrible shame," she giggled. "They're parked in a clearway, so we keep ringing to report them and the truck keeps towing them, but they keep coming back."

"Lucinda, Niamh and I will discuss the situation and hopefully, we can think up a solution. We'll keep you updated," said Tarren.

"Great. Thanks. I love you, Niamh. See you soon," said Lucinda.

"Love you too, Mum. Bye," Niamh responded and Tarren cut the call.

Tarren looked at his watch. "It's 3pm now. Why don't you have a shower and a quick nap? When you're ready, come next door and we'll have a discussion about the situation," said Tarren.

"Ok," said Niamh, thinking there was nothing more she wanted than a nice hot shower and a nap. She also had plans to ask Tarren a few questions about her Grimm heritage.

Chapter 51
MONICA

Monica shivered and pulled the hood of her coat down over her head to protect herself from the heavy rain. This was not how she had pictured executing a stake-out. In the movies, a stake-out involved watching a house in the warmth of your car and eating hamburgers and drinking coffee, not freezing your arse off in the rain.

Gunther had insisted he wanted them 'in your face' visible to the witch family which meant standing outside the car. They were all being forced to take a shift of eight hours around the clock and this had been in action for well over one week now. It didn't seem to make any difference as they had not once seen anyone who lived here, not even to take the bins out.

Reports from the other house were the same. They were wasting their time as her father and his woman were clearly not here. If her father was here, he would have come out by now and she would have sensed him. No one was brave enough to tell Gunther his plan hadn't worked and so they remained bored and freezing, and now it was hailing. Big, hard lumps pummelled at her hood over her head, forcing her to seek shelter inside the car.

Cold and wet, but at least out of the weather for a little while, Monica sat and fumed. She knew she was more intelligent than 99% of the Grimm males yet because she had been born female, she was relegated to the position of a mere incubator, housemaid and slave. This was the way it was, the way it had always been, but it still riled her. If she were in charge, she would have a completely different tact to what Gunther had ordered.

He had that weird guy with the goo-goo eyes, Hans, running the investigative side of things, and Monica knew he was only looking at the easiest to find data, like credit card usage and mobile phones. Her father was not a stupid man and would also have thought of these things, hence they were not receiving any information on his whereabouts. If she were in charge, she would be checking the finer details such as his car's registration plate and where it had shown up on road cameras and speed cameras, whether he had used any of his other cards such as fuel card, discount cards, loyalty cards, post office box footage, IP address on his laptop and not only her father's data but also his woman.

Monica was the one who had brought all her father's sins out into the light, and yet she had not been rewarded for coming forward. Her spot in the limelight had really only lasted fifteen minutes or so before being pushed back into the shadows and disregarded, treated as very inconsequential and unimportant.

She retrieved her phone from her coat pocket and called an Uber. When it arrived ten minutes later, she wound down the window just a small amount, less the hail hammer her.

"Beaton, I'm going home," she said, simply.

"You can't do that. You're rostered," said Beaton, alarmed.

"The roster can get fucked."

Chapter 52
NIAMH

Niamh finished reading the article on Tarren's laptop and sat back slowly, deep in thought. She was sitting at the desk in Tarren's room which looked remarkably like hers, and he was filling her in on the latest developments with the Grimm family. This article had now been shared and published by most of the major newspapers and many of the minor ones around Australia. There had even been a brief mention on the primary news channel at five pm.

Niamh looked at Tarren for a few minutes before speaking. "Is it true? Is it true that I inflicted a brain injury on your son?"

Too late, Tarren realised that she didn't know this and with everything happening in their lives, he had overlooked telling her. "Yes ... sorry, I was going to tell you today. I should have told you before you read the article."

She nodded and looked away, then looked back at him, her eyes unreadable. "I didn't intend that to happen, but I lost control."

"I know," said Tarren.

"I killed two men in Ireland and I don't feel regret or upset about it, though I know I should. Why do you think that is?"

"Well ... you knew those men were in Ireland with the intent of capturing or killing you, so in some ways, you could see it as pre-emptive self-defence," said Tarren, cautiously.

"My grandmother also caused the death of people, as you well know. Your family caused the death of my grandfather and May. I have murderers on both sides of my family so what hope do I have?"

Tarren stared at her as she stared at the wall. He opened his mouth to counter what she had just said but closed his mouth again, unsure what to say. What she said was true. What could he possibly say at this point? What did she need him to say?

"It's a terrible thing between our families, the absolute worst. I cannot deny that. What your grandmother did was inexcusable, but she was beside herself with grief and sought revenge. What my family did to your father was inexcusable as he was not a witch and had done nothing to upset them. They did it to unnerve your grandmother, flush her out so she would make a mistake, and it backfired on them. This witch hunting obsession is in the blood and we are indoctrinated with the idea from the time we are born. I doubt it will ever change."

"Why are you different? Why aren't you chasing witches? I don't understand because you say it is in the blood and you are indoctrinated with it from the time you are born, but you are proof that it's achievable," said Niamh, turning to face him.

"Yes, good point. I don't have a solid answer to that. I could say that I fell in love with your mother accidentally, but the truth is I was questioning this feud well before I met her. I can't tell you why I am different when I grew up in the same environment as the others. Most of my family are ruthless, dogmatic and ... nasty." He looked away at the last word. "I see it and I know it. My own children are the same, and I can't change it."

She nodded. "I am not the same as other witches. I met three witches in Ireland, and they knew immediately that there was something different about me. I seem to be some sort of mix of the two. Emma calls me a witchy Grimm." She grinned at the memory of that conversation. "I'm not really a true witch but I am still a witch."

"In the Grimm education there is just witches, not the possibility of something in-between. A Grimm mixing with a witch family was not something ever considered." He gave a short laugh at the ridiculousness of it.

"I want to ask you some questions about the Grimm heritage. Is that OK?" she asked.

Tarren nodded. "If I know the answers, sure."

"One of the witches in Ireland told me she heard of a magic family in Europe that were descended from an animal. It sounded very strange to me, but I sometimes growl when I'm having intense emotions, animals are drawn to me and there's a few other small traits that have an animalistic lean to them. Would that be possible ... that Grimm's are descended from an animal?" she asked.

She saw his eyes widen, and she couldn't quite identify what the expression on his face meant. After a moment, he shook his head and looked over at her.

"Well ... yes. It's sort of a family legend and some of us have doubted the authenticity of the story. When I was young, my mother used to read a bedtime story to us but it was not the usual nursery book from a bookshop. It was a very old, tattered and home-made book with fancy script writing, and scraps of things glued to the pages. Looking back now, I guess they were bits of fur, hide and maybe, skin. I wish I could remember it clearly, but I was very young."

"The main story was about a hunter called Grimm and his adventures in the woods of Europe. Once, he was so hungry that he killed and ate a large wolf and it turned out a witch had cast a spell on the wolf just previously that caused the wolf to be caught. After that, the wolf spirit came to him sometimes and made him do evil things. He killed children mostly, throwing them in the wood-fired oven and attacked women on their own. His biggest quest was to hunt down and kill witches and sometimes he was completely human and other times he had characteristics of a wolf. He married and had children and two of his sons put down his adventures into a book."

It was Niamh's turn to stare at him wide-eyed. "Are you talking about Grimm's Fairytales?"

"Yes. Apparently, rumour is we are from the same family. The book was burned in the fire when I was four years old but I remember being terrified to go to sleep at night in case Grimm the hunter came after me and put me in the oven to eat. I had forgotten about it until now."

"If I tell Emma that I have werewolf in my blood, she'll never come near me again."

"It's not werewolf as you know it, as you've seen in movies. There is no shape shifting or suddenly sprouting hair all over your body and a hunger for eating people."

"Oh, thank goodness for that," said Niamh and chuckled. "I have enough problems."

"It's ... like a sort of instinct takes over and you suddenly feel a bit like a wild animal," said Tarren.

"That's exactly how it feels," admitted Niamh. "I'm glad I have a better understanding of it now. I thought I was just a little crazy."

Tarren sighed and looked uncomfortable as he cleared his throat. "Niamh, I don't know what's going to happen and I can't tell you what to do, but … I want to ask you … umm … "

"Spit it out!" said Niamh, wondering what he was going to ask.

"I want to ask you not to … harm my children." He finished the sentence in a hurry.

Surprised, she stared at him and could see the torment. On one hand, his children were evil Grimm family members who wished to kill her and her family and possibly him, but they were also his own flesh and blood, his children and he loved them.

"I … I don't want to harm anyone," said Niamh, hesitantly. "I didn't realise I had permanently damaged your son. I was angry and wanted to hurt him, but I didn't realise my own power. I will try not to harm your children, but it depends on them too. If they do something and I lose control, I don't know what will happen." It was the truth, and she owed it to him. All she could promise was that she would not purposely set out to harm them.

He nodded, satisfied that she understood. After a moment's pause, Tarren collected his phone and turned to Niamh.

"Why don't you go and get a good night's sleep? You must be tired after the travelling. Tomorrow, we'll discuss what we are going to do from here on. I'm just about to phone your mother and wish her a good night. Do you want me to wish her good night from you?" he said.

Niamh stood and collected her things to make the move back to her own room. "No, it's ok. I'll tell her myself."

Tarren nodded thinking she meant she would be calling her mother as well, but that was not what Niamh had in mind.

Chapter 53
GUNTHER

Gunther's face flushed with anger and his eyes bulged. Hans and Ingrid, who were in close proximity to him were convinced he was about to have a heart attack and then he exploded in outrage.

"WHAT DO YOU MEAN YOU MISSED THEM?" Gunther screamed at Hans.

Hans appearing flustered, stepped back a little from the line of fire and stammered.

"Well, we weren't ... expecting her to ... leave so quickly ... from Ireland. We thought we would at least have another day to worry about it, but she had left the very next day."

"AND you missed her when she landed at Melbourne airport?"

"Yes."

"Have you viewed the CCTV footage of who picked her up, since then?" Gunther asked.

"We have, and it was Tarren Grimm."

Gunther exploded again and saliva flew from his mouth in all directions as he ranted and raged at Hans and prattled on about how useless he was.

"What now?" Gunther calmed a little and wiped his mouth with his handkerchief to sop up the spittle.

"The girl will want to visit her mother and we'll be watching," said Hans, smugly.

"Really? WE DON'T KNOW WHERE HER MOTHER IS SO HOW ARE YOU GOING TO BE WATCHING?"

A deep red flushed Hans face and he looked down at his notes. "Well, we suspect it is one of her sister's houses so we will keep watching both houses day and night. We'll grab the pair of them as soon as we see them."

"When is the boy's wedding ... you know ... the one with a brain injury?"

"Justin?" replied Hans.

"Yes. Justin," Gunther rolled his eyes.

"Umm ... errr ... it's next Saturday," replied Hans.

"Make sure the media know and get a good photographer there. We can milk this situation with the press. Poor Justin, permanently damaged from this monster of a girl and his sweetheart still marries him to look after him. Tug at the heart strings, won't it?" Gunther said, grinning at his own sheer brilliance.

"Great idea, sir," said Hans, smiling.

"Hans, you do have good security on me at all times, don't you? I wouldn't want that witch hybrid to come find me and fry my brain in my sleep. You understand?"

"Yes, sir. I have hired extra security guards and they are stationed outside the hotel and at the entrance to the suite you've booked. No one can get through here. Don't worry," said Hans, confidently.

"I'm sure the two Grimm victims in Ireland thought the same," said Gunther.

"I'll be sleeping next door so I'm on call and we'll keep you safe. That little witch can't get past any of us and especially, me."

Chapter 54
JONTY

Jonty Grimm kicked at the kerb with the toe of his shoe, partly to see if his toes had any blood left in them and partly out of boredom. Melbourne in August was so damn cold that his breath exhaled as vapour and he was wishing he had worn gloves.

This was supposed to have been his night off as he had worked the night shift the previous night, staking out the house of one of the witch family. The plan was for him to stay home and look after the two young children for the night while his wife, Monica, performed her duty and sat here in the goddamn cold and froze her arse off.

Nothing could have surprised him more than Monica suddenly arriving home only hours into her shift, announcing that everyone could get fucked and she wasn't going to be rostered on anymore. She made her way to the shower to warm up her frozen body, and he had been forced to take her place, lest they get in trouble with the rest of the family. Monica abandoning her post in the middle of an operation was seen as a very bad lapse and one that he didn't wish to face the repercussions of. Better that he just quickly head out to the location and take her place.

The other three Grimm family members on duty were Beaton, his brother-in-law, Jock who was Shera's husband and Annastacia. He had taken Monica's place and no one had said a word which was an incredible relief to him. Why did he have such a temperamental wife? Why couldn't he have a simple, kind and subservient wife like Beaton did?

It was 11pm and the night was pitch-black other than a few streetlights with the occasional drizzle of rain from overhead clouds. The house in front of him was dark with a few night lights on, glowing through the windows. Oh, how he wished he was curled up in bed right now, toasty and warm. It was going to be a long night.

Beaton had informed him when he arrived that Hans had called and the young witch was back in Melbourne now and to be extra vigilant. Two Grimm members had died in Ireland trying to locate her and he didn't have the whole story yet but surely, it could not have been her responsible for their deaths? She's just barely out of being a teenager and they were two grown Grimm men. Surely, she was no match for them. It must have been coincidental and bad luck.

Jonty felt a sharp pain hit his lower abdomen and he grunted slightly in protest. He tried to remember what he had eaten for dinner that may not have agreed with him. Monica had left a chicken casserole and there couldn't have been anything in that to upset his stomach. He felt another sharp pain and looked around the neighbourhood, wondering where the nearest toilet may be located.

Suddenly, he became aware of other sounds and looked over to see Annastacia bent over double, holding her stomach and groaning. Another cramp hit him and he also bent over involuntarily, holding his stomach as if just the touch of his hand would alleviate the pain. Hearing moaning, he turned to see Beaton walking in circles at a fast pace and muttering to himself and Jock, holding on to a nearby young tree in the nature strip with a strange look on his face, visible in the streetlight.

Without a chance to do anything about it, Jonty felt his bowels release and with a gushing sound, his pants filled up and ran down his trouser legs into his shoes and socks. He stood in shock and couldn't believe what had just happened. He hadn't pooped his pants since early primary school and here he was in front of his family, emptying his putrid and stinking shit for all and sundry to see.

Hearing groans and sobs, he looked at the other three sentry guards and realised that each of them had also soiled their pants. Annastacia was sobbing and wet squirting noises could still be heard issuing from her rear end as she tried walking over to the car that was parked next to them. Each step, another wet squirt and another sob erupted from her. She opened the back door of the car and jumped in where she launched into full sobs.

Beaton, Jock and Jonty stood on the nature strip in the foul-smelling aftermath of their digestive eruptions and stared at each other, embarrassed and unsure what to do. Each was aware that this had occurred to each of them, and later there would be time to wonder if they had all eaten the same thing or been exposed to a chemical that had caused this to happen to all three at the same time.

For now, they knew they had to go home, shower and change, then return for the rest of their shift. The three of them agreed that none of the family need know what had just occurred and they were positive that Annastacia would be of the same mind. They should be able to race home on the quiet and be back in thirty minutes. No harm done.

Gingerly, each man walked to their vehicle, Jock and Beaton to the front seats of the car containing Annastacia in the back, and Jonty to his own car he had driven to the location after Monica's untimely arrival home. Jonty drove home, aware that his own excrement was seeping out his trouser legs and onto the carpet on the floor of the car, and on to the car seats. How would he ever explain this to Monica?

He almost laughed out loud when he thought of the other three sentry guards all in the same, stinky vehicle with three of them seeping shit on to the seats and floor. He may be able to have his car cleaned but the car containing three shitting Grimm's needed to be burned.

Chapter 55
TARREN

Tarren's eyes fluttered open and he stared into the darkness. He'd been staying in this hotel for weeks now and yet, he still opened his eyes in the night and wondered where the hell he was. Had something woken him? He glanced at the bedside clock noting it displayed 12.03am in bright red numerals.

TAP TAP TAP

Tarren sat bolt upright and blinked a few times. Someone was knocking on his hotel door and with a prickling over his body, he knew it was Niamh. Was she ok? Why would she be knocking on his door after midnight? Something must be wrong.

He flung the covers off and raced over to the door, dressed in just his boxer shorts and a t-shirt. Opening the door with the expectation of seeing Niamh standing there, he was shocked to be looking into the face of Lucinda. She had a huge infectious smile on her face and flung her arms around his neck.

"SURPRISE!"

Tarren embraced Lucinda and lifted her into his arms, touching foreheads and seeking to bury his nose in her neck and wallow in the scent of his red gold girl. He hadn't seen her for a few weeks and the time had been excruciating for them both.

Pulling apart, he saw Arabella, Robbie and Niamh standing behind and trying to look inconspicuous as he and Lucinda reacquainted.

"But ... how?" he asked, confused how they were standing in front of him.

"We'll explain," said Lucinda as they all made their way into Tarren's room.

He quickly donned his trousers and a jumper as everyone sat around on a chair and couch. Tarren look suspiciously at Niamh and she smiled sweetly at him.

"They're ok. No one's hurt," said Niamh, allaying his fears.

"How did you do it? How did you get them out? Were you followed?"

"The four security guards out the front of Aunt Bella's house suddenly had an attack of gastro or something similar and were desperate to go to the bathroom. Alas, they didn't make it," Niamh said, so calmly and sweetly with a little smile at the end.

"They didn't make it? What, to the bathroom?" asked Tarren and then the realisation dawned on him.

"Oh, they wet themselves?" he asked.

"Oh no. Much worse than that," said Niamh, still smiling. "So, anyway ... what a coincidence. They drove away in two different cars just as I was about to visit my mother and aunt. I knocked on the door and Uncle Robbie answered. They were happy to leave the house before the security guards arrived back so, here we are!"

Tarren shook his head smiling. "Good job but you could have told me you were going," he admonished Niamh.

"Well, I did tell you that I would talk to Mum myself," Niamh said in justification. "I hope you don't mind that I used your car. Oh, you know what? The funny thing is that the security guards will be watching an empty house and not realise it." Niamh laughed.

Tarren shook his head again. "Ok. Tonight, we'll make do with sleeping in these two rooms but tomorrow, we need to find a better location for everyone that's safe, and Niamh and I need to discuss what we do now."

Chapter 56
MONICA

Feeling flustered, Monica opened the front door to discover Beaton standing on her doorstep, wearing a slight grin at the unannounced visit. She wasn't in the mood for pleasantries and didn't return the grin or indulge in a greeting. She turned and stomped back into the kitchen where her young son, Claus, was sitting in his highchair, merrily tipping his bowl of banana custard all over the floor.

"AAHH, STOP THAT YOU LITTLE CRETIN," she yelled at the perplexed child as she snatched the spoon and small bowl from his grasp.

Beaton, who had walked in behind her, laughed ungraciously. "Ah, the joys of children."

"No kidding," Monica replied as she wiped the yellow sticky mess from the child's face and used magic to clean up the mess on the floor.

"So, any after-effects for Jonty since the night we all suffered the sudden attack of gastro?" Beaton asked.

"No," she replied, finding the topic distasteful.

"Coincidence don't you think - that the same thing happened to the four guarding the other witch house the next night?"

She had thought it very coincidental and was quite sure that magic must have been involved. "If I had to guess, I would say the young witch did it to both groups and helped the occupants of the house escape," she said.

"Yeah, that's what I've been wondering."

"What are you here for anyway, Beaton? What do you want?" she asked, gruffly, her patience worn thin.

"Well, I've been thinking about something and I need help from you," he said.

"That would be right," she said, unenthusiastically.

"Our little brother is getting married tomorrow, as you know, and ... his brain is so addled now that I don't even think he realises what's happening, who Natasha is, or what is about to happen."

Monica nodded as she tried to spoon the left-over banana custard into the pink cherubic mouth of Claus.

"Well ... I ... don't think he knows ... about sex anymore, if he ever did."

"WHAT? What do you mean?"

"I'm sure he once knew all about it but his brain doesn't work anymore, and I don't think he knows the basics," said Beaton.

"Ok," Monica said slowly. "What can I do about it?"

"I'm planning to sit down with him later today and try to talk to him, see what he knows and explain things. Hell, I might have to draw pictures." Beaton laughed but it was a short, tense laugh.

"I was hoping you ... would talk to Natasha."

"I'm sure she knows what to do," Monica said, cutting him off.

"Yes, but ... she might have to take the reins firmly in hand." Beaton looked at the puzzled look on Monica's face. "You know ... take control of the situation."

"Seduce and guide him?" Monica asked.

"Yes," said Beaton, relieved he didn't need to go into any further detail.

"Hmmm ... she is inexperienced so that is a tough thing to talk about," said Monica.

"I know it would be but otherwise, I think they would spend the next fifty years playing Playstation all night," said Beaton.

"His body still works, doesn't it? Like ... if he has the right ... stimulation, he can still ... perform?" asked Monica, hesitantly.

"Yes. Yes. Well ... I think so. I'm sure the doctor would have told us if he couldn't."

"I've just thought of something," said Monica. "Natasha's mother, Queenie, is here for the wedding. I'm going to explain things to her and let her talk to Natasha. Easier coming from the mother, I think," said Monica.

"Good idea," said Beaton.

"Is he going to be ok? Justin?" she asked, in a rare moment of caring.

Beaton sighed. "I hope so. I think he will once he has a routine and someone to look after him."

"Does it bother you that Dad won't be at the wedding?" she asked.

"Yes. It does but he doesn't deserve to be there," said Beaton, fiercely.

"Do you think about what will happen to him when Gunther catches up to him?"

Beaton paused and leaned back against the wall. "Gunther will execute him, for sure. How do I feel about that?" He was silent for a few minutes. "I'm distressed about it. I am, but that is the Grimm way. He has committed a very serious breach of our values, of everything we believe in and we can't turn our backs on that, even if he is our father."

Beaton looked at Monica, waiting for her thoughts.

"I still can't accept that he is lost to us forever. I don't believe he is. I certainly don't want that puffed up, narcissistic man, Gunther, to take him away from us. I feel that if we remove the woman he's with, and the witch family altogether, he will come back to us. He'll be upset, of course, but he will eventually come back into the fold." She looked at Beaton for his reaction.

"You maybe right, sis."

"We need to do something before it's too late," she persisted.

"I'll talk to Anton and see what he thinks," said Beaton.

Monica turned back to feeding her child, knowing she had planted the seed.

Chapter 57
JEANNE SHAPIRO

Jeannie Shapiro sat at her desk in the open plan office and stared at the media release that had been published a few weeks earlier. She had been tasked with following up on the story, investigating the matter further and writing a few follow-up pieces.

It was not that she was unhappy with the task but she really had no idea where to start. It seemed like a plot straight out of a fantasy novel. Witches? Rich family? Murder? Arson? She liked to think that she was a serious journalist, a seeker of truth and justice, a woman of the times, but this seemed flowery, frivolous and as if it were written for a reality television show.

Ah well, she concluded. She would be fair and treat it as a real and serious article, and who knew? Maybe it would end up being more comprehensive and complicated than what she imagined. The best start was to break down the story into an understandable narrative in chronological order. Sentence by sentence, she analysed and wrote notes.

1. Around 1980, Dora Heidi Grimm accuses two witches of fraud and obtaining money by deception. The two witches are Maybelline Sarah Connor and Agatha Caitlin Flynn.

Note: How does Dora know they are committing fraud unless she was a victim of the fraud or knew someone who had been a victim of the pair?

2. As a result of the accusation, Agatha Caitlin Flynn sets a fire that kills a man in a car and a father and two children in a house.

Note: It seems extreme for a person to murder this many people in such a horrible way due to a fraud accusation. Did the police interview Agatha? Was she ever a person of interest? Why was she never charged?

3. *Forty years later and after Agatha Flynn has died, two grandsons decide to go to Maybelline Connor's house to ask her about the incident with the fire.*

Note: This seems strange that they would wait until Agatha had died. Why wait? Why not ask Agatha when she was alive? Maybelline would be an old lady by now and the two grandsons would be young men. How threatened must Maybelline have been to produce a knife and try to stab the two grandsons?

4. During the altercation, Maybelline was stabbed in the chest and died.

Note: Two young men could easily outpower an old lady and unarm her. Why was she fatally stabbed in the chest?

5. The granddaughter of Agatha, Niamh Flynn, arrives and assaults one man with a broom and the other with burning water and a saucepan.

Note: Again, two young men should be able to outpower a young girl. How old is Niamh Flynn?

6. The two young men are arrested and charged with murder and attempted murder, and a number of other charges while Niamh flees to Ireland to escape charges.

Note: Australia has a extradition treaty with Ireland so if charges were to be laid on Niamh Flynn, she would be extradited to Australia. Is there an application for extradition? Is Niamh Flynn still in Ireland?

7. Justin Grimm has a traumatic brain injury as a result of the assault by Niamh Flynn and cannot remember   the   incident.

Other Notes:

What stage is the legal process up to?
Is there a date for a court hearing?
Who is the Grimm's legal representative?
Who is Niamh Flynn's legal representative?
Can I obtain the reports of Justin Grimm's condition?
What are the terms of bail?
What information has been released by the public prosecutor?
Who is the lead investigator?

Is there an old appointment book belonging to the witches so I can see if Dora Grimm was ever a customer?
Is there more Flynn family who I can contact to ask questions? There was a granddaughter, so there must be a daughter or son, at least.
The article published mentions fifty years on two occasions yet 1980 to today is forty years. Why the discrepancy?
The Grimm family have called the press conference that resulted in this published article. Why? Why now?
Review newspaper articles from the 1980 fire.
Speak to investigating police of that time, if possible and view what reports are publicly available.
Search for any mention of Agatha or Maybelline in newspapers.
Search for any mention of Grimm family in newspapers.
Search for marriage certificate for Agatha, and birth or death certificates for any children to build a family tree.
Search for marriage certificate for Dora, and birth or death certificates for any children to build a family tree.

Jeannie sat back in her chair and exhaled loudly. Ninety minutes had passed since she had put her head down to study the published article and begin taking notes. It only felt like five minutes ago and she thought it incredible that she had so totally absorbed her mind in the story.

This investigation may be more exciting and intricate than what she had originally thought.

Chapter 58
NIAMH

Three weeks had flown by and despite the beautiful surroundings of the Dandenong Ranges and the lovely large house on short rental from AirBnB in the name of Arabella's brother-in-law, Niamh was restless and bored.

Sitting around looking at the scenic view, listening to the bellbirds and walking through the fern gully's is only mesmerising for a certain amount of time, and then it becomes boring and all looks the same. Niamh was missing the company of Emma, her school friends, Lee and Maddie or any semblance of her normal life. Hiding and not able to leave a digital trail was driving her crazy., not even being able to check Facebook or any of her usual social platforms.

The only fun and exiting time had been the first afternoon when the local animals turned up at the house to welcome her. She had sat with wallabies, koalas, wombats, echidnas, goannas, snakes, kookaburras, lorikeets, cockatoos, galahs - all native animals as well as a few exotic animals that were in the area and now lived feral including foxes, dogs, cats, rabbits and an African parrot. Usually, the animals visited at night when she first arrived at a new house but this time they arrived in the afternoon.

"Tarren, we NEED to find a solution. I can't live like this forever," Niamh pleaded in desperation as she flopped down on the couch.

"You could call him 'Dad' you know," said Lucinda, a sentence she had repeated many times in the past seven months, invoking the same blank look from her daughter.

Bethany, Arabella and their two husbands were out walking on a mountain side trail and the three of them were alone, so Niamh thought it the best time to confront Tarren again.

"I know. I know. I wish we had the magic available to us to wave a wand and the problems would all disappear," Tarren said.

"We need a fairy," said Niamh, antagonistically. "Mum, any chance of fairy in our bloodline? We already have witch, Grimm and wolf."

"Niamh," her mother scolded. "Don't be rude."

Niamh shrugged angrily and a crash of thunder was heard outside, rattling the windows. Tarren and Lucinda glanced out the window, noting the sun had disappeared and dark clouds were forming. Both looked at Niamh realising where the threat of bad weather was originating from.

"Oh, I'm sorry. I'm just bored. What are we waiting for? Are we waiting for the Grimm family to suddenly decide they like us after all? Are waiting for this Gunther guy to kick the bucket? Would that even change anything? We need to roll the dice and meet with them or do something." Niamh's frustration was tangible and Tarren sighed, sinking into a chair near her.

"You're right. We can't sit here forever and think things will change. We need to force a change, force their hand. I'm just so hesitant about putting your mother and the baby at risk in any way," Tarren said.

Niamh nodded. "I agree. Can we leave Mum here with the others, and you and I go and sort this out?"

"NO," said Lucinda.

Tarren turned and put his hand on her arm. "Babe, we have to sort this. We have to, you understand that don't you? I want our family to live in peace and not be worrying who's watching and trying to harm you or our little one. Niamh and I – we'll look after each other. Don't worry."

Niamh was nodding at her mother. "We'll be ok. Trust us."

"Babe, I have a plan and we won't be gone long, just a few days ... possibly. You'll be safe here with the others. Ok?" he asked, rubbing her arm.

Lucinda looked like she was about to burst into tears but she held them at bay. "Ok. Promise me that you'll look after each other. I couldn't bear to lose either of you."

Niamh held her hand up with three fingers up, in the boy scout salute. Tarren nodded. "Of course," he said.

Niamh jumped to her feet ready to prepare for leaving. Her mother looked surprised. "You're not leaving now, are you?"

"We are. If we wait for the others to get back from their walk, Robbie and Stuart will want to play hero and come with us. Let's avoid that," said Niamh and she raced out of the room to grab her bag.

Within fifteen minutes Tarren and Niamh had packed a bag, farewelled Lucinda and were driving down the winding, narrow road of Mt Dandenong Tourist Road back to Montrose and back toward Melbourne.

"So, you told Mum you have a plan worked out. What's the plan?" asked Niamh.

Tarren gripped the steering wheel more firmly and stared straight ahead as he responded. "I have no fucking idea."

Chapter 59
MONICA

Monica struggled with her current situation in life but could only admit it to herself. The last six or seven months had progressively worsened, and her outrage and anger had grown to boiling point. She had no experience or idea of how to handle the rage or how to hide it.

She couldn't say she was happy in her Grimm life, but it was the only life she had known and she accepted it as all the Grimm's did. The men were the dominant ones, the leaders and the women were subservient, and that's how it had always been. She knew that. Everyone knew their place in the hierarchy of the family. She had accepted this fact and not even thought about it.

Until recently.

When had it all changed for her? Was it when her father had left the family and gone to live with another family, start another family and not only that, but had the sheer nerve to be happy in his new life, happier with his new family than he had been with the old one? Why did he have the option to choose what life he wanted? Why could he choose who he wished to spend his life with? That was so unfair.

Her husband, Jonty, had been chosen for her, selected for their complementary characteristics and not being too closely related in blood, of course. A small committee in Sydney studied the family trees to ensure the marriage unions were not too closely intertwined. She had not been given a choice, had not asked for a choice as you just didn't do that. You accepted whatever it was that the family wanted of you.

Jonty was satisfactory as a husband and father, but so damn boring and not terribly intelligent. She could run rings around him in the smart department, and she struggled to accept his decisions on various household projects without calling him a total fuckwit. Good Grimm wives didn't call their husband a 'fuckwit'.

Now that her father had removed himself to chase his dream, it had made her think about her dream. Did she have one? She knew she was not supposed to have one, not allowed to have one. Good Grimm wives didn't think of anything other than reproducing, keeping the house clean and catering for the husband. She definitely was not a good Grimm wife, and when she pondered her purpose in life, she didn't see the domesticated goddess as her end goal She saw Monica the intelligent businesswoman, organising, scheduling, communicating, improving and running the show. That is what she would be best at and what she felt she had been born to do.

The only one in Grimm leadership was Gunther, her great grandfather and a total authoritarian male who could never remember her name and thought of her as unimportant in the scheme of life. She hated him. Wrinkled up, ugly old man who didn't have the good grace to die of old age. Hardy was supposedly in charge of the Melbourne family but everyone knew that was more of a token role. He was Mr Nice Guy lacking a strong backbone for decisions and ideas.

In some ways she regretted being the one to bring her father's indiscretions to the family's attention. Why had she done it? She had been shocked at what she saw, her father having a baby with another woman and her carrying a magic baby, a girl. She had always been her father's little girl and she hated the thought that there could be another baby girl claiming her father's love and not her. It was bad enough that her father had a witch daughter not much younger than herself, but at least there had been no contact with her in the past twenty years until now. A brand-new baby girl was more than Monica could bear to think about.

Other than the jealousy, she thought informing her family in such a spectacular fashion would gain points with the family, put her in the spotlight and she would be seen for the intelligent person that she was. She imagined that the Grimm males would look at her with awe, that she had leadership qualities and it may turn the situation around.

Now she could see that her hopes were in vain. The Grimm family thought nothing of her other than she was a messenger, delivering information to the people who mattered. She felt the anger rise again and tried channelling the anger toward a small lamp on a side table in the lounge room. After a few minutes, the light bulb shattered, tiny shards falling to the table and floor. It gave her some small satisfaction to see the chaos and destruction, and she imagined it was Gunther's head she was shattering.

If Gunther was no longer in charge, then she was sure the family would not go ahead with executing her father, because that is what everyone thought was going to happen. Gunther had not exactly made it public what his plans were for her father, but everyone knew.

Her discussion with Beaton had gone nowhere after she had asked him to speak with their other brother, Anton. She had hoped the two boys would agree that they cannot allow Gunther to execute their father and that between the three of them they would come up with a solution, but when she had later queried Beaton, he had shrugged his shoulders dismissively and said Anton was sorry about it but we had to follow Grimm rules.

She was not prepared to accept this response from her brothers or from anyone. She resolved to be the one and only Grimm to prevent the execution of her father, and in her dreams, she would execute Gunther and take on the leadership role herself.

She just needed to come up with a plan.

Chapter 60
ANNE RILEY

One month had passed since Niamh left Ennis and Anne still felt a tug at her heart when she thought of it. She couldn't comprehend the strange feeling when she had spent her entire adult life alone, as well as much of her childhood life. She didn't know where she would have been without Byron and Jerry before him. There had been four dogs since she had been alone, and each had found her at the right time when she was at her lowest point and most in need.

There had been no one else, no friendly neighbour, no male attention, no girlfriends ... no one. People turned away when they saw her coming or crossed the street as if she smelled to high heaven, but she knew it was not her odour. She was very particular and made her own soaps, bathing in warm water every few weeks. The truth was the local folk were afraid of her. She knew it and had even encouraged it. It was her only defence against people, and she did it without thinking. Ward them off, repel them, scare them so they would leave her alone and not send her off.

She told Niamh her family were Cailleach and they were and seen the surprised look on Niamh's face as it was a word that had been used for Niamh's own ancestors. The difference was that the Cailleach's of Anne's world were old hags, the aged, ugly hags and crones who the public were afraid of yet sought their assistance with love potions or curses on enemies, not the Cailleach's of Niamh's world who were beautiful witches.

Anne had walked away from that life when she had barely reached teenage years, not wishing to follow her female ancestors into the life of being a wrinkled up old hag, stirring the boiling cauldron. She'd never seen her mother again and it didn't mean anything to her. She didn't feel regret, grief or affection for that cranky old biddy who had birthed her. She had never felt affection for anyone other than the dogs who had chosen to keep her company. They were the only ones who had looked out for her, wanted to be near her and shown her affection.

Ennis was the town where she had ended her travels and she loved Ennis. The town folk didn't love her but that was ok. She had learned to live with that and figured every town needed an older woman to act as the evil witch and keep the villagers on their toes. They left her alone and she left them alone. Sometimes, they blamed her for bad things that happened in town but she rarely touched magic these days. She wasn't even sure she still knew how to do anything other than small tricks.

Everything changed when Niamh arrived and Byron warned her of the witch's arrival. Anne had been terrified for those weeks of what was going to happen to her. Would the witch exile her from her home of Ennis? Would she curse her and make her suffer? Would she take Byron away?

Anne suffered sleepless nights agonising over her fate, and Byron watched the witch as much as he could, even coming home with a body crawling with fleas on one occasion. She had been so concerned that she had worked up the courage to venture out to the cottage on the other side of Ennis at Claureen, and meet with the witch. She figured that she may be able to convince the witch that she meant no harm and they could live in harmony, but the witch had not been home and the young woman she spoke to seemed very nervous. She also felt something had been blocking her from touching or entering the witch's gate and concluded the witch must have a spell on the boundary.

The first time she met Niamh had not gone well or to plan. Anne put it down to her own lack of courtesy, lack of etiquette and lack of communication skills. Niamh had caused storms and rain in the sky above her and soaked her to the skin, frightening her enough to race back home where she felt safe. It had taken her a while to build up her own courage to try again, and this time, she had been successful in befriending the witch.

She'd never had friends and that day had been an immense awakening to her. Not only the witch, Niamh, but also her friend and three other local witches. They had all been so polite, friendly and warm to her, that she had felt tears in her eyes ever since. Anne had never known this feeling, had never experienced the warmth and love of others. The feeling had overwhelmed her and changed her life. Suddenly, she felt like the protector, the defender of witches everywhere and the one who would fight to the end for her friends.

She was heartbroken to learn that Niamh had left town and returned to Australia, feeling her heart was going to break from grief and loss. Emma had told her the story of those Grimm people and that they had tried to wipe out witches for centuries. Two men had arrived at Ennis with ill intentions of Niamh's demise on their agenda and Niamh had taken care of them, burned them to a cinder in a hotel fire.

Then Niamh had left for her home to protect her own family and Anne thought that very honourable. She was pleased Emma was still here as it meant one day, Niamh may return. There was still that connection here from her newfound friend and she called on Emma once a week to check if there was any news and if Emma was doing ok. She had even met the young man from the village who played the guitar so sweetly and he had been welcoming too.

Byron had come home this morning, upset and agitated and wanted Anne to follow him. Her first thought had been that something must be wrong with Emma or the other three witches, so she grabbed her bag and coat, tied a scarf around her head and rushed out the door following her companion.

Anne walked a few metres behind the wobbling white backside of her beloved Byron as he tried to increase his pace, eager to show her what he had seen.

"Slow down, boy. I've only got two legs, not four like you," she growled and chuckled at him.

They walked into the centre of town and across to the next parallel street where the fire in the hotel had been. She had seen the official looking men sifting through the ash and ruins, investigating the cause of the fire and trying to understand the event. They had been there for weeks now, and she had calmly walked past, paying attention to any words she could hear from them. She was positive there was no link to Niamh and that there was no way they could determine that she would be involved in any way.

As they were about to turn the final corner where she would see the ruined hotel on the opposite side of the road, she stopped walking and stood stock-still.

Something bad was happening. She could feel it crawling all over her body, a creepy, crawling that sucked the breath from her lungs. She had slightly felt this once before when she had finally met Niamh and the three witches, but that tingling had been mildly pleasant, this sensation was like someone was dragging a sharp pencil all over her skin and it was tearing the top layers of her skin.

Byron had stopped and was looking back at her, worried. She looked at him wide-eyed, wondering what he had planned to show her. Slowly, she stepped the last few steps to turn the corner and view the burned hotel. She heard Byron give a few soft whimpers as if he wanted to show her but at the same time, didn't want her to see.

Across the road she was confronted with the collapsed building, black and charred with a modular, wire fence erected around it to keep people out. What caught her eye immediately, was the group of people standing in front of that fence, three men and a woman in dark clothing. All four of these people were staring across the road and straight at her. They knew she was coming.

Anne turned back the way she had come, feigning innocence and no awareness, but she knew she was not fooling anyone. Without needing to look back, she knew from Byron's face and whimper that the four people were after her. She quickened her pace, fearful now that these people could easily gain on her and capture her. That was the last thing she wanted to happen.

These people were the dreaded Grimm's that Emma had told her about, the ones that had been trying to kill Niamh and had come to Ennis to kill her. Now, there were more of them and as she raced down the street, running for the first time in at least forty years, she knew they were here to find Niamh, and they knew she had magic.

They would have felt the tingling to alert them to someone of magic nearby and were waiting for her to turn that corner.

She could hear their footsteps as they ran on the cobblestones of the road, nearer and nearer. Byron was still whimpering as he scurried along next to her, her little shadow. She couldn't let them take Byron or hurt Byron and she knew they would do whatever it took to make her talk and give up Niamh.

Her breathing was already laboured from the exertion, and it was only a matter of time before someone grabbed her shoulder. Ahead was a shortcut she usually took, down a narrow lane. She focused and for the first time in forty years, summoned up her magic abilities, hoped they still worked and she still knew how to use them.

She turned the corner into the lane with Byron and disappeared, vanishing into thin air, both suddenly appearing back in their home in the sitting room. Anne squealed in delight at the success and Byron looked around puzzled. She imagined that the four Grimm people would have almost felt themselves touching her and would have been smugly expecting to capture her in that lane, only to turn the corner and find empty space.

She laughed at the thought and knew the laugh sounded like a cackle. Unperturbed, she cackled away, feeling good for having outsmarted them and that her magic had worked after all this time. Suddenly, she stopped cackling and stared at Byron. The thought had crossed her mind that it was only a matter of time before they found Emma at the cottage, or her friend Collins. From there, how long would it take for them to find the three other witches and that Niamh was in Australia. She didn't own a mobile phone and panic set in as she realised what they were looking for.

She had to warn Emma.

Chapter 61
EMMA

Although having exchanged a multitude of text messages with Niamh in the weeks since Niamh had been in hiding, they hadn't spoken on the phone since she'd left Ireland. Emma was aware Niamh was struggling with remaining in hiding and itched to confront the Grimm's and bring issues to a head. No one seemed to know how to do that safely and successfully and so, they remained in hiding, twiddling their thumbs.

Now, she had no choice but to fill Niamh in on the current situation in Ennis as much as she hated further adding to Niamh's troubles. Emma wandered outside into the garden away from the others so she could talk in private.

"EMMA!" exclaimed Niamh, excited to hear her friend's voice. "I'm so pleased to hear your voice. I've missed you."

"Yeah, me too," said Emma. "It's not the same here without you."

"How's Collins ... and the others?"

"Good. They're ... all good," said Emma with a slight hesitation.

"What's wrong? I can tell by the tone of your voice. Something's going on. Is everything ok?" said Niamh, worried.

"Yeah ... everyone's ok. I just wanted to fill you in on the current situation."

"Fill me in on what?" Niamh was becoming worried.

"Ok, so … I'm at Asher and Mauve's place at the moment, and I'm here with Molly, Maureen, Anne and Byron."

"Ok," said Niamh, cautiously, trying to analyse the sentence.

"We're in hiding too."

"WHY? WHAT'S HAPPENED?" asked Niamh, jumping to her feet in alarm.

"We think the Grimm's have sent more people over here, maybe to check out what happened with the fire … and I suppose, look for you."

"How do you know that? Have you seen them?" asked Niamh, panicked.

"Well … no but Anne has. They chased after her and Byron, but she managed to give them the slip. She said they knew she was magic and she could tell they were."

"Is she ok?" asked Niamh.

"Yeah. She's fine but she sent Byron to the cottage to let me know there was a problem. You see, if they can tell she's magic then they'll find her house easily and may decide she's a witch and …" Emma said quietly.

"Yep," said Niamh, understanding that Emma meant they might choose to exterminate her on the spot.

"Or … they may … find ways of getting her to talk about you. Obviously, there are a few issues here … we don't want the Grimm's to harm Anne or the four witches in any way, and we don't want them to find out where you are, so we are all at the house of Asher and Mauve, determining our next move."

"Where's Collins?" asked Niamh.

"I haven't spoken to him yet," said Emma. "He's not magic so they shouldn't know who he is."

"Ok," said Niamh, thinking frantically through the possibilities of the Grimm's finding out who Collins was.

"We think they would ask around the village and sooner or later, someone will direct them to the cottage. You've been away for a month now so the border protection might not be strong enough to keep them out," said Emma, voice trembling.

"That's true," said Niamh, mind racing for a solution. "So, Molly and her daughter, Maureen are with you, but her husband and the rest of her family are still at their house?"

"Yes."

"Hmmmm," said Niamh, concerned whether the Grimm's would take hostages in an attempt to find what they were after.

"SHIT! WHY IS THIS HAPPENING WHEN I'M NOT THERE TO PROTECT YOU?"

"It's ok, Niamh. It's not your fault," said Emma.

"I'm sorry, Emma. Plus, I've put the other witches in danger." Niamh could feel tears of frustration spring to her eyes.

"Do you want me to ask the witches to collect their pee, and maybe Collins could tip it around the fence at the cottage?" asked Emma.

"NO," said Niamh, immediately. "As much as I love that cottage, it's only a house. I don't want any of you put in harm's way. I wish I could just put the damn lot of you on a plane to Australia, but of course, that's not possible."

"No," said Emma.

"Stay where you are for now. Please let Collins know what's happening and maybe, he can discreetly keep an eye on the Grimms in town?" said Niamh, feeling useless.

"Ok. There are four of them."

"It's clear to me that I need it made public that I'm here in Australia. Maybe then they'll leave Ennis."

"Ok, please be careful, Niamh."

"I will. Give me love to the others and tell them I'm sorry and I'll try to right it."

Chapter 62
JEANNE SHAPIRO

Jeanne sat at a small table in the historical Yarra Glen Grand Hotel and it felt surreal to be there, sitting opposite a real-life witch and hearing a tale that was going to be the story highlight of her career. She could barely believe her luck and fiddled with her recording device on the table, checking that it was still working.

After weeks of investigating the story of the Grimm family and the witch family, she had discovered so many flaws in the current narrative and had so many questions, which surprisingly, this girl could answer. Jeanne, the hard-nosed journalist who could smell bullshit from a mile away and had caused many hardened criminals to shake in their boots with her words was almost speechless with what she was hearing.

The girl in front of her was a beautiful girl, not classically beautiful like Sophia Loren or Brigitte Bardot, but intensely interesting with those steel grey eyes, flecked with amber, that thick, dark red hair that appeared to be hastily tied behind her head in a ponytail, though wisps and curls had escaped their confinement and her smooth, lightly freckled skin. Sometimes she appeared innocent and naïve like a teenager on the cusp of becoming a woman, and other times she seemed fierce and strong, a warrior woman. The mix was electric and fascinating, and Jeanne found herself mesmerised and captivated.

"So, can I summarise what you've told me?" she asked, and the girl nodded.

"The Grimm family are in fact, a European family with magical abilities who have a long-standing vendetta against witches and have spent centuries hunting and killing anyone suspected of being a witch?" She looked up at the girl for confirmation and the girl nodded. "What sort of magical abilities do they have?"

The girl shifted uncomfortably in her seat. "Well, I don't know. I'm not a Grimm but they can control objects and manipulate markets so they remain rich."

"You, are from the Flynn family who have a long line of female witches, originally from Ireland?"

"My mother was not a witch. Not every female is a witch but yes, there is a line of witches and the family originated in Ireland."

"But ... you said you are not a Grimm and yet, didn't you also tell me your father was Tarren Grimm?" Her eyes bored into the young girl in front of her. She thought she saw the girl's eyes flash an amber colour but decided it must have been the lighting in the dimly lit room.

"Yes. My father is Tarren Grimm."

The girl's head moved just a fraction to the side as did her eyes and Jeanne realised that her father was in the room somewhere at that moment. He was protecting his daughter and the thought that he was in the room sent a shiver up her spine. "I have Grimm blood in my veins but I am NOT a Grimm. I have inherited the witch characteristics of my mother's side of the family."

"So, the Grimm's want to find you so they can execute you like they have always done with witches? Is that correct and likewise, is that what happened with the two Grimm boys who have been charged with the murder of

Maybelline Connor?" she asked, again seeing the amber flash in her eyes.

"Yes. They would like to kill me as they consider me a witch and not half Grimm. They would also like to kill my mother as she is pregnant with a witch, and you are correct that Justin and Beaton Grimm broke into May's house for the purpose of killing her and probably killing me too."

Jeanne saw the girl's eyes fill with tears and knew this line of questioning was very personal and difficult for her.

"How do the Grimm family feel about your father now that he is living with a witch family and soon to father another witch?" Jeanne asked.

"I can't speak for them, but my understanding is that they're not sending out baby shower invitations." The girl smiled and Jeanne chuckled at the joke. "In fact, my sources indicate that their intention is to eliminate all of us including my mother AND father, which is why we have all been in hiding for the past month."

"Have you spoken to the police?" Jeanne asked.

"No. The Grimm family are powerful and we cannot be assured the police have not been bought or compromised."

"The article published last month said that you had escaped being charged by fleeing Australia for Ireland. For the readers of this article, is that true?"

"No. There are no charges pending against me. My friend and I flew to Ireland for a few months break and to see where my ancestors came from. My friend was also present when the Grimm brothers killed May and attacked me. She was traumatised as well, so the trip to Ireland was for both of us to relax and heal."

"And did that happen?" asked Jeanne.

"Well, not exactly. We did love Ireland and were enjoying our trip, however, the Grimm family began hassling my mother, aunts and even my father. I was terrified they would be harmed, as May had been so I flew home to see if I could find a way of resolving this conflict, and that is why I'm speaking with you, to set the record straight and find a solution."

"What do you think the solution is?" Jeanne asked.

The girl paused and pursed her lips in thought. "In a perfect world, the Grimm family would forget this ridiculous urge to kill witches and learn to live alongside them. They would accept that my father has now found happiness with my mother and have a new baby on the way."

"Just a few more questions if that is ok ... did you try to kill Justin Grimm?"

"He had just killed May and was mocking me. I did try to hurt him in anger but not kill him."

"Did your grandmother burn the Grimm family in the car and house many years ago?"

"I wasn't born then but I know the Grimm family caused the death of my grandfather and that my grandmother was beside herself with grief so there is a good chance she did that terrible thing at a time of extreme distress."

"Why did you ask to speak with me today?"

"Because I don't want my family to live in hiding for the rest of our lives. I want everyone to know that we are being persecuted, a witch hunt I guess you could say, and I want to reach out to the Grimm family and tell them to let it go. Let us live in peace. I will not make threats, but I will not allow my family to be hunted either. It's their choice." The girl looked at Jeanne, eyes penetrating. "I want you to immediately publish a teaser saying you have spoken with me and the article will be following shortly."

"Why?"

"Because I want them to halt anything they are currently doing and wait to see what's in the article. It may save a life."

Jeanne looked at her stunned for a moment. She blinked to bring her mind back to the task.

"One more question ... your father, Tarren Grimm ... he's here, isn't he? Can I meet him?"

Chapter 63
NIAMH

Niamh stood across the room and watched as Tarren stared out the window of their dingy hotel. He had been sitting at the small, scarred desk, paper in hand and staring out the window for at least thirty minutes and she felt for him. She had already read the paper left on their doorstep as she had risen early, eager for the day to begin. Reading a physical paper was so much more enjoyable and relaxing than trying to read the news on a laptop monitor.

The small teaser Jeanne Shapiro had added at her request was exactly as they had spoken about.

DON'T MISS SATURDAY'S EDITION FOR AN INTERVIEW WITH NIAMH FLYNN

The witch at the centre of the murder/mystery plot, the granddaughter of the witch accused of burning members of the Grimm family and the one accused of assaulting Justin Grimm resulting in a traumatic brain injury. Who is telling the truth? Read the interview on Saturday.

Niamh explained to Jeanne Shapiro that the Grimm family had the power to prevent the article from ever reaching publication and that she should safeguard herself and her article in any way possible. As far as she knew, Jeanne had gone to ground, and the article would be published remotely.

When Jeanne had asked her why she wanted the teaser published immediately, she had replied:

"Because I want them to stop anything they are currently doing and wait to see what's in the article. It may save a life."

That had been the truth however, she had refrained from explaining anything to Jeanne regarding the situation in Ireland, that she had killed two European Grimm family members and now there were other Grimm members in Ennis looking for her. She wanted word to reach the Grimm's in Ennis that she was currently in Australia so they would leave Ireland.

She could imagine members of the Australian Grimm family reading the teaser this morning in a panic and the ensuing uproar when Jeanne Shapiro was unavailable and they were unable to have the article shelved. She almost smiled at the chaos this small teaser would create, but she looked at Tarren again and the smile slipped from her face. The teaser was nothing to do with his despair this morning.

Further back in the same paper, in the social column had been a photograph and small article regarding his son, Justin's wedding to his bride, Natasha. The photo had captured the bride and groom cutting the huge, tiered cake, with a look of sheer delight on her face and a wide-eyed look of surprise on his. There had just been a sentence mentioning that the wedding had been held at the Mont Blanc Gardens with a reception at the Mont Blanc Reception Rooms.

From across the room she watched as Tarren read the sentence and stared at the photo for a few minutes, then quietly put the paper down and stared out the window. He didn't say a word, just stared out at nothing, and she wondered what was going through his mind. Did he regret his decision to renew his relationship with her mother? Did he wish he was back with his family? She knew he was hurting and wasn't sure how she could help, or even if she wanted to help.

She sent a text to her mother suggesting NOW would be a good time to phone Tarren for a chat. Moments later she heard Tarren's phone ring, so she walked outside to give him privacy. It was a good time for a brisk walk around the block, and she relished the fresh spring air as she walked. She giggled at the growing number of birds flying and swooping about above her head and the dogs barking a welcome as she past them.

There had been a plan brewing in her mind since Tarren had mentioned he thought Gunther was staying at Mont Blanc Hotel which was the same place where Justin Grimm had just married. It appeared the Grimm family were very involved with this venue including accommodation, a venue for special occasions, conferences and meetings. Niamh had no doubt the Grimm family-owned Mont Blanc venue and businesses.

With her elimination of the threat at Ennis, Ireland due to the hotel fire, she was contemplating sneaking into Mont Blanc Hotel at night and doing something similar to Gunther. She'd never met him, and was aware he was an old man in his eighties, but she felt confident he would not be as powerful with magic as she was. Niamh also knew that she was a direct descendant of his which seemed bizarre and unbelievable. It was difficult enough to accept that her father was a Grimm but at least he was a good Grimm, whereas her great grandfather, Gunther, was the essence of pure evil according to what she heard from Tarren.

If she could successfully enter the premises, then Niamh was confident she could eliminate this leader who was such a bad influence on his family. Perhaps, the rest of the Grimm family would be more easily negotiated with and a solution found once this crazy old man was out of the way. That was her hope and the only scenario she could come up with. They had been in hiding long enough and no one was coming up with any scenario that would resolve the conflict and keep her mother out of harm's way.

Tonight, as soon as Tarren fell asleep, she planned to sneak out and use his car to head over to Mont Blanc Hotel. She could barely wait.

Chapter 64
EMMA

Niamh, how are you?" Emma asked. It had only been a few days since they had last spoken on the phone.

"Good. Good. Is everything ok?" asked Niamh, concerned she was phoning again so soon.

"Yes. I just wanted to let you know we're positive the Grimm's have left Ennis. Collins has been snooping and saw them leave the Jacksons Hotel this morning with small suitcases."

"How is he snooping? How's he been doing that?" Niamh asked.

"Well, when I told him there were Grimm's in town and we were hiding out at Asher and Mauve's place, he did some fishing around and found they were staying at Jacksons. Don't forget he's lived in this town his whole life so he knows lots of people. He knew the receptionist at Jacksons so he asked her to let him know when they check out, and today, they checked out. She sent him a text message and he arrived just in time to see them putting their suitcases in the boot of a car and leave," said Emma.

"That's great," said Niamh. "I spoke to a journalist a few days ago and she published a teaser in the paper this morning announcing an interview with me will be published on Saturday. I wanted the Grimm's to realise that I'm here in Melbourne, and it worked."

"Well done," said Emma.

"How are the girls? I bet they're driving each other crazy by now."

"Well, no. I guess Anne's a bit different and not very au fait with the whole social thing, but she's trying and she's actually quite sweet." Emma smiled thinking of how Anne had tried so hard to fit in and be one of the girls.

"We are so lucky to have found these lovely ladies. Please thank them from me."

"Oh, I will," said Emma.

"Also, one more thing. Can you ask the witches to start peeing in containers so you can make a new boundary at the cottage?"

"Already on its way. We've a little stash of containers collected already," said Emma and she laughed. "How are things there, Niamh?

"I won't bore you with the gory details but I have a plan. I hope things may change after tonight."

"Promise me you'll be careful, Niamh. I know what you're like," said Emma.

"Of course."

"How's your Mum and Tarren?" asked Emma.

"Mum's hiding with my aunts up in the Dandenong Ranges, and I'm in this hotel with Tarren. He's a bit upset today as his son got married recently and he obviously, wasn't invited. He saw a photo in the paper today."

"Oh, that's sad. This all must be so difficult for him. You know, loving you and your mother, and yet loving his own horrible children as well," said Emma.

"I did feel sorry for him when he read the paper."

"What, you ... show emotion? Feel sorry for Tarren? Surely not," said Emma, teasing.

"I may be a witch, but I do have a heart too, you know."

Chapter 65
NIAMH

Dressed in all black with her hair tied back, Niamh felt ready for the task ahead. She'd heard Tarren lightly snoring as she had listened at the door to his bedroom. The hotel suite they were in, though dingy and bleak, had two bedrooms so it was easy to locate the car keys in the main lounge area and sneak outside.

The Mont Blanc Hotel involved a thirty minute drive from where she was staying and it was close to midnight so the roads were quiet. There was a sense of déjà vu as it was only a month or so earlier since she sneaked out at night, took the car and drove to another hotel to perform the same task she was planning for tonight. The plan was to be warm and snug back in her bed in the next few hours and tomorrow morning she would look forward to hearing news of the fire and reading the article Jeanne Shapiro had written regarding the interview with her.

Night lights were visible around the hotel and solar garden lights lit a pretty display as she made her way around to the back of the building. There was no sign of security at the front of the hotel which she had almost expected to encounter. Her plan for any security was to gift them a severe case of gastro. Entering via the back entrance had worked for her in Ireland so she quietly made her way past commercial sized rubbish bins and a kitchen herb garden until she found a door used mostly by staff. Peeking around the corner of the building, she located the CCTV camera above the back door and it was motionless, facing straight ahead. Puzzled, Niamh watched it for a few minutes expecting it would rotate but it didn't. It remained facing ahead and even with a wide-angled lens would not capture anyone walking up from the side.

Niamh crept along the side of the building to the back door and as she was about to touch the door handle, she realised the door was slightly ajar. Frozen in place, she waited and listened for any sound. Had a janitor come outside for a cigarette break, a smoko? Is that why the camera was offline? She couldn't see any lights on inside or hear any noise, so she gently pushed open the door and walked in.

Edging her way cautiously down the corridor, Niamh watched for any other security cameras, lights, guards or unexpected movement or noise, but all was quiet and dark. Perhaps, a staff member left for the day without checking the back door or setting the alarms. That would make her life easier tonight if that was the case, but there was no way of knowing? Still cautious, she made her way up the stairs to the first floor, shivering as the tingling careered through her body. She had expected this sensation as she neared this man named Gunther Grimm, and she hoped he was asleep so wouldn't sense her. If he did sense her and she was confronted, then she had no doubt there would be a battle of magic power between them.

This was not the standard hotel with a book of guests but a boutique resort which hosted special functions and only an elite few stayed at any one time. She wasn't expecting to find other guests on the premises except possibly, Gunther's security, bodyguard and a secretary. They would be Grimm's as well so the tingling of being in the vicinity of someone magical was inevitable. There was also the possibility of being confronted by someone magical other than Gunther Grimm.

In Ireland, she had searched for a guest list to identify the room she was seeking but this time, she needed to hurry and get this over and knowing the hotel didn't cater for many guests at once meant, she felt confident of finding his room.

Reaching the first floor, all was quiet and dimly lit. Again, she was aware that there was a CCTV camera but there were no lights or movement, and somehow, she knew it wasn't working. Again, she wondered if the staff member in charge had left in a hurry, leaving the back door open and security off. Why was this hotel so quiet and dark? It had been too easy to get to this point without encountering a single security person or working camera. At least it was in her favour, she reasoned and continued her stealth mission down the corridor.

The corridor stretched for another twenty metres in front of her with doors off to each side. She saw signs on the doors as she passed including Conference Room, Projector Room and Tea Room. Tarren had mentioned this was the venue where Gunther organised an interview that never happened, and she wondered if had been planned for the Conference Room on the first floor.

She stopped and shook her head to clear her thoughts of non-important matters, needing to be clear and concise and have full faculties on this mission. The crazy tingling up and down her spine was difficult enough to ignore, and she just hoped her quandary was not awake and feeling it too. Creepily, she heard a few creaks now and again, and it startled her each time though she chided herself that it was just the structure of the building creaking like they always seem to do at night.

She was just reaching the corner where the corridor turned sharply left and continued down the next side with the building structured as a large square around a courtyard. Although feeling the tingling for some time now, she still felt confident that Gunther was going to be on this last side of the building, with a good view of the elaborate courtyard garden. Niamh was still not sure what she was going to do when she reached his room but her first goal was to work out where he was.

She turned the corner and came face to face with someone.

In shock, she froze and stared at the person in front of her. Her steel grey eyes were exactly the same height as the blue eyes that stared back at her. The person looked as shocked to see her as she was to see them and neither party knew what to do next. Time ticked by as the two stared at each other, wide-eyed, each taking in the black clothing the other wore and the shocked expression.

Niamh had seen this face before in a photo that sat in Tarren's office. This was Monica.

Suddenly, an arm snaked around and grabbed her around the neck from behind with great force and held her in a tight chokehold. The pressure was so intense, she had no chance of conjuring any magic or planning an escape. Her only thought was surviving and easing the pressure that was preventing her from breathing. Her vision was slipping and vaguely, she saw Monica in front of her, still looking shocked and saying something which she couldn't hear. She fought in vain against the powerful chokehold as felt herself slipping into darkness.

'I'm going to die' her mind told her. 'I can't breathe. I'm going to die'. She tried to see Monica and her mind told her that Monica would be the last sight she saw.

Then the world went black.

Chapter 66
MONICA

Monica stared down at the crumpled body on the floor in shock and then up at the tall hulking figure of Hans, her great grandfather's solicitor and henchman. Her heart was thumping, adrenaline was racing around her system and when she opened her mouth to speak, it took a minute to find her voice.

"Is she dead?" Monica asked, her voice high pitched from shock.

"No. I hope not," came his deep voice with a slight laugh as if the whole thing was humorous.

"I hope not too. Gunther will have your balls for breakfast if she is," Monica responded, again staring down at Niamh prone on the floor.

Hans appeared unsure what to do, glancing at Monica then down at the witch. Eventually, he bent down to check the pulse in her neck.

"You're in deep shit if she wakes up. What are you going to do with her now?" she asked.

"Ummm … I'll go find something to tie her up with," he said, standing up straight and looking at her more closely. "Why are you here and why are you dressed in black?"

Monica opened her mouth but nothing came out. He had caught her off-guard and her mind snapped back to find a good excuse for why she was there.

"I heard the witch was back in Melbourne and I had a hunch she would come here so I've been waiting for her." Monica knew the explanation had been accepted as Hans nodded once and then looked at the witch again. "You'd better get a doctor quick because tying her up is not going to stop her magic. She needs to be sedated. Hurry! Before she wakes up."

Hans fidgeted for a few seconds, hands in pockets as if the solution could be found in there, then raced off down the corridor. Monica looked down at the figure on the floor and for a moment, wondered what to do if the witch woke up. Would she run? Would she hold her ground? Who knew what to do in that situation?

Monica squatted down and stared at the girl's face, taking advantage of her unconscious state. Her face was on the side and a few wisps of her dark red hair had escaped the confines of a hair band and were across her face. Monica reached and out and moved the strands of hair out the way so she could see her clearer. She touched the hair ready to let go in an instant if the girl moved, or the hair was electrified.

She hated to admit it but the girl had a pretty face, pale smooth skin with a few small hints of freckles across her nose. Her eyebrows were dark red, well defined and a medium thickness, not dark and heavy like the Grimm eyebrows. This was her half-sister, her father's child from another woman. Monica hated this girl.

She pulled her hand away, wiping it on the side of her black jeans as if she could wipe off the witch scent. She hated what this girl had done. She had taken her father's love away from her, assaulted and harmed her brother permanently and as if that wasn't bad enough, the damned girl was a witch.

A witch!

She looked back at the prone figure and thought the girl didn't look like a witch, the thought giving her a little chuckle as she had never seen a witch before so how would she know what a witch looked like? It didn't matter whether she looked like a witch or not, the fact was that this girl was a witch and it was in her blood to hunt and kill witches so this girl was the enemy and to be hated.

Monica looked down at her own hands. Could she kill the witch now? Could she place her hands around the witch's neck and squeeze the life out of her? Then it would be over and she would have revenge on the one who had hurt her brother and taken her father away. Somehow, killing the witch now was not going to bring her father back to her, though it would feel good, her mind reasoned.

She almost laughed out loud when she thought that the two of them were most likely here tonight for the same reason. This witch must be here looking for Gunther to kill him like she had most likely burned the men in Ireland. She would want Gunther dead which was exactly what Monica wanted and why she was here. She had planned to find a way of getting inside Gunther's room and murder him, escaping before anyone realised he was dead. No one could know that though so she would stick with the excuse she had given Hans and that would be enough.

Gingerly, she put a finger out and moved it closer to touch the witch's face. Ready to pull the finger back at the slightest movement, she reached out and touched her finger lightly to the witch's cheek. It felt smooth and a bit cool, and Monica hoped the coolness was just the temperature and didn't mean she was on death's door. What was going to happen now?

She didn't have further time to ponder that question as she heard footsteps running down the corridor. Hans appeared, puffing slightly and with links of chain in his hands. He squatted down and chained the witch's hands behind her back and her feet together.

"Chains? Really? Chains? That's a bit dramatic, don't you think?" said Monica, derisively.

"Harder for her to escape from or use magic on than rope," Hans answered. "I've phoned the doctor and he's on the way."

Monica didn't need to ask which doctor as the Melbourne Grimm family only used a medic that was on their books and handsomely paid for his troubles.

"Watch her and I'm going to go wake up Gunther," said Hans and he took off down the other side of the corridor.

"Good luck with that," said Monica.

She turned and looked back at the chained witch and wondered how long the chains would hold her for.

Chapter 67
GUNTHER

In the deep dream state he was in, Gunther ran through the forest, a deep, thick forest with tall pine trees and the scent of pine filled his nostrils. As he raced across centuries of fallen pine needles composted into mulch, he looked down at his feet and they were the paws of a dark grey wolf. Feeling excited, he ran faster, darting among trees in the dark forest where he knew there was prey ahead and he needed to catch up to it. He could almost taste the succulent flesh of the deer he was chasing, ripping the meat from its bloody bones.

KNOCK … KNOCK … KNOCK

Gunther jumped and his eyes snapped open, staring at the dark ceiling. What on earth had woken him up?

KNOCK … KNOCK … KNOCK

There it was again, someone knocking furiously at the door. He glanced across at the bedside clock and saw it was 12.20am. Who on earth would be knocking at this time of the morning? Was the hotel on fire? Had the world ended? There had better be a damned good excuse to wake him from such an intense dream.

He swung his legs to the side of the bed and sat up, groaning at the discomfort from his arthritis which was always worse in cold, Melbourne than when he was home in Sydney. Feeling a wet chin, he grabbed a fist full of tissues from the side table to wipe the saliva off his chin and mouth, marvelling that it must have been a hell of a dream to have salivated in real life.

KNOCK ... KNOCK ... KNOCK

"Yeah, yeah, I'm coming," he yelled out, feeling the anger build.

He pushed his feet into his slippers, donned the thick dressing gown from the chair and walked in a stilted gait toward the door. It generally took time in the mornings to loosen up his joints so he could walk freely.

"This had better be good," he called out as he flung the door open.

Hans was standing there with an odd expression on his face and Gunther couldn't help noticing his purple pyjamas which looked strangely like a onesie.

"We got the witch," Hans said quickly, almost breathlessly.

"You got her?"

"Yes. Chained her up. Down the corridor." Hans gestured off to the right.

Gunther realised the appearance of Hans being breathless was ... excitement. He'd never seen Hans excited before as he was always such a robotic, nondescript type of person.

Gunther followed Hans down the corridor in the semi-dark, tying his robe tighter as he walked. His mind racing to wonder how they could catch the witch in the corridor of his hotel, and he briefly wondered if this was a joke or trap.

Ahead, he could make out movement and dark shadows, and as he drew closer, he saw it was one of his family members. He knew her face but couldn't remember her name, sitting on the floor next to a girl with arms behind her back and chains around her ankles. Gunther stopped and stared down at the figure on the floor. It was difficult to see with the darkness.

"Turn some goddamn lights on," he snapped at Hans.

Hans turned and felt around the door frames hunting for a light switch, and after a few minutes, the lights in the hallway blazed on. Gunther looked back down and could see the dark red hair of the witch, dressed in black clothing.

"Is she alive?" he asked.

"Yes", said the Grimm girl on the floor. "Unconscious."

The girl stood up and Gunther noted that she was dressed in black as well. He turned his attention back to the unconscious witch, kneeling down to take a better look at her.

"She doesn't look very fierce, does she? She looks like a strong wind would blow her over. Are you sure you have the right girl?" He looked back up at Hans, eyebrows raised in question.

"Yes, sir. This is her. I've seen photos of what she looks like, and this girl was sneaking down the corridor, looking for your room."

"MY ROOM?"

"Yes, sir. I guess she was planning to sort you out like the martyrs in Ireland," Hans said.

Gunther gulped. Had he really come that close to death? How could she have managed to get so close to where he was staying?

"Where's my security detail?" asked Gunther, wondering how this witch could have got so close to him.

"I don't know," said Hans, looking puzzled.

"I was awake and felt the magic nearby, so looked out into the corridor and saw her. I followed her and when she nearly ran into this one." He gestured to Monica. "She was distracted so I sneaked up and grabbed her, knocked her out."

Gunther looked at Monica again. "What's your name?"

"Monica."

"Ah, yes. You are Tarren's daughter, are you not?"

"Yes. I am. I heard the witch was back in Melbourne and thought she would come here so I was here, waiting." She thought she'd get in first before he asked why she was here.

Gunther looked at her, studied her as he would a science experiment, then just as quickly, dismissed her and turned his attention back to the witch. He felt excited for the first time in a long while at the thought that they had caught a witch. It had been at least fifty years since he had the pleasure of capturing a witch and he fondly remembered driving the young witch out to the middle of nowhere and setting her alight. He had sat for hours, watching her burn and at first, she had screamed and even when the screams ended and her body burned, he had eagerly watched every sinew and piece of her turn to ash. In the morning, he had taken a piece of her bone as a souvenir and left the remains of her to be found by a farmer one day.

"I sent for the doctor as we're worried when she wakes, she could use magic to free herself. We thought it best to keep her sedated," said Hans.

"Excellent. Excellent," said Gunther.

Right on cue, they heard knocking on the front door downstairs and Hans raced off to let the doctor in.

"What are you going to do with her?" asked Monica.

Gunther looked at Monica, forgetting her name already then looked down at the chained girl. "We are going to use her for bait."

Chapter 68
TARREN

Tarren rolled over in bed and sat up, forgetting for a moment where he was and feeling confused. A sound had woken him and groggily, he looked around to orient himself. Ah, the hotel room. It was still dark so it surely wouldn't be Lucinda sending him a text message as she liked to sleep in until a reasonable time in the mornings.

According to the beside clock, it was 6am and Melbourne was still dark at that time in early spring. As not many people had his burner phone number, his curiosity peeked, and he picked up the phone to check who the message was from.

The message was from Hardy and suddenly, he was wide awake and swung his legs over to the side of the bed. Why would Hardy message him at 6am in the morning?

You need to come to Mont Blanc at 7am. They have the young witch.

Tarren stared at the message as if it could not be real and he was misreading it. They have the young witch … Niamh? They have Niamh? He jumped out of bed and threw open the door to the other bedroom where Niamh slept but her bed was empty.

Panic hit and he felt like vomiting. It could not be real. Surely? He opened the front door and stared out at where the car should be parked, but the spot was empty.

Frazzled and with panic setting in, he sat back on the bed to clear his thoughts, aware he was not thinking clearly. Ok. Calm down, he told himself. He had retired for bed at the same time as Niamh, around 9.30pm. She had seemed normal with no sign she had planned to do anything after he was asleep. Obviously, she had left at some point and taken the car and … and … driven to Mont Blanc? Is that where she had gone? Why had she gone there? Gunther was there and now he remembered that he had mentioned that to her at one stage. She must have decided to take matters into her own hands, as she had in Ireland.

Ok.

They have her, the message said. 'They' would mean the Grimm's and in particular, Gunther. He could just imagine the glee Gunther would feel capturing a young witch. She must be still alive, mustn't she? He couldn't imagine Hardy would tell him the wrong thing. Gunther was trying to get him to come to Mont Blanc and he was using Niamh to get him there. It was a win – win for Gunther. He had Niamh and now, he was dangling the carrot to capture Tarren as well. The guise would work, of course, as there was no question he would do whatever it took to save Niamh. He felt physically sick at the thought that they had her in captivity. She must be incapacitated in some way because they would never be able to contain her otherwise. He just hoped she was still alive.

What would he tell her mother? Nothing. What could he say? He didn't know anything.

Grabbing a pen and notepad from the drawer next to his bed, he quickly wrote a note to Lucinda. This note was intended to be read by Lucinda only if the worse should happen and he never returned. He lifted the paper to his lips and kissed it, hoping a small part of him would implant on the sad note.

He ordered an Uber and dressed while waiting. He had no plan of attack and didn't know what to expect. He would be flying blind and there was no other way. He needed to walk into that hotel, and he knew it would be the conference room as Gunther liked a spectacle. He also knew that many of the Grimm family would be present and waiting for his entrance. They wouldn't want to miss the execution of a witch, just like in the olden times, when people had flocked into the streets to witness the executions.

A tooting horn heralded that his Uber was outside and ready to go. With a deep breath, he left the hotel room and entered the Uber with instructions on where to drop him off. He didn't feel nervous, oddly. In fact, he was quite calm and relaxed about his own fate. He had determined that he would not be returning or leaving that conference room alive this day but as long as Niamh did, then that was ok.

He just couldn't bear the thought that Lucinda could potentially lose them both today and be on her own once again with his baby. If today turned out badly, the chances were high that the Grimm family would seek out Lucinda and her sisters and wipe the slate clean of witches and anything to do with witches.

Whatever happened on this day, Niamh must survive.

Chapter 69
MONICA

The large conference room was beginning to fill up with her family members as Monica took her seat in the front row next to Jonty. The room had been assembled with rows of seats on both sides and an aisle running down the centre up to the stage where Gunther planned to stand at the lectern, master of all he surveyed. From his vantage point, he would be high above everyone else in the room and anyone entering was forced to walk straight toward him. Monica recognised the grandiose behaviour for what it was and it made her angry.

An unconscious Niamh had been placed on the stage in front of the lectern, lying on her side and facing the audience. Her hands and ankles were still shackled with chains, and the doctor had ensured she would remain sedated for some hours to come. The doctor had been booked to return in a few hours to dose the witch again to ensure she did not wake.

Monica had not returned home after the capture of the witch and she wasn't sure why. Perhaps she had not wanted to miss any excitement as it was not every day a witch was captured. Perhaps it was the mistrust of Gunther and what he would do with the young witch if left alone with her. Perhaps it was wanting to be instrumental in the action and not wishing to miss anything. Perhaps it was all of these things.

She had called her husband, and asked him to arrange babysitters for their children, collect a blouse from her hanging wardrobe and meet her at Mont Blanc, which he had done, arriving at 6am. She had changed her top, not wanting family members to see her all in black and ask questions. Better to discuss her presence at the hotel on the quiet and only if asked. She had found it best to keep to minimal answers when telling an untruth. Jonty had sounded puzzled as to why she was there but she had shrugged it off, promising to tell him later.

From the front row, she enjoyed watching each family member walk down the centre aisle and react when they saw the young witch lying on the stage. There had been exclamations of shock, surprise, horror and excitement and most interesting, had been the reaction from Dora, her grandmother.

"What? Is this Tarren's child? Is it?" Dora looked around at Gunther, at Hans and anyone nearby. "Is it? That can't be right. She doesn't look like Tarren. She looks like the old witch. She looks like Agatha."

Someone quickly steered Dora to her seat in the front row, and Monica guessed Gunther didn't want the Grimm's to think too much about the fact that this young witch had Grimm blood herself and was related to them. It would make it harder for them to execute her.

Monica was not sure exactly what was going to happen this morning because as far as she knew, no one was able to contact her father, Tarren. She had tried a few times but he was no longer using his phone. Gunther had said he wanted to use the young witch as bait, but bait was useless if the person being baited could not be contacted. She guessed that if no one could contact Tarren then they would all be present to witness the destruction of the young witch. That would keep the family happy and satisfied, leaving her father for another day.

Jonty walked over and sat in his empty seat next to her. He'd been speaking with Beaton, Hardy and Anton in front of the stage while staring at the young witch. She was such a novelty to the family that they couldn't take their eyes off her. For most, it was the first time they had ever seen a witch.

"Hardy said he thinks he can contact Tarren. He's going to send a message to be here at 7 and see if it works. He said he doesn't want anything bad to happen to his little brother but now they have the young witch in custody, this issue needs to be sorted, once and for all."

Monica nodded slowly, and glanced over at Hardy, Beaton and Anton who were still standing near the witch. Beaton would remember her from the day he and Justin had killed the other old witch, and the young witch had harmed Justin. Did he harbour enough anger to want to kill her himself? Monica had thought she did but when sitting on the floor next to the unconscious witch last night, she had found the anger strangely subdued.

She shivered and smoothed her hair, to calm her nerves. She was aware she looked cool, calm and collected but inside, she was a whirlwind of emotion, each emotion vying for a prime position. She wanted to see her father and yet, she didn't want him to appear at all if it meant he was going to be harmed. She wanted the young witch executed and yet, she was half-blood Grimm and her sister, and she was not sure at all how she felt about that. She looked up at the lectern where Gunther was speaking with Hans and making final arrangements. More than anything else, she wanted her great grandfather gone and out of the picture entirely.

A low growl escaped her throat as she looked up at Gunther and Jonty turned to her quizzically.

"Are you ok, Monica?" he asked.

"Oh, yes. Sorry. Just clearing my throat."

She heard muffled whispers in the room and then the room became eerily silent. She knew immediately what this meant - her father had arrived and had entered the conference room. She stood and turned, wanting to see him and there he was, standing in the doorway, silhouetted by the light behind, not moving, just staring at the stage where his daughter lay chained and unconscious.

A tear escaped and slid silently down Monica's cheek and she had no control over it.

Chapter 70
TARREN

The crumpled object on the floor of the stage could only be Niamh and Tarren couldn't take his eyes off his daughter. The spotlights above the stage had been positioned so one was on Gunther standing at the lectern and one was on Niamh, lying on the floor in front of the lectern. She wasn't moving and from where he stood, he couldn't identify whether she was breathing or not.

His eyes took in the chains on her ankles and although he couldn't see her arms behind her back, he assumed they were also chained. This was a small relief as his brain reasoned that they would not need to chain a dead girl. If they were chaining her, then they were worried that she could harm them with magic if she were loose.

He stepped into the room cautiously, one slow step at a time, wanting to be prepared for any possibility. It was difficult to look anywhere else but he forced himself to glance around, taking in the family members sitting on both sides watching the spectacle like trauma junkies. How could they? How could they gather to watch the pain and death of another being? Were they here to watch the execution of a witch, or to see him fall from grace, or was it both? He didn't care. In that moment, he hated them all.

He continued his slow walk down the aisle, alert and wondering where that large attack dog, Hans was. Hardy had told him about Hans when they met in the city. Was

Hans about to jump out and wrestle him to the floor and put him in chains like his daughter?

Tarren drew closer to his daughter and found he needed to regulate his breathing, feeling the emotion building and potential sobs banking up in his throat. He couldn't let them explode at this time, in front of these people. It was not the right time.

Gunther stood staring down at him as he approached like a ghoul or a semi-god waiting for the subservient subject to reach the desired distance. He heard a slight noise as he reached the spot where Gunther had decided he should stop, and totally ignored it, continuing his walk to reach his daughter and check on her welfare.

He could vaguely hear sounds of disapproval and Gunther conversing with Hans, and he didn't care. Tarren reached the edge of the stage and could see Niamh in front of him lying at the same height as his chest. She looked pale and still, but he could see her nostrils moving and her chest slightly heaving so he let out a sigh in relief. He wondered why she was not conscious and guessed there must be drugs involved as he couldn't see any signs of trauma to her body or head.

He didn't know what he would have done had she been deceased and he didn't want to think about that. Today he was here to try to save her and that was all. For Lucinda and for Niamh, he had to find a way of protecting and releasing Niamh, even if it meant his own demise.

Gently, he reached out his hand and touched her cheek, whispering to her.

"It's ok, baby. I'm here and no one's going to hurt you. Can you hear me?"

There was no response to his words and he sighed, in some ways relieved, because if she was not conscious then she couldn't be a threat to the Grimm's and he had more time to come up with something. Eventually, after satisfying himself of Niamh's well-being, he stepped back and looked up at Gunther.

"Ah, I see you're ready for us now. Are you ready to face the Melbourne Tribunal and account for your sins?" Gunther's voice boomed out, designed for theatrics.

"I am," said Tarren.

Chapter 71
GUNTHER

Gunther revelled in Tarren's slow walk down the aisle and up to the stage. Finally, he had managed to ensnare both him and the young witch. Well … Hans had but it remained Gunther's victory. The family which he considered his audience, were totally silent and watched every movement Tarren made. The atmosphere was electric, and he couldn't have scripted it more perfectly.

He gave Tarren time to check the unconscious young witch before addressing him to ask if he was ready, and he felt Tarren's response was a tad arrogant. Gunther admired arrogance over weakness and looked forward to the coming hour. He looked down to refer to his notes placed in front of him on the lectern.

"Tarren Forsyth Grimm, you appear before the family today, accused of the following offences:

- Placing a magic block on two Grimm family members, Justin and Beaton Grimm,
- Failing to adequately secure a release or pardon for the same two family members,
- Consorting with a witch and a known witch family,
- Protecting a witch,

- Conspiring to bring a witch into the world on two occasions,
- Siding with a witch family over the Grimm family, and
- Failure to attend an explanation meeting with myself.

How do you plead?"

Tarren looked up at him, again with a certain arrogant look about him. "I plead guilty." He said it strongly and without hesitation, standing tall and maintaining eye contact.

The guilty plea threw Gunther for a moment as it was not what he had expected. He thought Tarren would waiver and hesitate and try to explain his actions, not just outright plead guilty as he had. Gunther stared at him for a moment and their eyes locked.

"Would you care to explain to the tribunal why you have taken this course of action and why you are pleading guilty?" Gunther demanded, raising his arms to indicate his audience.

Tarren stared at him defiantly then turned to face his family, eyes scanning from the left to the right but settling on the area where his children sat. "I wish to make it clear that I do not condone this witch hunting business. I know we have been raised to think that is what we are supposed to do, and maybe there was a reason for that centuries ago, but that time is over. IT IS WRONG AND IT NEEDS TO END!"

"Witches are people with magic just the same as we are, and they deserve to live the same as we do. This feud with the witch family began around fifty years ago with two witches who were minding their own business, they never came after us, or anyone in our family." He looked directly at Gunther's daughter, Dora, his own mother. "We targeted them and started this war which resulted in deaths on both sides of the fence."

Gunther put his hand up. "The family does not need a lecture from you. Are you going to address your actions?"

Tarren continued without looking up at Gunther. "I have been attached to the witch family over the past twenty years or so and fell in love with a normal person from that family, not a witch. Our union has resulted in the birth of a witch." He pivoted and looked back at the unconscious witch on the stage and then back at the family. "Plus, we are soon to welcome another magical baby into the world. These two children are blessings and are half Grimm blood. They are not technically witches, but a cross between witch and Grimm. It wouldn't even matter if they were full blood witches, they are people and we need to let them be."

"What about this young witch who hurt Justin and damaged his brain?" called out Hardy's wife.

"Justin and Beaton broke into an old woman's house and stabbed her which ultimately, killed her. They then attacked Niamh, when she arrived at the house. She fought back in self-defence and to protect her friend. Also, she had only learned of her magical abilities weeks earlier so did not have a good grasp on control. The harm to Justin was accidental on her part and his own fault for being there when he shouldn't have been."

Tarren looked over at the other son involved, Beaton. "I love my sons, just as I love all my family, but I will not sit back and let them harm or kill a witch, and especially, their own sister. I followed through with their time in remand and blocked their magic as they needed to be punished by the public legal system for the crimes they committed."

"You left your Grimm wife to go live with this witch family. What do you say about that?" asked Gunther.

"That is my right. There is no Grimm law that forces me to stay in an unhappy marriage. I am grateful to Marion for giving me four beautiful children, but I chose to follow my heart and live with the one person that I am in love with and have been since I first met her."

A slight muffled, groaning sound was heard and Tarren turned to look at Niamh. She was still unconscious but had stirred slightly.

"Before this tribunal makes any decision or you continue with your lecture on how Grimm's should behave, you will remove the magic blocker from Beaton and Justin Grimm. Do you understand?" Gunther thundered his order down to Tarren and could see the pleased look on the face of his audience. Oh yes, they were enjoying this theatrical performance and his strong authoritarian position.

Tarren hesitated, then nodded his head and looked over where Justin and Beaton were sitting behind each other.

"STAND," called out Gunther and the two boys rose.

Tarren stared at them for a few minutes then closed his eyes, bowed his head and raised his hands in front of him. His arms trembled as if a great force was tugging at them and his breathing was rapid and loud. After a few more minutes, he let out a loud gasp and lowered his arms, opening his eyes. Beaton looked back at Justin who had no idea what was happening, then sent magic to a light sconce on the wall and a tinkling of glass was heard as the light shattered. Satisfied, Beaton sat down.

"Do you have anything else to say?" Gunther asked, looking down at Tarren.

"Yes. Let my daughter go. Let Niamh go. She is an innocent young girl with her whole life ahead of her. Do what you like to me but I want the tribunal to agree to let her go and leave her family alone from now on."

Tarren's words were forceful and sounded like an order to Gunther who took offence.

"She killed two Grimm men in Ireland. She is not innocent as you say."

"There is no proof she did that, and what were the Grimm men doing in Ireland anyway? They had been sent there to kill her, so if she did cause their deaths, then it was self-preservation." Tarren almost spat out the sentences in anger.

"She has blood on her hands, just as you do." Gunther looked up at his audience who were hushed and leaning forward in their seats. "This tribunal sentences you and the witch known as Niamh Flynn to death."

There was a hush throughout the audience and dead silence as the family sitting in front of the stage held their breath. Even though this sentence had been whispered about and half-expected, they still appeared shocked. Gunther peered around the room at the faces, waiting to see if there would be any push-back but no one said a word. As far as he was concerned, his decision was the tribunal's decision. He wanted the audience to feel included in this sentence and it would help instil the Grimm values on them.

Gunther, enjoying this moment and all attention riveted on him, leaned forward and said loudly, "I think we will make a return to the old days today. LET'S BURN THESE TWO AT THE STAKE."

'THAT IS RIDICULOUS," Tarren yelled out, facing his family. "Are you all so callous and unfeeling that you could kill a young girl not even out of her teens and your own family member?" The room was silent, staring at Tarren.

Gunther thought this pleading from Tarren helped create the atmosphere and he relished the desperation in Tarren's voice.

"HARDY ... ANNASTACIA ... ALL OF YOU. You're my family and Niamh shares your blood. We are all family. I beg you to stand up and reconsider. Let my daughter go."

Gunther looked around at the audience, of how they were reacting to Tarren's pleas. He saw most faces showed distress at the sentence with tears and tissues, but he expected that. Tarren was a son, a brother, a father, and uncle and a grandfather. This was their own family member who had broken the sacred rules of the family and must now pay the price. It was an unfortunate event and set of circumstances, but it was a fact of life. The Melbourne family would mourn but they'd get over it.

Gunther turned to Hans, who was standing to the side of the stage waiting for what he knew would be inevitable. "Hans, set up the stakes in the courtyard and find wood and accelerant. Get help from a few others and do it quickly."

Hans nodded and disappeared.

Tarren turned back to Niamh and placed his forehead on her cold and unmoving shoulder. He remained in that position, as preparations for their execution were carried out.

Gunther on a personal level, was looking forward to the spectacle.

Chapter 72
NIAMH

Niamh dreamed she was physically lodged in a long tunnel which was so narrow that she was jammed in tight. She could feel the pressure of someone pulling at her arms and her legs but she wasn't budging. She opened her mouth to tell the appendage puller that she was stuck but nothing came out except garbled moans. She could hear the garbled noise emitting from her mouth but was unable to speak clearly. Her mouth didn't want to work and neither did her vision. She could vaguely see blurred and moving shapes, but she had no control over her vision, speech or body.

Niamh had no idea how much time had elapsed before she opened her eyes again and this time, the blurring was not as bad. She was looking at palm trees, tall, pale coloured trunks reaching up to the sky. She tried lifting her head up to see how tall they were, but giddiness forced her head back down. Nothing made any sense so she decided she must be still dreaming.

"Niamh, Niamh, sweetheart. Can you hear me?"

She heard Tarren's voice, penetrating her dream state and she opened her eyes again. Where was he? Was he in her dream? She turned her head to the left and could make out his blurred face only metres away. She couldn't quite identify the expression on his face or any details, but she knew he was there.

"Tarren?" She asked and could hear her voice was thick and almost incoherent.

"Niamh. Wake up. You've been drugged. Wake up!"

Niamh blinked a few times to try to banish the blurriness, but it remained. Drugged? She was drugged? She turned her head from side to side and the movement made her feel nauseous. Ok, maybe she was drugged. Her mind tried to work through the fuzziness and remember where she was and what had happened. Why would she be drugged? All she wanted to do was return to sleep.

"NIAMH, open your eyes. Stay with me. Come on."

She heard Tarren's voice again, firmer and made an extra effort to turn toward him and keep her eyes open. He was still there, his face turned toward her. She couldn't feel her arms and legs. Where were they? She tried looking down and around and realised she was restrained, arms bound behind her back and ankles bound together with what looked like chain. Why was she bound in chains?

She looked over at Tarren and he appeared to be bound in chains the same as she was. What was going on? Her brain tried to focus and she kept repeatedly blinking to clear her vision.

"Niamh, I'm sorry."

Tarren was telling her he was sorry. What was he sorry for? His voice sounded low and upset and with a loud grunt, she pulled herself out of the tunnel and into a slightly more alert consciousness.

Her nostrils twitched and she could detect the odour of smoke. Looking down, there were timber logs around her feet and scrunched up paper. Looking over at Tarren, he had the same, timber and paper around his feet. What the hell was going on? She and Tarren were standing in the middle of a large fire pit of some sort. She could feel a pole behind her and the chains holding her wrists, looped around the pole. She guessed Tarren was in the same predicament.

Swinging her head around, she saw a large area with palm trees, shaped hedges and colourful bushes. With a start she realised it was the courtyard at Mont Blanc which she had only glimpsed in the dark where night lights lit the path areas. Now it was broad daylight and there were people standing and sitting around, watching.

WATCHING?

Niamh didn't need to look twice to realise this was a large group of Grimm's and they were about to burn her and Tarren to the stake. Now adrenaline was facing through her veins, she was becoming more alert by the minute. She swung back to look at Tarren, her eyes wide and full of the terror of knowing what was happening. He was still staring at her and the expression on his face broke her heart.

"I'm sorry, Niamh. I'm sorry."

She wanted to scream at him to stop it. Shut up. Don't be sorry. Just fight. Fight it.

The smoke increased as the fire took hold of logs. She couldn't see the flames or feel the heat yet as it was behind her but she heard the crackle new fire makes and she knew it was coming.

Niamh's head ached and her vision was still fuzzy, and damn it, her magic wasn't working. She was not alert enough and couldn't seem to raise it. She focused and tried repeatedly, but nothing happened.

FUCK IT! Of all times, she really needed her magic now and it had failed her.

She could hear more crackling and feel some heat against the back of her legs so she knew the fire was taking hold and spreading through the logs. She was going to die and there was nothing she could do to stop it. Frantically, she looked around and at the people in front of her watching the scene unfold. How could they sit and watch two people burn? A few women had their hands across their mouths as if feigning horror, but they still watched.

Someone stepped across in front of her, and she squinted to see who it was. It was an old man, silver grey thinning hair and thick silver eyebrows. This must be Gunther that Tarren had told her about, her great grandfather, her executioner. He looked her over and walked a few steps to do the same with Tarren, then stood between them and looked out at the assembled people.

"This is step one of this mission. We are cutting the snake off at the head but now we must eliminate the risk from the dangerous body. Next, we eliminate the rest of this witch family and especially, the woman and unborn witch child."

"NOOOOO," yelled Niamh. "You stay away from my mother."

Her voice came out strong and fierce as she pulled and tugged at the chains, desperate to find an escape but the chains held firm. Niamh looked over at Tarren and he was also tugging and pulling at his bonds. They both stopped and looked at each other at the same time, both knowing the struggle was useless, and both beyond distress at the thought of her mother and little sister's fate. She tried magic again but other than a flicker, nothing was working.

A tall, solid man stepped forward from the side and addressed Gunther. "The doctor is here. Are you sure you don't want him to quickly sedate the witch again?"

"No. I want her awake so I can see her pain," said Gunther, grinning.

"You'll pay for this, you despicable piece of shit. If not me, then someone, somewhere will rip your fucking head off," she spat at Gunther.

Tarren cried out suddenly and she squealed in fright, swinging her head around to see a flame flare against the back of his leg.

"DAD!"

He took a few deep breaths and looked across at her, his eyes soft and grateful. She had never called him dad before. He continued gazing at her and she saw flickers of pain across his face as the flames heated up the back of him. She could start to feel the flames at the back of her legs too and knew it wouldn't be long before the heat would become unbearable.

"NOOOOOOO!"

A scream rang out, a blood curdling scream that lasted a long time until the person ran out of breath. It rendered the room silent with shock as heads spun around to identify where the scream had originated from. Niamh turned to see a blonde woman pushing past everyone in her row of chairs to get to the front of the group. Niamh recognised her as the blonde woman she had encountered only last night in the hotel corridor before she had been rendered unconscious. Niamh knew her face, although a younger version of it from a photo framed in Tarren's office. This was his daughter, Monica.

Monica's face was distraught and angry as she marched up toward Gunther with a man pulling her arm to try to stop her. She furiously pulled her shoulder out from his grasp and screamed at Gunther.

"STOP IT! STOP THIS RIGHT NOW!" She turned to the men around her who had positioned themselves at the front of the group for the best vision of the execution.

"GET UP THERE AND PUT THE FIRE OUT. NOW! DON'T LET THIS HAPPEN." The men looked nervously at each other and up at Gunther, unsure what to do and deciding to do nothing.

She addressed Gunther. "YOU CRAZY FUCK! WHAT ARE YOU DOING? YOU CAN'T JUST KILL PEOPLE LIKE THIS."

Monica bowed her head, eyes closed, and all was quiet as she invoked magic. Niamh heard the flames sizzle behind her as if they were being doused with a water can. The fire flickered but flared up again, the dousing not strong enough to quell the flames.

"COME ON," she urged the people around her. "HELP ME. DO IT! HELP ME!"

Monica bowed her head again, and the flames sizzled. Niamh glanced over and saw Tarren had his head bowed as well. Looking around she saw a very small number of Grimm's with bowed heads but the great majority were looking in horror at Monica and then at the fire.

Gunther's face was red with fury, eyes popping and salivating at the mouth and Niamh could see he was about to explode at Monica. Once that happened, there would nothing dousing the flames so Niamh put all her concentration into trying to resurrect her magic against Gunther. Her head still ached and her vision was still slightly blurred, and she knew the drugs were still affecting her ability to use her magic in any real sense, but if she could just slow Gunther down in some way, then there may be a chance.

She focused and pushed, throwing her magic at Gunther without any real instructions or proposed outcome, and saw Gunther stumble midstride and appear confused. He looked around at the group of Grimm family as if forgetting what he was doing and why he was there. Niamh focused again and pushed, she saw his eyebrows furrow and his eyes squint, and he stood still momentarily then raised his two hand to his chest and pressed. A minute later, he fell to his knees and toppled sidewards, landing prone on his side in front of the pyre with his head touching Niamh's feet.

Niamh looked down at the old man with the crown of his head touching her foot and decided there was only one thing to do in this situation, what any witch would do.

She pissed her pants.

Chapter 73
JEANNE SHAPIRO

The emergency services had finally arrived at the front of Mont Blanc Hotel and people were running everywhere, like ants before a rainstorm. It was a chaotic scene as a policeman held Jeanne back from racing into the hotel entrance. She had been monitoring the recording device she had planted on Tarren prior to him attending Mont Blanc Hotel at 7am that morning and spent a frustrating time frantically calling 000 and her phone wouldn't work. Of all times to forget to charge her phone, this had been the worst possible day. Flagging down a motorist and using their phone, she had eventually reached the emergency first responders. The police, ambulance and fire brigade had all dutifully arrived but not fast enough for Jeanne's liking. She had nearly lost her mind in the meantime.

Knowing she could not confront the magical Grimm family on her own and lamenting her own shortcomings with her lack of phone charge, and for not arranging backup with something so serious, she had paced and sobbed and almost pulled her hair out, positive she was too late and Niamh and Tarren would be burned to death long before emergency reached the venue.

Even now, authorities wouldn't let her attend and declared the entire Mont Blanc Hotel a crime scene. She wasn't even sure who was alive or dead, the last thing she had heard on the recording device was a female screaming 'help me' then there had been some strange noises and an eerie screeching sound like a male in immense pain, the screeching made way for howling and then screaming from a group of people as they tried to stampede out of the hotel. The police and fire brigade entered the front doors at that time, and no one was allowed to walk away. People were shepherded into an adjoining room and were being held.

Jeanne paced outside and desperate for news of Niamh and Tarren. Emergency workers moved aside as the medical attendants carried out two stretchers and loaded them into waiting ambulances. She raced over to glimpse the faces to see if it was Niamh and Tarren, so positive it would be that she was already sobbing before she reached them. The first face was an old man and he appeared to have severe burns over his face that were visible even with his oxygen mask on. The skin had peeled back and blistered and was an angry and swollen red colour. An attendant mentioned the patient had also had a heart attack and she guessed it to be Gunther.

The face on the second stretcher was a middle-aged man with a very Germanic look about it, even though his facial skin was blistered and peeling. He was conscious and making strange noises which she found difficult to listen to. She backed up and looked toward the doors to the hotel. She was desperate to know the fate of Niamh and Tarren.

"Please let me see if they are ok," she pleaded to a police man standing guard at the door. He looked at her and sighed, having stopped her from entering for the past hour. "Oh ok. Just for a minute and don't touch anything or ask any questions."

She nipped past him and into the foyer where people were moving about in various directions. She located Niamh, huddled in a silver thermal emergency blanket, sitting in a chair with a medic dabbing disinfectant on her wrists where she would later learn that chains had bit into her flesh.

"Niamh, oh thank goodness," Jeanne cried out as she saw her and raced to sit next to her. "Are you ok, love?" She reached out to gently hug Niamh.

"Hey Jeanne. I'll live. They're making me go to hospital to check me out as the Grimm's drugged me and I have some minor burning on my legs but I'm ok."

"Is Tarren ok?" Jeanne asked, almost too afraid to ask.

"He's over there. A bit of burn to the back of his legs but he'll live."

Jeanne looked over and saw Tarren over the other side of the room with a medic sitting on the floor next to his legs, dabbing something on that made Tarren wince. He was also wrapped in a silver thermal emergency blanket.

"Why is he all the way over there and not near you?" asked Jeanne, confused.

Niamh laughed. "Oh, he's staying away from me," and she laughed again. "Do you remember what I told you about my urine?"

"Hmmm, yes. You said it was a good deterrent around the boundary of a property to ward off Grimm's."

"Yep. You should see what it does when it touches their skin," said Niamh, pulling a face.

Jeanne thought about the two men she had seen on stretchers and how their faces looked burned. Is that what she was referring to?

"NIAMH, NIAMH" A female voice called out and the two of them looked up to see Lucinda standing at the doorway signalling to her and waving, her face wet from tears and worry.

"Mum," Niamh called out. "Can she come through?" The police at the door let Lucinda through and she raced over to Niamh and wrapped her arms around her.

"Oh, darling. What has happened? Are you ok?" Lucinda asked, fussing over her daughter.

"I'm ok and Dad is ok."

Lucinda stopped and stared at her daughter, the word 'Dad' hanging in the air. A tear streaked down Lucinda's face and she leaned forward to kiss her daughter on the top of the head.

"Mum, did you bring the change of clothes like I asked? I've peed my pants."

"I did," Lucinda said and threw a small bag to Niamh.

"Oh, this is Jeanne." Niamh indicated the journalist sitting beside her.

Lucinda smiled at Jeanne and then kissed her daughter on the top of the head again and made her way over to Tarren.

Jeanne watched her, a beautiful woman in her late thirties with golden red hair, a flowing dress and a pregnant stomach. She watched as Lucinda bent down to Tarren's level and the two of them touched foreheads for a minute or so. She had never seen anyone do that before and it was so endearing, it took her breath away. Maybe there was another story here after all, a love story.

"You know," said Niamh to Jeanne. "Mum and I are lucky Dad wasn't around when I was a baby because he never would have been able to change my wet nappy. It would have burned his fingers."

Chapter 74
NIAMH

"Oh, they're not in the same hospital as me, are they?" Niamh had summoned her best frightened little girl voice and pulled a terrified face.

"Now, don't you worry. They're on a totally different floor than you, in intensive care, and there's a police officer stationed in the corridor outside their rooms. They're not going anywhere. You're safe," the more senior of the two investigators assured her, patting her arm gently.

Niamh hadn't tendered an argument at all when the doctor ordered she stay in hospital overnight to ensure the drugs were out of her system. Her mother had reacted with surprise expecting Niamh would fight to be released immediately but she had just nodded and smiled. Her mother had assumed she must be still drug affected or possibly in shock so staying in hospital overnight was the best place for her.

Tarren was released from hospital after protesting that his burns were treatable and he hadn't been drugged but was aware he would need follow up medical attention. Her mother and Tarren ... her father ... Dad ... were staying at a hotel near the hospital tonight as they were not yet confident it was safe to return home to Coburg, and it was the same with her two aunts and their husbands. Until they knew for a certainty that they were all safe from the Grimm's then they would remain cautious.

Her father had spoken at length with police investigators, and they had a recording of the entire incident. Her father had the foresight to contact Jeanne Shapiro the moment he received a text message from Hardy telling him they had Niamh and to come along to Mont Blanc at 7am. Jeanne wired him with the device so she could listen and record in real-time then positioned herself outside the hotel. Jeanne also notified the police about the situation but there had been a delay that Niamh was not clear on, resulting in the police forcefully entering the hotel almost too late. She could barely contemplate what would have happened had the police been another five or ten minutes later. With all certainty, her father and herself would have been toast ... literally.

Niamh had only spoken briefly to the police with a commitment to participate in an in-depth interview tomorrow. With the possibility of the drugs still in her system, her police statement would not have been valid and she wasn't ready to speak with them yet. As far as Niamh was concerned, the incident was not yet over.

According to the police, Gunther Grimm had suffered a mild heart attack and then acquired burns to his head and face when he fell into the fire. Hans Grimm had also suffered burns when a liquid, possible accelerant, had splashed on his face and caught alight. Niamh had listened and nodded thoughtfully but not said a word. How was she going to tell the police that her urine had dribbled on to Gunther's head and burned him, and then when Hans had come to Gunther's aid, he had managed to get it all over his ugly face?

She didn't even know how much her father knew about that part of the incident as he was participating with Monica in dousing the fire and had his head bowed. Even when Gunther collapsed and was burned, he would have assumed Gunther was suffering a stroke or heart attack. The eerie and blood-curdling screaming that emitted from Hans mouth after his face had been burned by her urine, had gained her father's attention and probably the attention of everyone within a ten kilometre radius of the Mont Blanc Hotel. But again, her father may have assumed he had burned himself with the fire.

The police had stormed the hotel right at the same time as the group of Grimm's in front of the pyre had realised there was witch urine burning Gunther and Hans and hit the panic button. People and movement blurred for Niamh as she had listened to the screeching of Hans, the screaming and crashing of the Grimm's trying to exit the courtyard and the police ordering everyone to halt. What a crazy scene it had been.

When the police were releasing her from the pyre, she knew then that her father could smell she'd peed her pants. She saw his nose wrinkle, and his eyes widen in recognition of what the pungent odour was. No doubt he realised at that point what had happened, but she doubted her would be telling the police.

No. This would be their little secret, her urine being a weapon of mass destruction.

Note to self: tell Jeanne not to publish anything about urine.

Chapter 75
NIAMH

"Yoohoo, Gunther. It's your favourite great granddaughter," Niamh said with a small laugh. "Yoohoo."

Only yesterday, he had been tall and imposing, screaming orders at people, and sentencing her and her father to death. Yet, here he lay in the hospital bed, looking old and frail with an oxygen tube, an IV in his arm and monitors beeping his readings to the nurses who were watching the measurements from the central desk. Well … they had been there earlier.

Gunther's face had an angry, swollen redness to one side of it, like a slab of veal that had been well hammered in preparation for crumbing a schnitzel, and it had a greasy look as if an ointment had been applied. Looking down at his sleeping face, it was surreal to imagine that this frail man ran the Australian chapter of the Grimm family and had tried almost successfully to execute herself and her father. She wondered what part he played in the devastating events that happened fifty years ago.

His eyelids fluttered and opened as her voice penetrated his sleeping state, and he stared up at her, not comprehending. She gave him her most beatific smile and fluttered her eyelids innocently.

"Oh, there you are." She noticed his eye colour was a dark brown and nothing like her steel grey which was a small satisfaction. "Do you remember who I am?"

She saw his eyes move from side to side as he tried to place her and work out where he was and what was happening.

"I'll let you in on a little secret, shall I?"

She leaned in closer to his face so her mouth was just centimetres above him. Her voice came out in a threatening whisper. "I'm a witch, but don't tell anyone." She laughed.

"I heard they still burn witches to the stake. Have you heard that? Sad affair, really."

She saw his eyes widen with recognition, realisation and then, fear. Now he knew who she was and that made her happy. "You were going to execute your own grandson. That's a bit harsh, don't you think? Killing family members."

She reached out and ran her hands gently down the IV line noticing that the sound of his heart monitor was beeping faster than it had been when he was sleeping. What a shame no one was around to hear the speed-up of his heart, she thought. Placing her hand in her robe pocket, she drew out the syringe and held it up to the light shining through from the hallway. The full syringe shone like liquid gold and she smiled at the illusion.

"Do you know what this is?" she asked him.

His eyes were so wide they looked ready to pop from his damaged face as he stared at the syringe, then his head started shaking from side-to-side. Niamh understood this movement to mean 'don't do it', and surely if he was not wearing the mask, he may have said those words.

"This is witch piss. Do you know what that does to a Grimm?" Then she laughed ironically. "Oh, of course you do. Your face was burned yesterday with witch piss, wasn't it, great grandpa?"

She reached up to hold the IV line, watching as the saline bag dripped liquid down the line and into the patient's arm. She saw Gunther throwing his head from side to side and frantically moving his body in a vain attempt to escape.

"Oh, what was that? You don't want to die? That's a shame, isn't it? I'm sure all the people you have killed over the years wanted to live as well. Well, we won't have to worry about that any longer. Will we? This witch is going to ensure you never harm another person EVER."

She pushed the needle tip of her syringe through the IV line and injected half of the witch urine into the line. Without another word or look, she withdrew the syringe and left the room, knowing that his heart monitor was about to go ballistic. She needed to hurry now and locate Hans before the nurses and doctors returned from the bathroom and came running.

Chapter 76
NIAMH

"Ms. Flynn, you have a visitor," called out the nurse from the entrance to her room.

Niamh was sitting on the edge of her bed, packed and ready for her parents to pick her up. She'd spoken on the phone with her mother earlier and announced her release time so when she felt the tingling feeling, she expected to see her father. The visitor was not her father.

Niamh sprang to her feet in surprise, unsure whether to fight or flee. Monica Grimm stood in the doorway, eyes on Niamh and waiting for her reaction. The two women stared at each other wordlessly, before Monica took another step into the room. She didn't appear hostile and if anything, she looked conciliatory.

"I wanted to see you," Monica said as she made another step. "... and I wanted to talk to you." Her voice sounded calm, and her expression was friendly enough, though wary and slightly nervous.

Niamh sat back on the bed and indicated to the chair across the room. Monica walked over and dragged the chair closer so the two women were only metres apart. Monica sat down and leaned forward to give Niamh her full attention.

"I'm sorry for what happened to you yesterday. I really am. I'm sorry for what happened to your family ... for all of it. My thinking has ... changed recently and I don't want to harbour this grudge against you ... or witches anymore."

Niamh studied Monica's face as she spoke and thought she sounded genuine. She was maintaining eye contact, but Niamh still felt tense. What if it was an elaborate trap set by the Grimm's to finish her off for good?

"I tried to stop Gunther ... to stop what was happening ... and to be honest, the reason you saw me at Mont Blanc the night before was because I'd gone to the hotel in the middle of the night to kill Gunther. So had you, it seems."

Niamh still watched Monica silently and let her talk.

"I probably wouldn't have been successful and the whole thing would have ended up a disaster, but I had to try. I didn't want him to hurt my father ... not at all ... and I didn't want him in charge of our family anymore."

Monica opened her handbag and brought out a tissue to wipe her eyes. The emotion was affecting her eyes and they were becoming watery.

"I spent last night agitated and awake all night, hoping Gunther had died of his heart attack and trying to work out what I was going to do to end his life if he survived. This morning, I hear the news that he and Hans mysteriously died overnight, and the doctors are not sure what happened."

Niamh maintained her steady, calm gaze back at Monica, not wanting to admit to anything.

"When I heard the nurse station was vacant at the time because the staff all had stomach upsets, then I knew it was you. I wanted to thank you ... I wanted to thank you for getting rid of that revolting man. Thank you."

Monica and Niamh remained eye locked, and an understanding passed and a truce.

"I want to know my family will be safe," said Niamh, the first words she had spoken to Monica.

"There has not been time since the incident to talk to everyone in the family yet, but I'm hoping this incident may have opened their eyes to how wrong it is. What Gunther was trying to do to you and to my father, was despicable and inhumane. I aim to find out how everyone is feeling after this has happened. I would like to work at changing things so the family can quit this ridiculous family legacy of chasing witches, but I am only a female. "

"What do you mean you're only a female? You're what the Grimm family needs. You could lead them out of the dark ages."

"Well … they're old-school … males are the leaders and females are the house maids and incubators." Monica gave a wry smile at her lot.

"Change it. YOU can change it. Please try. I'm sure our father would do what he can to help you," said Niamh watching as a tear trickled down Monica's face.

Her phone pinged as a text message arrived and Niamh looked down to read the screen.

"My parents are downstairs to pick me up," she announced to Monica and stood up to collect her bag.

"I'll walk with you. I want to see how my father is today," said Monica and the two women left the room.

Chapter 77

TARREN

Tarren and Lucinda stood in the hospital waiting area downstairs near the café watching the two elevator doors just a few metres away. It was more convenient to collect Niamh from this location than walk up to her hospital room, due to Tarren's burned legs stiffening up overnight.

The police had requested an interview with Niamh at 10am this morning and wanted to clarify a few details in Tarren's statement, so Tarren and Lucinda were heading straight to the police station after picking up Niamh. Lucinda would then drive off to their home in Liddle Street which they hadn't seen for over one month, before they had been forced into hiding. None of them could estimate how safe it was to stay there but after the events of the last couple of days, a decision had been made that they would not hide any longer. Lucinda would pick up the two of them once their interviews were over and they were going to return to their home.

Just this morning, Tarren had read Jeanne Shapiro's article from the day before on the interview with Niamh and thought it was excellent. Jeanne had captured the playfulness and softness in Niamh which she didn't always reveal to people. He felt confident the public would fall in love with Niamh after reading the article and realise she was not the evil witch portrayed by the earlier Grimm article.

Today's newspaper headlined the incident from yesterday as their primary story, that Niamh had been captured, drugged and chained allegedly by the Grimm family. The news item went on to summarise that the victim's father, had attempted a rescue and been captured and restrained. Emergency services were called to attend the Mont Blanc Hotel where the father and daughter were located chained to a post in what appeared to be a fire pit receiving minor burns. An investigation was ongoing.

Jeanne Shapiro planned to publish a follow up story in the coming weeks and Tarren hoped that would help end the dilemma they had found themselves in lately. He had not even spoken to any of his Grimm family since the episode and was determined to make some calls later in the day to his children, his brother and sister and his mother. He needed to know how everyone was feeling and reacting to the events of yesterday and satisfy himself that they didn't all wish to see him dead. He had nearly died along with his daughter, and if it wasn't for Monica, then there was a good chance they wouldn't have survived.

The police phoned him earlier that morning to report that Gunther Grimm and Hans Grimm had died overnight in separate rooms at the hospital with the exact cause of death unknown. Tarren would question Niamh later of her involvement and he predicted she would act innocent, but he knew better, and was pleased they were gone. Lucinda and the family deserved to be safe and the world would be a better place without those two evil men.

A ping drew his attention to the elevator reaching the ground floor and he turned expecting to see Niamh disembark. The doors opened and out stepped two women who halted a few metres in front of the elevator and smiled at him, enjoying the shocked look on his face. He was speechless with mouth agape as he stared at his two daughters who were standing next to each other and grinning as if it were the funniest thing ever. He glanced at Lucinda who was also looking shocked although she had never met Monica, she still knew the woman standing with Niamh was a Grimm.

The two women walked over to the stunned pair and Niamh laughed. "Surprise!"

Monica stepped forward and kissed her father on the cheek. "Hi Dad, are you ok?"

He still couldn't speak as he looked down at Monica and then across at Niamh who was still laughing. Monica turned to Lucinda and nodded her head. "Hi, I'm Monica," she said, her voice a little cautious and stilted but it was a start and Tarren couldn't believe it.

"Pleased to meet you, Monica. I'm Lucinda."

Having finally acknowledged that he wasn't dreaming and these two were not apparitions, Tarren's face broke out into a huge grin as he looked from Lucinda to Niamh to Monica.

"I'm great. I'm better than great. This is the best day of my life."

THE END

About The Author
L.J. FOX

L.J. Fox holds a Bachelor of Adult Education, Master of Business Administration (Internet Marketing), as well as qualifications in Information Technology. She has worked as a computer programmer, taught business computing at a TAFE College and managed the online presence for a number of corporates as well as the State Library of Victoria in the role of Web Manager. She has now retired to the mid-north coast of NSW where she grows Clivia plants and independently publishes novels in the light fantasy/paranormal/horror genre.

'I am a storyteller from Australia and my primary writing goal is to entertain you, to keep you turning those pages not anticipating what will come next, not to mention - the story must involve something a little morbid or downright weird. If you found the stories easy to read, fast-paced, interesting, enjoyable and little bit quirky then my work is done.'
L.J. Fox

For more books and posts, visit the website and join the mailing list - https://ljfox.com.

www.ingramcontent.com/pod-product-compliance
Lightning Source LLC
Chambersburg PA
CBHW070430170726
48291CB00002B/443